I SPY WITH MY LITTLE DIE

A RIGHT ROYAL COZY INVESTIGATION MYSTERY

HELEN GOLDEN

DREW BRADLEY PRESS

ALSO BY HELEN GOLDEN

A Right Royal Cozy Investigation Series

Tick, Tock, Mystery Clock (Free Novelette)

Spruced Up For Murder

For Richer, For Deader

Not Mushroom For Death

An Early Death (Prequel)

Deadly New Year (Novelette included in Vol 1 of Riddles, Resolutions and Revenge cozy anthology)

A Dead Herring

I Spy With My Little Die

Dying To Bake

ISBN (P) 978-1-915747-14-3

ISBN (E) 978-1-915747-11-2

Edited by Marina Grout at Writing Evolution

Published by Drew Bradley Press

Cover by Helen Drew-Bradley

First edition September 2023

To my darling Squid,
You make my heart swell with pride when I look at the
beautiful, funny, and caring person you are. You make me
smile every day, and I'm so grateful to have you in my life. I
love you, and you will always be my best girl.

NOTE FROM THE AUTHOR

I am a British author and this book has been written using British English. So if you are from somewhere other than the UK, you may find some words spelt differently to how you would spell them, for example Scottish whisky is spelt without an e. In most cases this is British English, not a spelling mistake. We also have different punctuation rules in the UK.

However if you find any other errors, I would be grateful if you would please contact me helen@helengoldenauthor. co.uk and let me know so I can correct them. Thank you.

For your reference I have included a list of characters in the order they appear, and you can find this at the back of the book.

1

3 PM, MONDAY 25 JANUARY

Waiting for the familiar wave of nausea to pass, Detective Inspector Ethan Preece of City Police leaned back into the large white pillows. The nurse had told him he could expect to feel dizzy when he got up or did anything too quickly for at least another few days. She'd pointed out he'd been very ill and his confinement to bed for much of the last month while they'd patched him up made him weak and vulnerable to infections.

He sighed. *At least I'm alive. But how much longer will I need to be here?* Opinions varied. One doctor had vaguely said, "A few more weeks," while another had told him it depended on how well his rehabilitation, due to start tomorrow, went. His stomach fluttered. He was safe here for now, but what would happen to him when he left? They'd tried to kill him once. They wouldn't just give up, would they? *I need to get out without them knowing. Just run. Mexico? Isn't that where people go to hide? Or South America?* He could dye his greying brown hair black and grow a beard. Along with the weight he'd lost since he'd been in here, it might be enough.

He shifted slightly and winced as the sharp pain in his side took his breath away. Glancing at the clock on the wall opposite his hospital bed, he frowned. It would be two more hours before the nurse was due in with his medication. He took a deep breath, and the pain reduced to a dull nagging ache.

Would Beth come to visit today? He'd been gobsmacked when the nurses had told him his wife had been by his side during the first few crucial days after the shooting. It had been touch and go, apparently. Had she hoped he would die, and that her attempt to play the devoted wife would result in support from his colleagues, hopefully of the financial variety? Since then, he'd only seen her once. After greeting each other and discussing their teenage boys, they'd had an awkward fifteen minutes of silence until she'd remembered her free parking was running out. With a throwaway, "I'll come back again in a few days," she'd left. That had been ten days ago.

Money! It had always been about money. Money and status were all that mattered to her. The new cars, the five-star holidays abroad, and the boys' school fees. Constantly having to compete with her snooty sister and her wealthy brother-in-law. How had she expected him to afford it on a copper's salary? No wonder he'd had to... He shook his head. *I was never enough for her. I'm such a stupid fool! There's nothing that will make her care again, not even my brush with death.*

He smiled wryly. She was unaware of the stash of money he'd stored away in an offshore bank account. He had no plans to tell her. That was his running away fund. He needed it now more than ever. *If only I can get out of here...*

The door to his private room opened, and a tall doctor he didn't recognise walked in. "Good afternoon, Mr Preece." The man closed the door, and moving to the end of his bed, he unhooked the chart from the bottom rail and raised it to his face. "How are you feeling? Still in pain?"

"Only when I laugh," Preece quipped.

The man didn't smile. "Good, good," he mumbled, walking around the bed towards the monitor and drips.

What is it with these doctors? They never seemed to hear what you said. *It's as if they're robots.* He suppressed a smile. *Is that how they're getting around the shortage of doctors these days, by cloning them?* This one looked especially inhuman as he pressed a few buttons on the machine. It was obvious the man's slicked-back black hair had been dyed. When Preece looked closer, he could tell the man was older than any of the other doctors he'd seen previously. He must be one of those evasive senior consultants the nurses discussed in hushed tones. Preece craned his neck to see the doctor's name tag. *Where is it?*

"So I have something for you to help with the pain," Doctor No-name said, taking a vial of clear liquid out of one pocket and a needle from the other. He took the plastic tip off the needle.

Why isn't he wearing a name tag? Preece glanced at the security pass hanging from the doctor's neck. The picture showed a much younger man. *That photo must have been taken when he was a junior doctor...*

"This will make you feel a lot better," the man said, plunging the needle into the vial.

Unless that's not him. Preece's stomach churned. *What's going on?* The room was quiet. Too quiet. A hole opened up in the pit of his stomach. A tightness squeezed his chest. He tried to turn his head to look at the door, but the pain in his side shot through his body, and he froze.

"You'll just feel a sharp prick in your arm."

"No!" Preece cried. He attempted to lift his shoulder off

3

the bed and roll away, ignoring the pain ripping through his body.

Fingers grabbed his wrist and pinned his arm to the bed sheet. "Now, Preece, no need to worry about the injection. It will all be over soon."

His insides quivered. What had happened to the refined tones the man had been talking in before? Preece recognised his accent. *East London!* He swore under his breath. *How could I have been so stupid? Of course they can't risk me talking. But I wasn't going to...*

A stabbing sensation in the crook of his arm made him squeeze his eyes shut. *Ouch!* He wanted to move, but his limbs were heavy, like they were made of lead. He screamed, but no noise came out.

"Cheers, detective inspector. Thanks for your service."

The voice was almost drowned out by the sound of his heart beating out of his chest. He tried to catch his breath. He gasped. *Air. I need air!* He couldn't swallow. *Please don't let me die like this.* He wanted to move, but one side of his body was now paralysed. *I'm going to die.* After everything he'd been through over the last month... *It's all been for nothing...*

A picture of his wife dressed all in black flashed in his mind. Her blonde locks dangled over her shoulders. One hand held a white handkerchief to her heavily made-up face; the other was outstretched towards him. Her mean blue eyes narrowed.

You're never getting another penny out of me, you greedy cow!

A wave of tremors from his head to his feet overcame him. He took one last desperate breath, then the tension left his body. He felt light, like he was floating. There was no pain anymore...

AFTERNOON, TUESDAY 26 JANUARY

The Society Page online article:

Police Officer Shot in the Attempted Kidnapping of the King's Brother Dies

Detective Inspector Ethan Preece (43) from City Police died in the hospital of a suspected heart attack on Monday. He had been there recovering from a serious injury he had sustained during the failed attempt to kidnap Prince David (61), the Duke of Kingswich, back in December.

A spokesperson for City Police made the following statement earlier today: "It is with great sadness that we announce the death of Detective Inspector Ethan Preece of City Police. DI Preece was a valued member of the organisation since he joined as a trainee police officer twenty-five years ago. Our thoughts are with his wife Bethany and his two children, Marcus and Oliver."

Intelligence gathered by PaIRS, which protects the royal family, resulted in the duke being taken to safety and replaced by a decoy to catch the kidnappers in the act. A confrontation between the kidnappers and law enforcement officers resulted in DI Preece and a PaIRS operative sustaining injuries. Preece was rushed to the hospital where he underwent a series of operations to save his life. We believe the PaIRS officer sustained a broken leg. City Police and PaIRS have been running a joint investigation into the incident but have no suspects so far.

In other royal news, Lady Beatrice (36), the Countess of Rossex, and her business partner Perry Juke (34) have arrived at Gollingham Palace in Surrey to begin a refurbishment project of several guest suites at the King and Queen's official residence. Mr Juke and his partner Simon Lattimore (39), the crime writer and celebrity chef, recently got engaged and are expected to get married at Francis Court, Lady Beatrice's parents' stately home in Fenshire, in the spring.

3

LATE AFTERNOON, WEDNESDAY 27 JANUARY

"So you're really going to move back to The Dower House then?" Perry Juke cocked his head to one side as he examined a pair of elaborately decorated nineteenth-century Japanese Imari vases standing on a tall varnished walnut side table along the wall of the sitting room of the Blue Guest Suite at Gollingham Palace. He shook his head and slapped a yellow sticker marked 'storage' on the left one.

Lady Beatrice, the Countess of Rossex, straightened up from popping a blue 'keep' sticker on the small Chinese money plant in a sturdy white lotus leaf marble planter she'd been studying. She tucked her long auburn hair behind her ear and walked towards him. Daisy, her West Highland terrier, trotted beside her. "I think so. It's time I moved on, isn't it?"

But am I really ready? Ever since the notion of moving back to The Dower House had taken root in her mind, she'd been asking herself this same question. She was ready to be independent again; she was sure of that. When her husband James had died fifteen years ago, she'd been only twenty-one and twelve-weeks pregnant. When her mother Her Royal Highness Princess Helen had suggested she leave her and

James's marital home The Dower House within the grounds of Francis Court and moved back to the main house, Bea had been easily persuaded to return to the home she'd lived in since she'd been ten. There, she'd have her parents to support her and protect her from the press and public scrutiny. She'd thought at the time it would only be for a few months while she came to terms with James's unexpected death, but time had passed and she'd felt safe and secure at home, surrounded by comforting childhood memories and people who loved her.

Then her son Sam was born, and he hadn't slept for the first two years of his life. Looking back now, she didn't know how she would have survived without the help and support of her mother, her mother's maid Naomi, and the family staff. She'd tried hard to do it all on her own, but when she'd been so exhausted she'd barely been able to put one foot in front of the other, someone had always been there to step in, take Sam, and put her to bed, leaving her to sleep until she'd been able to function again. So she'd stayed. And Sam had thrived. Although he'd been missing a parent, he'd always had either her father Charles Astley, the sixteenth Duke of Arnwall, her elder brother Lord Frederick Astley, or Harris, the family butler (who Sam thought was the bee's knees and vice versa) around to provide a bit of male guidance when needed. Happily cocooned in love and support, there had been no pressing reason to leave. But now...

Bea grimaced. "I'm thirty-six, and I'm still living with my parents."

Perry grinned. "Yes, but in your own apartment in their grand and beautiful stately home. You're hardly taking up their spare room, are you?"

She smiled back. "No, you're right. But I'm ready to be independent now." She plucked a 'storage' tag from the pad and slapped it on an ugly red dish. Sometimes she couldn't believe how much her life had changed over the last year since Sam had gone away to boarding school. Back then, she'd been unsure of what to do with herself. Now there weren't enough hours in the day, with her and Perry's interior design business going from strength to strength. And, of course, she had Perry and his partner Simon in her life now. Her best friends. Always there to make her laugh and give her support and encouragement. They wanted nothing from her other than friendship. They had become such an integral part of her and Sam's life now, she simply couldn't imagine it without them.

"And how do you feel about going back to The Dower House?" Perry asked cautiously. "Are you okay with that?"

She nodded. She'd even been to visit it just before they'd left to come here. She'd wanted to see how strange it would be to go back to the house she'd shared with her husband before his death. And it had been fine. In fact, she'd felt a sense of coming home that had been unexpected. As she'd moved through the house, noting that she would need to spruce it up a bit as it looked tired and a little dated, there had been a lightness in her chest as she'd thought about how she would put her own stamp on the place. She was now impatient for the time when she could go back and get started. "I'm good, Perry. Honestly. The house is light and airy. It gets the sun for most of the morning. It has a good feeling about it." She rocked her head and shrugged. "It needs a bit of TLC, but the bones are good. With Sam growing up so fast, I can't wait for us to have our own space. Something less formal. You know, somewhere he can invite his friends to stay without being worried about breaking something priceless or making too much noise."

Perry nodded. "And how does Sam feel about it?" he

asked, putting a white 'maybe' sticker on a small yellow Japanese plate with large blue flowers painted on it.

Heat rose up Bea's neck. She'd been putting off talking to Sam, worried he wouldn't want to be removed from the environment he'd grown up in and the people he'd had around him all his life. He would miss her parents. He adored them and ate dinner with them most nights when he was home from boarding school. And Fred? He and her brother were so close. Sam loved catching up with his dashing uncle whenever Fred got away from London and came back to Francis Court for the weekend. Of course, Sam could still visit Francis Court. It was only a brisk ten-minute walk from The Dower House and even quicker if he used his bike, but it wouldn't be the same. Would he want to leave the hustle and bustle of Francis Court and move to a quieter area of the estate with just her? She suppressed a groan. Would she be enough company for him?

Perry looked over and raised an eyebrow. "You haven't discussed it with him yet, have you?"

She slowly shook her head. "What if he doesn't want to move, Perry?"

Perry shrugged. "Then don't." She raised an eyebrow. "No one is chucking you out, Bea. If Sam really hates the idea, then you can wait until he changes his mind or until you can persuade him otherwise."

Her heart felt like it was shrinking. *But I don't want to wait.* Now that she'd been to see the place, she wanted to plan the work so they could be in before Sam broke up for the summer. "But—"

Perry raised his hand. "I think he'll love the idea, Bea. I really do. He'll be closer to Robbie for a start."

Her nephew Robbie was not just Sam's cousin but also his second best friend. His first best friend was Archie Tellis, chatterbox and devotee of *The Society Page*. Perry was right. Francis Lodge, where her sister Lady Sarah and her family lived, would be their closest neighbours. Maybe they could reopen the gate that linked the two gardens? She'd have to talk to Sarah about it.

"And," Perry continued, "you can give him his own proper space. He'll really appreciate that."

Again, Perry was right. She and Sam had been quite happy to share their apartment all these years, but he'd been growing out of his bedroom for a while. As she hadn't wanted his enormous television and gaming paraphernalia in her beautiful and serene sitting room, at the suggestion of Mrs Harris, the family head housekeeper, they'd cleared an unused bedroom on the other side of the corridor to Bea's suite and had set Sam up a television and games room there. It was working well, but in The Dower House, she could give him a whole cluster of rooms on the other side of the house so he really could have his own space.

"But most of all." Perry grinned. "He'll have an entire kitchen to himself."

She rolled her eyes. *Of course! Why didn't I think of that?* Sam's love of food and cooking had been growing over the last year since he'd joined a cooking club at school. Aided and abetted by Simon, Perry's partner and winner of *Celebrity Elitechef* two years ago, he was turning into a half-decent cook. At the moment he was limited to using Simon and Perry's kitchen or trying to persuade Mrs Ward, the Astley family's cook, to let him squeeze into her kitchen between meal prep and cooking. *He will love his own kitchen!*

"Perry, you're a genius," Bea cried. "I think that might be enough to do it." Although slightly put out that a kitchen would have more appeal to her son than living alone with her, she recognised it was her best tactic. "I'll talk to him when he's home this weekend." She gave a deep, gratifying sigh. "I might even take him to the house."

"That's a good idea. But be careful. If he's anything like Simon was when we moved into Rose Cottage, he'll want to redesign the kitchen completely!"

Bea laughed. She would be happy to make whatever changes Sam wanted if it meant he would agree to the move.

Perry walked over to the window-end of the wall and stopped by a gold and silver-inlaid walrus ivory armchair. Bea and Daisy followed him. "It's beautifully made, isn't it?"

Perry nodded.

"But I'm afraid it will have to go into storage."

He pulled a face as he placed a sticker on it. "I guessed that, but it's such a shame. It would look good with the blue theme we're going for in here."

"I know, and when it was made back in the mid-nine-teenth century, it would have been fine to display in here. But these days, we can't have ivory in a guest room," she said, moving over to stand by a Louis XV red-and-gilt Chinese lacquer commode. She rested her hand on the marble moulded top and studied the busy gold figures in what looked like a courtyard market on the front. It was impressive, but it wouldn't fit with the look they were going for. She added a 'storage' marker to the heavy top.

"There's a real eclectic mixture of stuff in here," Perry said as he joined her, reaching down to pat Daisy on the head.

She nodded. "The sovereign receives a lot of gifts from dignitaries, ambassadors, governments, and heads of state. They end up being placed on display in various palaces. I think they were going for a vaguely oriental theme in here."

"So will they get sold now if we don't want them?"

Bea shook her head. "Remember, this isn't a private home, Perry. It's a royal palace. If someone has officially given an item to a member of the royal family in the course of their duties supporting or on behalf of the king, then it can't be sold. Instead, it becomes part of the royal collection. We'll send anything we don't want down to their storage area, and they will decide what to do with it."

"Can we also see if there's anything in storage that we want? Like we did at Drew Castle?" Perry asked.

"Indeed. I've arranged an appointment for us with the curator on Thursday. The collection is vast, so I'm hoping we will find some real treasures."

Perry's eyes lit up. "I can't wait." He looked at his watch. "Oh my giddy aunt, look at the time. We really have to get a wiggle on. I need to shower and change before we leave. Who knows what the traffic will be like getting to Clapham."

"Alright, let's call it a day," Bea said, glancing at her phone. It was kind of Emma and Izzy McKeer-Adler to invite them to dinner tonight. It would be inconsiderate to be late. "I'll arrange a car to pick us up in an hour."

"An hour?" Perry cried in a strangled voice. "But I need to—"

"We can't be late, Perry. And anyway, it's not a fancy do, just a casual dinner with friends."

He pouted. She smiled. "So as you so rightly said, you'd best get a wiggle on."

———

Lady Beatrice pulled the dark-grey jumper down over her head, and her skin prickled as it covered her body. Smoothing it down over her black jeans, she shuffled over to the wardrobe. She grabbed a pair of black boots and brought them to the sofa in her sitting room. Pulling on the knee-high leather boots, she zipped them up. There was an empty feeling in the pit of her stomach as she looked up and stared into the darkness. *Why am I so nervous?* She reached her hand over to the little white dog curled up next to her and rested it on her wiry head. *It's just dinner with Emma, Izzy, Perry...and Richard Fitzwilliam.*

It had only been a few weeks since the investigation they'd both been involved in at Drew Castle, and for a change, they had parted on good terms. She swallowed. *Will he revert to his boorish self now he doesn't need my help anymore? I hope not.* Although she was struggling to come to terms with their more collaborative work relationship, she certainly didn't want to go back to the sniping and one-upmanship that had defined their earlier association. Getting used to the relaxed and cooperative Fitzwilliam was taking some time. But there was also something more. She was beginning to enjoy his company — and it was freaking her out!

There was a beep on her phone from the driver telling her the car was ready. With a lightness in her chest, she kissed Daisy on her head and grabbed her coat. *Let's see what the evening holds in store...*

4

6:30 PM, WEDNESDAY 27 JANUARY

Izzy McKeer-Adler slowly shook her blonde head at Detective Chief Inspector Richard Fitzwilliam from the Protection and Investigation (Royal) Services as he entered the hall of the three-storey townhouse in Clapham and enquired after Izzy's wife. "Just be careful, Rich. She's a bit more emotional than usual. It's not just that they've told her she needs to keep the plaster on for at least another week, probably two, but I also think she's still processing what's happened to DI Preece and, of course, she's refusing to talk to the counsellor PaIRS has suggested she contact."

She sighed and led him down the wide corridor that he knew led to the sitting room. "I don't think she's sleeping either," Izzy continued. "I've woken up a few times and found her out of bed, having a cup of tea in the kitchen. She looks tired all the time, but when I suggest she take a nap…" She shook her head again. "I'm worried about her, if I'm honest. I'm glad you came early, before the others arrive. Maybe she'll talk to you."

Fitzwilliam shifted the bunch of winter flowers into the same arm already holding the bottle of Malbec he'd brought with him. Reaching out, he gently touched her arm. "I'll try to figure out what she needs."

Izzy cleared her throat. "Thanks, Rich."

The door opened ahead of them. "Fitz!" Detective Chief Inspector Emma McKeer-Adler hobbled into the corridor, her white teeth showing through a huge smile that spread over her face.

Izzy grabbed the wine and bunch of flowers from Fitzwilliam as he hurried towards the petite woman wobbling towards him. He swamped her in a bear-hug, holding her tight and upright at the same time. "It's good to see you," she mumbled into his chest before she pulled away. He leaned back and steadied her by grabbing her elbows.

He smiled down at his colleague. "Shouldn't you be sitting down somewhere with your leg raised?" he chided gently.

"You're as bad as Izzy," she huffed, reaching out to use the wall to keep her balance now that he'd let her go. "I'm fine. Anyway, I've only got another few days, hopefully, so I need to get used to moving. It's not good to sit around all the time. Come on through." She turned and shambled along the hall towards the open door she'd come from.

Fitzwilliam looked over his shoulder at Izzy, who rolled her eyes in return. "You go," she said. "I'm still getting dinner ready. Would you like a drink? Beer? Wine? Coffee?"

"A coffee would be great, Izzy. I'm driving back later, so I'll just have the one glass of wine with dinner." He followed Adler into the sitting room. She settled into a blue-and-white striped armchair next to the window, levering her plastered leg up to rest before her on a footstool in the same fabric. "You know I actually miss the snow we had up in Scotland," she told him, avoiding his gaze as he dropped backwards onto a brown dog-eared leather sofa opposite her. "It was proper snow, you know. It always turns immediately to slush in London." She leaned forward and adjusted her grey joggers on her other leg.

Fitzwilliam studied his friend as she stared out of the window at the small paved area surrounded by black railings in front of their house and out onto the path beyond it. The skin under her eyes was darker than usual, and there was a red patch on her bottom lip, as if she'd been biting it. Her arms, hanging over the chair, were twitching, her fingers on one hand drumming on the material on the side. Fitzwilliam frowned. This wasn't the Adler he'd seen last week. He acknowledged that she'd been fed up then, still waiting to hear when she could return to work. But she'd not been like this.

She gave a dry laugh and raised one hand to rub the back of her neck. "Sorry. I can't believe I'm talking about the weather so soon." She snorted. "It's a sign of how bored I am with this stupid leg." She thrust her finger at the plaster cast, then threw herself back into the chair as she let out a rush of air through her teeth.

Fitzwilliam remained unconvinced. He'd seen a bored Adler before. They'd done several jobs together in the past where they'd had to sit and wait for something to happen. He'd always been impressed by how relaxed she'd been then, 'just chilling' as she'd described it, seeming to enjoy the downtime. This Adler wasn't bored. She was buzzing like an electric razor.

"You look tired. Are you sleeping?" he asked. She shrugged. "Adler, Izzy is worried about you, and I can see why. You're a bag of nerves, and you look completely drained. Are you in pain?"

She hesitated, then sighed. "No, not anymore."

"Then what is it?"

She looked down at her leg and mumbled. "I want to get back to work, Fitz. I've got nothing to do here, and it's doing my head in."

"Read a book. Do a crossword puzzle. Watch TV. Make the most of the downtime. Chill. You're normally good at that."

She glared at him. "Don't you think I've tried all of those things? It's not working."

"Come on. I know you. There's more. What's really wrong, Em?"

She dragged her teeth along her bottom lip, tears welling up in her big brown eyes. "Were my reactions too slow, Fitz? Could I have stopped Preece getting shot if I'd reacted quicker?"

Fitzwilliam shuffled forward on the sofa, and resting his arms on his knees, he bent his head down and to one side to look into her face. "Adler, Preece died from a heart attack. It was nothing to do with the shooting."

She shook her head. "Come on, Fitz. He was young... Well, youngish and healthy. The stress of being shot or some complication with his treatment must have brought it on. He was still in a lot of pain according to someone I know who went to see him last week. He wasn't recovering as quickly as they'd expected. Maybe it was an infection or something. But I'm fairly sure if he'd not been injured during the attempted kidnapping, then he'd still be alive now."

Fitzwilliam shook his head slowly. "You can't know that, Adler."

Her brown eyes lifted to meet his. "Come on, Fitz. Don't tell me it's all a coincidence."

He looked away. She was right. It seemed likely they could link the heart attack to Preece's injuries or the trauma he'd been through. He shrugged and leaned back on the couch. "Even if the heart attack is related somehow, it doesn't change my view that Preece should have moved faster. I still don't know why he just stood there and did nothing." The investigation into the incident was still ongoing. Now Detective Inspector Preece from City CID was dead, it could even turn into a murder inquiry. "You had a badly broken leg, remember, but you still threw yourself at him and saved his life. You did an incredible job. Everyone says so."

"That's all very well, but what will the official inquiry say? Did I lead the team into a dangerous situation without the right backup or training? Did I have a full understanding of what we could face? Is it my fault Preece got shot at in the first place, Fitz? It was all such a mess."

So that was what this was all about. She blamed herself for what had happened to the DI that night. Fitzwilliam had read the preliminary statements, and when interviewed in the hospital, Preece had not been able to reliably recall the events of that evening when they'd foiled an attempt to kidnap the king's brother. The two other officers at the scene had said the same thing — after swinging the metal bar at Adler's leg and taking her down, one of the two masked men had taken out a gun and had deliberately aimed it at Preece. That Adler had dragged herself along the floor and yanked him off his feet just as the bullet had flown through the air, causing it to hit him in his side rather than in his stomach, had been a miracle, they'd said. And then, even with a smashed up leg, she'd directed her team to administer first-aid to stop Preece bleeding out while she'd called in descriptions of the men who had fled the scene so a search could start immediately.

If I can just reassure her she did nothing wrong, then maybe she'll stop beating herself up. He opened his mouth, but she raised her hand. "And don't just say no because you're my friend, Fitz. I don't want empty platitudes. I've had more than my share of them over the last month. What I want to know is, could I have done it better? Should I have done things differently so Preece wouldn't have faced weeks in the hospital while they tried to patch up the big hole in his side that ultimately led to his death?" She wiped a tear that had rolled down her face and sniffed. "I've replayed it dozens of times in my head, and I still can't figure it out." She bowed her head, and her body shuddered as she tried to get control of her emotions.

He averted his eyes, his throat aching. He wanted to pick her up and hold her tight, but he knew she would hate that. He tried to say something, but suitable words escaped him. *What can I say to fix this for her?* He'd been about to do exactly what everyone else had done — tell her she'd done an amazing job in the circumstances and ultimately, she'd saved Preece's life. But that wasn't what she wanted to hear. She wanted to work out how they'd got to that point in the first place. He cleared his throat. "Tell me exactly what you see when you close your eyes…"

———

Thirty minutes later, Fitzwilliam leaned back into the sofa and raked his hand through his short brown hair. Adler, cup of tea in hand, was staring out of the window, calm for the first time since he'd arrived. He leaned across the end of the settee and picked up his half-full coffee cup. At some point, Izzy had crept in and deposited a pot of tea and a cafetière of coffee on the low table between them, then tactfully retreated. He took a sip of the lukewarm beverage. Adler's description of the incident that had led to her and Preece's injuries had been consistent with the statement she'd made the day after the assault. *That's a good sign.* It meant her mind had added no embellishments to the tale in the weeks since it had happened. The overriding takeaway for him, though, was that it wasn't *what* had happened that was bothering Adler but *why*.

"I just can't understand why they shot him," she'd said when she'd finished relaying the chain of events to Fitzwilliam. "At that point, we were no longer a threat to them. I was down. Preece was close behind me, but he'd stopped when they'd attacked me. The other officers were too far away to catch them. We'd thwarted their plan. By then they knew it wasn't really the duke we had with us anyway, so why not just run?" Her brow had creased, and she'd shook her head. "When the taller man produced the gun, I remember thinking he was going to shoot me. I was on the floor and defenceless. I couldn't see much of his face. The mask covered his entire head and neck, but I could see his eyes. Not well enough to see the colour, but for a split second, he returned my stare, then he swivelled his head and raised his arms, looking directly at Preece, who was about five metres to my left. And I knew, in that moment, he was going to shoot him." She'd taken a deep breath. "I shouted to warn Preece and then sort of half-crawled, half-threw myself at his feet. Preece didn't seem to be reacting at all. I grabbed his ankles and yanked." Her expression had been grave. "I've relived it time and time again, Fitz, and that's what sticks in my head. Why did the shooter ignore me — a sitting duck and instead aim at Preece?" Exhausted, she'd slumped into her chair and closed her eyes. For a while he'd thought maybe she'd been sleeping, but then she'd slowly opened them, picked up her tea, and stared out of the window.

"So you think it was deliberate, do you?" he asked her, jolting her attention away from the outside.

She sighed. "I don't know. At the time I wrote my report,

I didn't. I just thought they were trying to stop us and it was their quickest way to put an end to it all. But now, having replayed it over and over in my mind, it makes no sense why they would do that. And—" She paused as if questioning herself again.

"And what?" he prompted.

She put her cup down on the side table and rubbed her hand over her bottom lip, wincing as she hit the raw patch. "There was something in that man's eyes that makes me think he knew exactly what he was doing."

5

7:30 PM, WEDNESDAY 27 JANUARY

Lady Beatrice could hear the doorbell ringing inside as she and Perry stood on the doorstep of the three-storey townhouse and waited. Holding a bottle of wine in one hand and a bunch of roses in the other, she pulled her coat around herself as best she could.

Next to her, Perry stamped his feet as he shoved his hands in the pockets of his cashmere overcoat. "It's freezing out here," he muttered.

Just then the door opened and Izzy appeared, a wide smile on her round face. "Welcome! Come in, come in!" she said courteously, ushering them both inside.

The warmth of the house hit Bea like a wave of bliss. She could feel it seeping into her very bones as she stepped through the doorway.

"Let me take your coats," Izzy said, holding out her arms.

Shrugging hers off, Bea handed her fawn-coloured full-length puffer coat to the blonde-haired woman. Perry, following close behind, gave a sigh of relief as he walked into the entranceway. Taking off his coat and mumbling thanks, he handed it to Izzy. Turning around and opening a door to what looked like a cloakroom, Izzy hung the coats up on hooks inside.

Bea smiled. "These are for you," she said, handing the dark-red blooms to her.

"They're beautiful, Lady Beatrice," Izzy said, smiling back.

"And this is for all of us." She gave her the bottle of red wine.

"Oh, and this is in case you'd rather have white," Perry said, thrusting another bottle at Izzy.

"Well, thanks," Izzy said, balancing both bottles and the flowers in her arms. She ushered them down a wide, airy hallway decorated with antique furniture and scenic water-colour paintings. "I'll put these roses in water right away. Go on through," she instructed. "Rich and Em are already in there. I won't be a minute."

Bea's cheeks flamed as she glanced at the open door ahead of them. *Rich.* Perry gently shoved her in the back. "Come on," he whispered.

The scent of spices filled Bea's nose as she walked into the room. The walls were painted an inviting shade of apple green, a colour that set off the deep-red velvet of the curtains on the other side of the room where Fitzwilliam and Adler were having a whispered conversation. Candles flickered in the subdued light, giving off a cosy feel, and a fire burned in the hearth over on the left, maintaining the warmth from the hallway.

Fitzwilliam hoisted himself out of a large low sofa, and Emma McKeer-Adler thumped her plaster-cast leg off a foot-stool in front of her and, using the arms of the chair, levered herself upright.

"Lady Beatrice." Fitzwilliam walked over and offered his hand. "Nice to see you again," he said, smiling. Bea looked into his smooth, slightly sallow face as she returned his handshake. There didn't seem to be a hint of sarcasm in his voice. She dropped his hand quickly and mumbled, "You too," before turning to Adler.

"My lady, welcome to our humble abode," Adler said, grinning as she, too, offered Bea a hand.

Bea grinned back as she took it. "I've noticed there's a distinct lack of armour," she said, continuing the joke they'd shared at Drew Castle the last time they'd seen each other. *She looks tired*, Bea thought as Adler chuckled and let go of her hand.

Perry, having greeted Adler and Fitzwilliam, immediately went over and warmed his hands by the fire. Lady Beatrice joined him, letting the comforting heat radiate around her body. Looking over at Fitzwilliam and Adler, she narrowed her eyes. Something about their expressions as they exchanged a brief glance made it all too clear that they'd been talking about something important — something secret — before she and Perry had walked in. Her pulse quickened. *Have they discovered something further about James's accident?*

When they'd all been together at Drew Castle a few weeks ago, she and Fitzwilliam had told Perry, Simon, Adler, and Izzy about the additional information they'd learned over the last nine months concerning her husband's accident fifteen years ago. She'd been excited when Adler had suggested that maybe Gill Sterling, the woman who'd been found beside James in the smashed-up car and who had later died in hospital, could have been paid by someone to get close to him. Bea didn't quite understand why it made her feel better to think her husband had fallen for someone being paid to seduce him, but it did. Hopefully, Adler and Fitzwilliam would share any discoveries later over dinner.

Izzy appeared in the doorway. "Shall we go into the dining room?" She smiled as she beckoned them to follow. Bea accompanied Izzy as she trailed down the hallway and into the adjoining room. The promise of delicious food wafted through the air, and Bea's stomach grumbled in anticipation.

The dining room was a well-proportioned space with large windows lining one wall. The other walls were painted a cheery yellow colour and adorned with family photos and some modern art. In the centre of the room sat a grand table, intricately carved out of dark mahogany wood, surrounded by six high-backed chairs. On either end of the table were vases filled with fresh blooms — calla lilies and blue eryngium, creating a feeling of a special occasion.

"This looks lovely," Perry said, taking his seat as he looked around the room.

Adler nodded. "I wish I could take some credit for it, but I can't. It's all Izzy," she said, giving her wife a smile.

Izzy blushed slightly. "Well, it's nice to have guests. Rich, will you pour the wine while I get the food?" She caught Bea's eye. "The food's nothing fancy, I'm afraid, my lady."

Bea smiled. "It smells amazing, and I'm sure it will be delicious."

Izzy returned her smile, then turned and left the room.

"You prefer red wine, don't you, Lady Beatrice?" Fitzwilliam asked as he moved to stand beside her, a bottle of red wine in one hand and a bottle of white in the other.

"Er, yes, please," she replied, surprised he'd remembered.

Leaning over her shoulder, he slowly poured the wine. Bea found herself acutely aware of his closeness. With his breath on her neck, a shiver shot down her spine. *Get a grip, Bea!* She tried to focus on the conversation Perry and Adler were having opposite her, but a warmth was spreading through her chest as Fitzwilliam continued to stand close beside her. She looked up at him, and he caught her gaze. For a moment, their eyes locked in an intense stare. Then Izzy returned to the room with dishes full of steaming food, and Bea rapidly looked away. *What's going on with me tonight?*

She took a deep breath to steady herself as Izzy placed them on the table. Roasted vegetables, herb-crusted lamb steaks, buttery roasted potatoes, and sautéed mushrooms all filled the room with delicious smells that made Bea's mouth water.

"Help yourselves," Izzy said as she placed two large gravy boats on either end of the table.

Perry, not needing to be told a second time, dived in while Fitzwilliam, wine duties completed, sat down next to her. As they both reached for the pile of bread just to her right, their arms brushed lightly against each other. Bea jumped back as if she'd been electrocuted.

"Sorry," Fitzwilliam said, a slow grin taking over his face. "Allow me." Bea leaned back as he picked up the bread board and offered it to her.

"Thank you," she mumbled as she grabbed the first slice she came to and dropped it onto her side plate. The smell of his aftershave — spicy and woody with just a hint of citrus warmed her senses, and she suppressed a sigh of relief when Izzy walked around the back of her chair and sat down on her other side. Thank goodness she now had something else to focus on other than Fitzwilliam's presence beside her.

"Thank you so much for all of this, Izzy," Bea said, turning to the blonde woman beside her. "You must have been cooking all day."

Izzy smiled. "I love cooking." She leaned towards Bea and whispered, "I love my wife, but she'll eat anything as long as it's hot. She's just as happy with baked beans on toast as she is with a spread like this! It's nice to cook a proper meal and have it appreciated…"

Not sure if she was joking, Bea turned to look directly at her. Izzy was grinning as she looked over the table at Adler. *It doesn't seem to bother her*, Bea thought as she helped herself to carrots, beans, and fat slices of lamb.

"Potatoes?" Bea whirled around as Fitzwilliam extended a large serving dish towards her.

"Er, thanks." She picked up the serving spoon and added two crispy roasties to her plate. *Why's he being so attentive?* Bea wasn't sure she was comfortable with this new Fitzwilliam — the one who seemed so eager to please.

Fitzwilliam smiled, and Bea felt her heart flutter. She quickly returned her attention to her plate, feeling embarrassed by the flush on her cheeks. Taking a bite of potato, its soft crunch and buttery flavour melting in her mouth, she worried Fitzwilliam had noticed her blush. Bea searched for something to say, anything to break the awkward silence hanging between them. She tried to convince herself she was just being paranoid, but deep down, she knew something had shifted in their relationship, and it made her uneasy.

As if sensing her discomfort, Fitzwilliam spoke first. "So how's the refurb project going?" His voice was light, inviting conversation.

Bea hesitated for a moment before responding with a small smile and told him of their progress so far. The two of them chatted as they ate. Bea told him of their plans while Fitzwilliam asked thoughtful questions and listened attentively. And no mention of wallpaper! Bea felt her worries melt away as they talked; it was nice to talk openly and honestly with someone who seemed genuinely interested in what she had to say. *What does this sudden change in his attitude mean?* Their conversation felt effortless and natural, which was strange given their previous awkwardness around each other.

Bea pondered the possibility of a new relationship between them, one based on mutual trust and understanding. Is that where they were heading? She didn't know, but either way, she was sure of one thing — this new dynamic was less stressful than being at loggerheads.

———

Following two delicious desserts — a decadent chocolate fudge cake with fresh cream and Izzy's signature apple pie that oozed with sticky cinnamon sugar and was topped with soft vanilla ice cream (unable to make a choice between the two, Bea was persuaded by Perry to do what he'd done and have a bit of each), Fitzwilliam helped Izzy clear the table, and they all moved back into the sitting room to have coffee.

"I'm so stuffed," Perry said as he gingerly lowered himself into an armchair next to Adler.

Adler raised her foot up onto the footstool and got herself comfortable. "Yes, love, that was a veritable feast," she said to Izzy as her wife placed a milk jug and sugar bowl on the table. "Fit for royalty," she continued, grinning at Bea.

"Indeed," Bea said, smiling as she avoided the sofa and sat in the third armchair surrounding the low glass coffee table. Fitzwilliam, having put the coffee pot and cups he'd been carrying onto the table, made himself comfortable on the leather sofa, propping up a few cushions and tucking his feet beneath him.

Izzy gracefully poured coffee into tall ceramic mugs and presented them to each person. The coffee was fragrant, its aroma tickling Bea's nose as she took her cup. Refusing milk, she glanced over to the sofa and studied Fitzwilliam as he held his cup in both hands, cradling it like an old friend. Dressed in a navy-blue striped shirt and dark-blue chinos, he looked like he'd come straight from work, but at the same time, he also seemed relaxed. She couldn't help but notice how handsome he looked as he sat there with a contented smile on his face. *Handsome? Where did that come from?* He looked up, and she glanced away, raising her coffee to her mouth.

Savouring the flavour of the dark and bitter beverage as it hit her tongue, she lowered the cup and looked at it properly for the first time. There was a beautiful swirl of bright colours running all around the sides and a deep-red lining inside. Recalling that Izzy was an expert in ceramics —indeed, she'd told Bea when they'd been at Drew Castle a few weeks ago that she'd met Adler at Gollingham Palace when she'd been working on a restoration project there— Bea said, "These cups are exquisite. Izzy. Did you make them?"

Izzy blushed and nodded. "They were a commission for the wife of the American ambassador, but I loved them so much, I kept them for myself and made her a fresh set."

Bea laughed. "Well, I'm not surprised you kept them."

"Thank you," Izzy mumbled as she poured herself a coffee and took the empty side of the sofa next to Fitzwilliam.

Bea looked over at Adler, who was showing Perry something on her phone. Perry recoiled with his hand to his mouth, and Adler chuckled. Bea had been disappointed neither Adler nor Fitzwilliam had said anything at dinner about the investigation into James's accident. Her stomach clenched. Maybe she'd been wrong. Perhaps that wasn't what Adler and Fitzwilliam had been discussing earlier. She stifled a sigh as she twirled the rings on her right hand. Although she'd accepted it when Fitzwilliam had said he'd come to a dead end when he'd spoken to Chief Superintendent Tim Street last year and he hadn't been able to find out anything, deep down she'd hoped Adler's new spin on things might spark Fitzwilliam into trying again. *Clearly not, or he would have said something, wouldn't he?*

She glanced over to where he sat, his arm resting along the back of the sofa as he chatted to Izzy. Had he really given up on the investigation? She'd been so sure he hated loose ends enough to carry on, especially when Brett Goodman, the CIA agent who they'd met at Drew Castle, had told them about James contacting him just before his death to tell him he'd had concerns about something he'd found out in Miami when he'd been on a recent trip there. She'd been convinced Fitzwilliam would want to follow it up. Her shoulders slumped, and she leaned back in her chair, suppressing a sigh.

She planned on having a good search through all the papers in storage at The Dower House when she was back at home this weekend coming. After James's death, she'd not had the heart to go through a lot of his things and had simply agreed with her mother that they could all go into storage until she felt strong enough. Six months after his death and heavily pregnant, she'd had a cursory sort out of his clothes and some personal belongings but had never attempted to sort through all his papers. *Is there any point now if Fitzwilliam won't follow it through?* She shifted in her chair. Maybe she'd see what she found before she said anything else.

She straightened up and looked at her watch. The car was due to pick them up soon. She rose. "I'm so sorry, but we need to make a move..."

Perry, who'd been deep in conversation with Adler, jumped up. He gave a deep bow towards Adler and Izzy and said, "Thank you so much for feeding us such a wonderful meal." He leaned in to kiss Adler on the cheek. "Don't get up," he said, grinning, and she made a playful swipe at his arm.

Bea, also smiling, walked over to her. "I really hope that cast comes off soon," she said, bending down and patting her on the shoulder. "It's been great to see you again."

"Likewise, my lady," Adler said.

Bea turned and followed Perry out of the room.

As she caught up with Izzy and Fitzwilliam in the hall, she turned to the shorter woman. "The food was delightful, Izzy. Thank you so much."

"You're very welcome. I hope we'll see you again before you finish at Gollingham Palace," Izzy said, handing Bea her puffa jacket.

Bea nodded. "I'm sure we will."

As Izzy held out Perry's coat to him, Bea turned to Fitzwilliam. "Goodbye, Fitzwilliam," she said, meeting his gaze.

He smiled warmly at her. "We'll have to have that coffee sometime soon," he said. He adjusted the collar of his shirt and straightened his back as he stepped closer.

Bea bit her lip, remembering when they'd been back at Drew Castle last month, and she'd told him about her next project being at Gollingham Palace, where he worked, and he'd suggested they meet up for coffee. She looked away for a moment before looking back at him. "I know you're busy, but if you get time, will you tell Chief Superintendent Street about what Brett told us regarding James's concerns about Miami?" she blurted out. *Why did you say that? You were going to wait!* Heat crept up her neck as she looked down at the wooden floor.

"You do like to tell me what to do, don't you?"

Oh, no. And it was all going so well. "I'm sorry. I just—" She looked up into his face and saw a twinkle in his eyes.

He winked. "I'm meeting him tomorrow."

She stifled a groan. Would she ever be able to read this man?

As their car arrived, its headlights illuminating the windows in the hall, she said her goodbyes and followed Perry out into the chill of the night.

Perry huffed as he got into the back seat. "I'm so full, I don't think I'll be able to eat again for at least two days."

Bea laughed as she buckled up beside him. "We both know that's not true."

6

10:50 PM, WEDNESDAY 27 JANUARY

Richard Fitzwilliam lounged on the sofa, half-listening to Izzy's and Adler's excited description of a movie they'd watched on television the night before. His eyelids felt heavy as he struggled to keep them open. *I need to make a move.* But moving felt like too much effort. He smiled to himself when he remembered the look on Lady Beatrice's face when he'd told her he was meeting Street tomorrow. A mixture of disbelief, pleasure, hope, and slight irritation. *It was good to surprise her.*

The distinct sound of Izzy's phone interrupted his thoughts. She stopped talking, and picking up her mobile from the table in front of them, she stared excitedly at the screen. "It's Liam! He wants to FaceTime in five minutes when he takes his afternoon break," she said, her face lighting up. "Do you mind if I take it in the kitchen?"

Adler and Fitzwilliam shook their heads.

"Send him my love," Adler said as Izzy rushed out of the room, clutching her mobile to her chest. "It's hard for Izzy to talk to her son when he's in LA. The eight-hour time difference is a pain. And he's working so hard at the moment. The music producing business is brutal when you're first starting out, but he seems to be making it work."

Fitzwilliam nodded. Oh to be young and just starting out again like Izzy's son... *Would I have done anything differently?*

"Fitz?" Adler closed the magazine open on her lap. "Do you think I should tell anyone about what we discussed earlier?"

He sat up straight and gave her his full attention. "You mean the team who's investigating the incident?"

"Yeah. Or maybe Blake. He's my boss, after all."

Fitzwilliam hesitated. Not that he didn't believe Adler's version of what had happened or that he was questioning the instincts that were telling her the kidnappers had deliberately shot Preece. It was more that he found it so unlikely in the circumstances that Preece had been a target. Why would three men who had planned to kidnap the duke want to kill an officer who hadn't even been chasing them at the time? If only they could find the potential kidnappers, but they'd gone to ground. Superintendent Blake would be skeptical, and it might reflect badly on Adler. Fitzwilliam didn't want her concerns dismissed as some sort of breakdown. What they needed to do was find out more about Preece and why he could have been a target. "What do you know about Preece?"

Adler shrugged. "Not a lot. He was one of the City CID contacts we worked with frequently, but he was also one of those guys who was around but you didn't really notice him. I always thought of him as a bit of a wet blanket, to be honest."

Fitzwilliam nodded. City Police, London's well-known police force, were often called upon to assist PaIRS in investigations, to provide additional resources for protection details, and to share intelligence. He, too, had come across Preece, but he wasn't sure he could have spotted him in a lineup. "Yeah. I saw him around in briefings a few times, but you're right; he wasn't very memorable."

"Why do you ask?"

"Well, I think it's worth finding out a bit more about him before you say anything to Blake or the investigators. If we can find out something that links him to this kidnapping or the people who did it, then it would give more weight to your suspicions."

Adler sat up straight, her eyes shining. "I can do some digging." She looked over at the door and then leaned in and whispered, "Don't tell Izzy, but I have my work laptop with me."

"Adler!"

"I know, I know. But I hate being out of touch…"

He sighed, then smiled. "Well, then yes, do a bit of digging and see what you can find out that might help us. Look at his career history first and see if that throws up anything."

"Yes, boss." She grinned.

It was good to see her a bit more relaxed. *Maybe this is just what she needs.*

7

MID-MORNING, THURSDAY 28 JANUARY

Detective Chief Inspector Richard Fitzwilliam strolled down the corridor leading to the Special Projects Department in sector three in the security wing of Gollingham Palace. The corridor was long and dark, the only light coming from flickering fluorescent lights that seemed dull and tired, as if they had given up the ghost. Security cameras lined the cold bare walls, their red eyes glowing ominously in the semi-darkness. Fitzwilliam hurried past the offices, fleetingly glancing at each doorway, but their occupants were engrossed in their work and unaware of his presence.

His stomach was tight, his fists slightly clenched. Would this meeting with Street take them any further towards finding out what had happened to Lady Beatrice's husband the Earl of Rossex, or would it be just a waste of time? He opened his hands and wiggled his fingers. *Am I becoming unhealthily obsessed with the earl's death?*

Fifteen years ago, he and Adler had been part of the PaIRS team investigating James Wiltshire's fatal car accident. In fact, it had been their first time working together after Fitzwilliam had been temporarily reassigned from the intelligence side of PaIRS. After the investigation, PaIRS had invited him to make the move permanently, and he'd readily agreed.

He suppressed a sigh. The investigation into the earl's death still preyed on his mind to this day. From the unsatisfying conclusion and the falling out with Lady Beatrice before the inquest, to the embarrassing delivery of a letter found nine years later from the earl to his wife, written the night he'd died, telling her he was leaving her for the wife of Francis Court's estate manager, he had dragged the whole sorry mess with him through his career at PaIRS. And, of course, when Lady Beatrice had discovered some additional information last year about her husband and Gill Sterling, who had died with the earl that night when his car had gone off the road and ploughed into a tree, it had only raised more unanswered questions about the original investigation. He knew he should let it go, but his dislike of loose ends kept it firmly on the edges of his mind, ready to drop in and disturb him at the slightest mention of the earl's death. *And now I have the added weight of Lady Beatrice's expectations to deal with!*

He'd reviewed the case in his mind yet again this morning before coming down here, and it appeared more likely that, as Adler had suggested while they'd been in Scotland, Gill Sterling had been paid by someone to either compromise or spy on the earl. Adler had pointed out it could have been the press, but a thought had been brewing in Fitzwilliam's brain ever since he'd talked to Brett Goodman at Drew Castle. Had the earl found out something when he'd been in Miami a few months before his death that had been so significant that someone had paid Gill Sterling to find out what he knew? *Is that too far-fetched?*

As he reached the glass doors linking sectors two and

three, he took a deep breath. *Am I onto something, or am I about to make a complete fool of myself?* Lady Beatrice's hopeful green eyes appeared before his, and he slowly shook his head. *I'll find out soon enough.* He grabbed the large metal handle and pulled the door open.

————

Ruth Ness, Chief Superintendent Timothy Street's executive assistant, was on a call when Fitzwilliam walked into the outer office. She raised her vibrant grass-green eyes to his face and mouthed, "Sorry," as she pointed to the headset nestled in her highlighted blonde hair.

Fitzwilliam nodded and smiled as he stepped away from her desk and took in his surroundings. Although he knew Ruth, this office was unfamiliar to him. They had added it after the recent expansion of the security operations based at Gollingham Palace. It was large and bright, a stark contrast to the dark musty corridors leading up to it. Sunlight streamed through the large windows that lined two of the four walls, casting its warm glow on the solid wood furniture populating the room. The carpeted floor was a soft shade of grey, and there were several armchairs and two small sofas scattered around for guests to sit in while waiting their turn to be seen. Two abstract paintings hung on opposite walls, each depicting vibrant swirls of colour along with shapes Fitzwilliam couldn't quite make out; they brought life to an otherwise mundane space. The air smelled faintly of vanilla, and he spotted a diffuser on the small glass table by the wall.

"Sorry to keep you, chief inspector." Fitzwilliam spun around as Ruth removed the headset, letting out a sigh of relief. She looked up at Fitzwilliam with an apologetic smile. "The chief superintendent has been called away on urgent business, so he isn't here right now. He should only be another fifteen or twenty minutes. You're welcome to wait, or if you want to go back to your office, I can ring you when he's back."

Just as Fitzwilliam was debating whether it was worth the ten-minute walk back to his office with the risk of having to turn back as soon as he got there, the door opened and Detective Chief Inspector Henry Bird entered. A tall and imposing man, he had an air of authority about him. *He hasn't changed since we worked together all those years ago*, Fitzwilliam thought. Bird smiled warmly when he saw Fitzwilliam and extended his hand in greeting. "Fitz, what brings you here?" he asked with genuine curiosity.

Fitzwilliam returned the handshake of his ex-colleague from Intelligence. "Oh, just a quick meeting with CS Street. Except he's been called away, so I'm waiting."

Bird nodded nonchalantly as he took off his coat and hung it on the coat rack near the door. "Great, then come into my office and have a coffee and catch-up." He turned to Ruth. "Ruth, DCI Fitzwilliam will be in with me when you need him."

"Yes, sir." Ruth's phone flashed, and she picked up her headset again.

"This way, Fitzwilliam," Bird said, motioning Fitzwilliam to follow as he headed towards an open doorway at the other end of the room. Fitzwilliam tailed Bird into a small office, which he worked out must back onto CS Street's much larger one. It was much more intimate than the outer office, with a single desk placed against one wall and two comfortable armchairs in the centre of the room. A large cabinet stood next to the desk, with a coffee machine on the top. Bird walked over and picked up two of the cups stacked next to the machine. "Do you still take it black?" he asked, pulling the steaming jug of black liquid off its heated base.

"Yes, please," Fitzwilliam replied, lowering himself into an armchair.

Bird handed him a mug of coffee, and after putting his own down on the table between them, he slumped into the chair opposite Fitzwilliam. "Did you hear the ceiling collapsed in my office two weeks ago?"

Fitzwilliam nodded. News travelled fast within the security block. "You were away, weren't you?"

"Yes, fortunately. It's a mess. They think there could be asbestos in it too, so the whole outer office has to be cleared as well. We've all been shipped off to other offices wherever they could find us a home." He grimaced. "So this is where I'm working for the moment," he said with a hesitant smile as he surveyed his surroundings. "It's much calmer than my old office, and I get plenty of natural light." He pointed at two large windows opposite his desk that overlooked a small courtyard garden below. "But I miss the hustle and bustle of being with the team." He looked at the closed door they'd come in through. "It's too quiet here."

Fitzwilliam nodded again. His office was within a busy outer office that his and Adler's teams cohabited. He enjoyed having his colleagues close at hand to discuss cases and exchange banter.

"So how's things in Investigations?" Bird asked. "I hear you were up at Drew Castle recently?"

"Yeah. I was actually on leave visiting Adler and got roped in to help."

"She broke her leg during the attempt to kidnap the Duke of Kingswich, didn't she? How's she doing now?"

Fitzwilliam shrugged as he took a sip of his coffee.

"Bored. She hoped to have the cast off by now, but they want her to keep it on for at least another week."

Bird's eyes narrowed. "Preece from CID got shot in the process, then died, I heard."

Fitzwilliam raised an eyebrow. Bird had a look on his face that said he knew more about it than his casual questions implied. "Yeah. A few days ago in hospital. Are you involved in tracking down the would-be kidnappers?"

Bird shifted in his seat, then leaned over and grabbed his coffee cup. He took a sip, then placed it on the table. He crossed his legs. "In a roundabout way."

Fitzwilliam gave a wry smile. If Bird was being vague, then something bigger was going on. "Any luck?" He might as well push and see what he could find out. Adler would be interested if nothing else.

Bird crossed his arms. "It's ongoing."

Ah, so it's top secret then. Fitzwilliam still knew the code from his early days in the intelligence arm of PaIRS.

"Do you know much about Preece?" Bird asked. "Ever worked with him?"

"Not directly. I saw him around in a few briefings but never really had anything to do with him. Why do you ask?"

Bird uncrossed his arms and leaned forward. "Did Adler say anything about him?"

Fitzwilliam stilled. Was Bird investigating Preece? He knew the DCI's remit was something to do with relationships between PaIRS and external agencies, but he didn't know specifically what that involved. It had been fifteen years since he'd been part of Intelligence, and although he occasionally still met up with a few of his ex-colleagues for a drink, they didn't discuss work.

"Do we have concerns about him?" Fitzwilliam could also defer questions.

Bird rose from his chair and picked up his cup. "Let's just say we're looking into his contacts," he said, walking around the oak desk, which had paperwork spread out in neat piles across its top, and taking a seat. He placed his mug on a blue glass coaster and leaned back in his black leather office chair. To his right, tucked in the corner against the wall and half hidden by an old framed landscape painting, was a door Fitzwilliam hadn't noticed when he'd first come in. "What's in there?" he asked, gesturing towards the door.

Bird shrugged. "This room used to be Street's dressing room, apparently. He *graciously* gave it up to accommodate me."

Fitzwilliam raised an eyebrow. Something in Bird's voice suggested he wasn't the chief superintendent's biggest fan. He tried to dredge his memory to see if he could recall any gossip about the two falling out, but he couldn't. Who did Bird report to now? Until recently, it had been his old boss, Superintendent Frances Copson. But hadn't there been a change after Street's promotion last year?

"So who do you work for now, Bird?"

Bird tilted his head away from the door. "Street," he said through a pinched mouth.

Oh dear, he's clearly not happy with the situation.

Bird's jaw clenched. "And he's—"

A knock on the door cut him off. Ruth Ness's oval face appeared around the frame as she flipped down the mouthpiece on her headset. Raising one thin eyebrow sculpted with pencil, she said, "The chief superintendent is back now, chief inspector, and ready to see you." She smiled and disappeared back around the door, leaving it ajar.

Fitzwilliam remained seated. He wanted to hear what Bird had to say about Street, but Bird rose. "You'd better not keep the boss waiting," he said, an edge to his voice.

Fitzwilliam stood and picked up his mug. "Thanks for the coffee," he said as he placed the empty cup by the side of the coffee machine. He held out his hand to Bird. "It was good to see you, Henry. Give Adler a shout. She's at home, but I'm confident she'll be happy to talk to you about Preece." Maybe they could help each other out?

Bird shook the offered hand. "I'll do that. Thanks, Fitzwilliam."

8

11 AM, THURSDAY 28 JANUARY

Ruth Ness gazed up as Fitzwilliam entered the outer office. "He'll see you now," she uttered, pointing at the office behind her. Through the ajar door, Fitzwilliam could make out Chief Superintendent Tim Street at his desk, flipping through some documents. Fitzwilliam rapped on the open door before entering. He squinted as he stepped into the office. Light filled the room, which was full of books and files. Its walls hung with certificates and awards.

"Ah, Fitzwilliam," Street said as he emerged from behind his desk. He moved closer to Fitzwilliam and extended his hand for a warm handshake. "I apologise for not being here earlier. I had some urgent business to attend to, but I'm glad we can finally talk without interruption."

"It's no problem, sir," Fitzwilliam replied politely.

Street gestured towards one of the plush leather chairs near his desk before taking his own seat again. He paused for a moment and then looked directly at Fitzwilliam. "So what did you need to speak to me about?"

Fitzwilliam took a deep breath and met Street's gaze. He

saw a look of understanding in the chief superintendent's eyes. *He knows what I'm about to say...*

"Is this about the Earl of Rossex's death, Fitzwilliam?" Street asked curtly as he leaned back in his chair. "I know there are still many questions *you* feel you need answers to, but we agreed there was no more to be done." His voice was soft yet firm. "I thought I made it clear it was time to move on."

Fitzwilliam could tell Street meant every word he said. "But, sir, has it occurred to you that someone hired Gill Sterling to get close to James Wiltshire?"

Street's brows creased deeply, his eyes narrowing to slits as if he was trying to see through the fog to an answer. "To what end?"

"To compromise him."

Street's expression was unreadable, his gaze drifting skywards as if lost in thought. His body remained still, his mouth set in a tight line as he weighed up the possibility of Fitzwilliam's suggestion. Fitzwilliam could tell Street was warming to the idea and continued, "Perhaps she was working for the press?"

Street leaned forward in his chair and folded his hands under his chin. Then he let out a long breath through pursed lips. He nodded slowly. "It's certainly feasible. It would explain the money you found in her bank account." He rubbed his chin thoughtfully. "In fact, it would explain quite a lot..." His voice trailed off as he made a move to get up from his seat. "Um, well, thank you, Fitzwilliam. It's food for thought, but—"

"I think there could also be another possibility, sir," Fitzwilliam blurted out as he shifted in his seat. Street dropped back down into his chair with a barely disguised sigh. Fitzwilliam was afraid Street was getting fed up with him and would dismiss his idea out of hand, but there was no turning back now. "Maybe she was being paid to find out what the earl knew," he said carefully, watching for Street's reaction.

Street's shoulders tightened. Then he cleared his throat and leaned back in his chair. "About what?" he asked, his voice level and controlled.

"Just before his death, James Wiltshire was concerned about something he'd found out in Miami when he was there in the October." Fitzwilliam paused, his heart racing as Street's eyes widened.

"What kind of something?" Street asked quickly, curiosity etched into every word.

Fitzwilliam shook his head slowly. "I don't know, sir," he muttered softly, feeling a twinge of disappointment in himself. He looked up to see the chief superintendent studying him thoughtfully and cleared his throat before continuing, "But according to my source, something the earl discovered in Miami was really bothering him."

"Who's this contact of yours?" Street asked, his words laced with a razor-sharp edge, each one said with a distinct authority.

Narrowing his eyes, Fitzwilliam tensed up at the question. Suddenly, he was hesitant to share the information.

"Well?" Street demanded, his expression stern and intense, his eyes narrowed and focused.

"It's someone who knew him during his early days with MI6." *Was that too vague?*

Street seemed to consider his words, his eyes still focused on Fitzwilliam. He sighed heavily and leaned forward in his chair. "You seem reluctant to give me a name, Fitzwilliam. I don't understand why."

Swallowing hard, a chill ran down Fitzwilliam's spine as

Street's gaze remained fixed on him. He fought the urge to lean back in his chair, away from the chief superintendent's powerful presence. *What's wrong with me?* He'd never felt intimidated by Street before. But now, as silence descended, thick and imposing like a blanket, Street's gaze held him motionless. Fitzwilliam was aware this man was one of the most powerful people in the organisation. He didn't want to get on the wrong side of him. But he couldn't ignore the feeling something was off. Taking another deep breath to steady himself, Fitzwilliam finally spoke up again. "I was told in strict confidence, sir," he said. Not technically true, but he just couldn't bring himself to put Brett Goodman's name out there. He didn't like the man's smarminess or his predatory behaviour around Lady Beatrice, but he didn't want to get him into trouble.

Street crossed his arms and nodded slowly. "Very well," he said firmly. "I respect your judgement, so we'll leave it for now. But be aware, if the need arises, I may have to pursue this further. Do you understand?"

Fitzwilliam nodded, then taking a deep breath, he relaxed his muscles. He hadn't realised until then just how tense he'd been throughout the entire exchange. He couldn't shake the feeling something was not right here, but he was relieved to have avoided having to give up Brett Goodman's name.

"So tell me what you know."

Fitzwilliam gave Street an abridged version of what Brett had told him before continuing. "He questioned if he could trust his MI6 contact. I think that implies the information was important and possibly concerned national security."

Street shrugged, now appearing to have lost interest. "That's not much information to go on, is it, Fitzwilliam?" He waved his hand dismissively. "Implications and possibilities aren't enough. The earl was in Miami as part of the preparations for our Olympic bid, wasn't he?"

Fitzwilliam nodded. "The bid team were there having a look at how Miami had done things four years before."

"So it stands to reason it was something to do with that, doesn't it?" Street crossed his arms and leaned back in his chair. "It was all a long time ago, Fitzwilliam. Whatever it was, it's most likely no longer relevant."

Fitzwilliam continued, determined to make him understand the gravity of the situation. "So why would he ask about MI6 if it was simply about the Olympic bid, sir?"

Street uncrossed his arms and leaned forward. "I don't know, Fitzwilliam." His voice was laced with exasperation. "But nothing you've told me is..." He trailed off and shook his head. "It's all just speculation."

"But Gill Sterling—"

"Was having an affair with the earl," Street jumped in. "That's still the most obvious reason she was in the car with him when they crashed." He placed his hands on the top of his desk and pushed himself upright. "There's nothing more to be done here, Fitzwilliam." He met Fitzwilliam's gaze. "It really is time to move on from this," he said firmly. "There's no evidence of foul play, and I fear we are only creating a tangled web of conspiracy theories that won't lead us anywhere. We must accept this and let it go now. Put it in the past where it belongs."

A heavy weight settled in Fitzwilliam's chest as he rose. He wanted so badly to make sense of what had happened, to have some sort of answer for Lady Beatrice when she inevitably asked. But now it seemed like all hope was lost. He'd failed her and let her down when she deserved to know the truth. "Yes, sir. Thank you." Fitzwilliam turned and trudged towards the door, his head bowed.

When he stepped outside into the dreary corridor, a wave of regret washed over him. *Should I have done more? Could I have pushed further to uncover the truth?* All his and Lady Beatrice's efforts had been in vain, and all that was left was an unanswered mystery. He huffed, then slowly made his way back to his office.

————

Chief Superintendent Tim Street cursed under his breath. Why wouldn't Fitzwilliam just let it go? He sat down, rested his elbows on the edge of his desk and interlocked his fingers. He'd underestimated Fitzwilliam's ability to dig beneath the surface for the truth. Sighing deeply, he ran his hands through his short grey hair. Fitzwilliam was getting too close. Street had done his best to throw him off the scent, but he was unsure if he'd done enough to put an end to his meddling.

He stilled for a moment as he entertained the idea of taking direct action against Fitzwilliam. Should he make a call? He quickly dismissed it as too risky. It would be too soon after Preece's demise. Anyway, he didn't want *them* to know there was an issue. He didn't want them getting any more jumpy than they already were.

He rested his chin in his hands and shook his head. He still couldn't believe they'd done such a sloppy job of silencing Preece. The man was a fool, of course. Preece should have known after all these years that they wouldn't pay him off and let him go just because he'd had enough. Street snorted. If it was that simple, he'd have taken the option years ago…

Forgetting Fitzwilliam for the moment, he unclasped his hands, and lowering his arms, he drummed the fingers of his left hand on his desktop. He needed to get back to the detective inspector from City Police. *What's her name?* He reached out with his other hand and flipped open his laptop. Tapping the mouse pad, the screen came to life. He stopped drumming and entered his password. His emails appeared before him. Madeline Carmichael. That's her. Detective Inspector Madeline Carmichael from City's Organised Crime Unit. *A routine inquiry about DI Preece*, he read. What did that mean? He had a bad feeling she wanted to talk about Preece and the recent rumours about his connections. *What happened to Preece?* He'd always been so reliable in the past — staying in the background, not bringing attention to himself. He sighed wearily. He'd have to smooth things over with this DI. *Maybe I'm worrying too much?* After all, if she had anything concrete, he would have heard about it by now.

His mind flitted back to Fitzwilliam. He should find out who had told him about James's worries about what he'd discovered in Miami. He might have to do some damage limitation there. Grabbing the handset of the phone just to his right, he pressed the green button. "Ruth?"

"Yes, sir?" The woman's voice was businesslike, as always.

A grin crept onto his face. It never ceased to amaze him how efficient his executive assistant of five years was, always ready for him when he needed her. "Can you tell me who the guests were at Lord Frederick Astley's shooting event at Drew Castle this past month? The one where that Rhodes chap was killed?"

"Yes, sir."

"Oh, and Ruth? Please be discreet."

"Yes, of course, sir."

9

8:30 AM, FRIDAY 29 JANUARY

"So he told you to go away and forget all about it?" DCI Emma McKeer-Adler's voice mirrored the frustration Richard Fitzwilliam was still feeling twenty-four hours after his meeting with CS Tim Street.

"Pretty much," Fitzwilliam confirmed. "He thinks it's all just speculation, and there's nothing solid enough to warrant any further investigation."

"Well," she huffed down the phone. "I'm disappointed in him. I thought he'd want to get to the truth too."

Fitzwilliam sighed and glanced out of the window of his office. He took in the well-manicured grounds of Gollingham Palace below. The sun was still low in the sky, painting the landscape in a glorious yellow hue that illuminated every detail. Staff arriving for work scurried around like ants on an anthill, all trying to reach their destination as quickly as possible. For a moment, Fitzwilliam felt removed from it all, isolated within his office.

"So have you told Lady Beatrice yet?" Adler's question dragged his attention away from the window, and he stared at the office phone on his desk, the amber light showing he was on speaker.

He sighed. "No, not yet. I'm not sure how to break it to her that there isn't much else we can do. Especially since we rather got her hopes up when we talked about it back at Drew Castle."

"Yes. I rather think that was partly my fault," Adler said apologetically. "But when she explained what you'd found out about Gill pretending to be abused by her husband and the money in her bank account, it just seemed to make sense to me that Gill was being paid to get close to the earl."

Or was she being paid to find out what he knew about Miami? Fitzwilliam, about to share his thoughts with Adler, remembered she didn't know the full picture. Only he and Lady Beatrice knew about James's conversation with CIA agent Brett Goodman the week he'd died. They'd agreed not to share Brett's position to protect Lady Beatrice's brother's role as an MI6 Special Observer. A position that, unbeknownst to Lady Beatrice at the time, James had also held until his death. Fitzwilliam closed his mouth. "I think we all got a bit carried away about maybe finding something new and significant. The issue is that without Street's support, we're back facing the same brick wall."

"You *are* going to tell her, aren't you?"

Fitzwilliam rubbed his hand over his chin, the slight stubble grazing his palm. He knew he would have to see her soon. She'd be waiting to find out how he'd got on. "Yes, of course. I'll see her this afternoon." Eager to ignore the problem for later, he changed the subject. "So how are you feeling today?"

"Great," Adler said eagerly. "I've found out some stuff about Preece. Do you have time for me to tell you?"

Fitzwilliam smiled. She'd listened patiently while he'd

unloaded his frustration about yesterday's meeting. The least he could do was return the favour. Plus, it was great to hear Adler sounding full of life again. Like the pre-accident Adler he knew so well. "Sure, let me have it."

"So, as you suggested, I started on his career. Now how's this for a coincidence... Preece was on the City team that helped with the investigation into the Earl of Rossex's accident."

Fitzwilliam, his hands on the armrests of his chair, about to lever himself up so he could stretch his legs, froze.

"Really?" He sank back into his black leather chair, its musty smell strangely comforting as it enveloped him. "That's interesting. What was his role in it?"

"He was a newly promoted detective sergeant back then. They sent him and a constable to gather the earl's belongings from the flat in Knightsbridge Court." James Wiltshire, the Earl of Rossex, had been planning to spend the night in London ahead of some personal errands he'd had to perform the next day. He'd left an overnight bag at the flat when he'd inexplicably driven back to Fenshire on that fateful night.

"According to the records, he delivered the bag in person to Fenshire CID." She sounded unsure.

Fitzwilliam frowned. He'd hand-delivered it? That was unusual. CID had had HQ return those contents to Lady Beatrice after the case had been officially closed, but someone had mistakenly stored that bag in the archives. That hadn't been known until nine years later when a letter had fallen out during the relocation of the items in the archives. And then it had been his sorry job to take it to her. He tugged his lip with his teeth. That hadn't been a pleasant task...

"So I did a little digging through the files from the investigation. I found a copy of a memo he'd written to Fenshire CID during the investigation, responding to the itemised contents list. He asked them if they'd listed everything. Written in pen on the copy is just one word — 'letter' with a question mark after it."

Fitzwilliam's skin tingled. The letter. Had Preece been looking for the letter James Wiltshire had written to his wife? But he wouldn't have known about it at the time. Had he or someone else added the word later, after the letter had surfaced six years ago? But even then, the only people who had known about the letter were him, the Fenshire police officer in charge of the archives, and Tim Street who had been a superintendent at the time. Street had been the PaIRS-MI6 liaison and had had a watching brief over the investigation because of the earl's secret involvement with MI6. Had Preece also known about it?

"Do you think he knew about the letter?" Adler seemed to be on the same track as him.

"It's possible. But I don't know how." He'd never told Adler or indeed anyone at the time about the letter. Lady Beatrice had eventually destroyed it, but it had been his and Lady Beatrice's secret that it had ever existed. That was, until last year when she'd told Perry Juke and Simon Lattimore and more recently when she'd told Adler and Izzy at Drew Castle a few weeks ago. "Until last year, the only people who knew about it as far as I'm aware were me, Lady Beatrice, and a Fenshire police archivist."

Adler pushed, "But it was all over the papers for days last year while you were investigating Alex Sterling's murder, wasn't it? So who told the press? Could it have been Preece?" Her voice had got louder.

Had Preece been Desmond Brooke's informant? The editor of *The Daily Post* had always been confident over there being a letter. He had just been unable to produce it. Even if it had been Preece, why would that make him a target eight months later? Desmond Brooke was many things, but he wasn't someone who would have an informant killed for giving him unsubstantiated information. No, the whole thing was crazy. They were going down a rabbit hole that wasn't going to do anything but get them stuck.

"I'm not sure any of this is relevant. It's interesting that he was on the investigation with us and we didn't know, but it has to be something more recent than a fifteen-year-old closed case that would lead to someone wanting him dead."

She let out a deep sigh. "Yes, I suppose you're right."

"Anything else about the jobs he did or his promotion reports, that sort of thing?"

"He did the usual stints in the drugs unit, murder investigation, and was a trained firearms officer. He was also involved in City's gang unit when it was first set up just before he made sergeant." She chuckled. "Oh, and there was something else. Guess who recommended him for a bravery award twenty-odd years ago when Preece was still a DC?"

"No idea, but I'm guessing it's someone we both know?"

"Yes. Tim Street!"

Fitzwilliam's head spun. So Preece had known Street? Was that how Preece had known about the letter? Had Street told him? But why would he have?

Adler continued, "Street was an inspector at City back then. Small world, isn't it?"

Is it? Fitzwilliam didn't know what to think. He sighed. "Anything else?" He hoped not. He needed time to process all this.

"Not at the moment, but I'll keep digging."

"That's a good idea."

"Okay. Well, I guess I should go. Unless, of course, you think I should be there to help with—"

"No! You've got a few more weeks before you're allowed back. You're supposed to be resting, remember?"

"But if I just—"

"Adler, I swear if you come anywhere near this building—"

She huffed. "Okay. I get the message."

"Just carry on with your digging and get some rest. I'll speak to you later."

After the call ended, he reached for his mobile phone and opened up the text app. He typed a message to Lady Beatrice suggesting they met for coffee later that day. Hitting the send button quickly, he dropped his phone back on the desk with a short *thump*. He would have to tell her now. Leaning back in his chair, he stared out of the window, his mind turning over what Adler had just told him about Preece. He shook his head. *It's all just a coincidence that Preece knew Tim Street and was involved in the earl's accident investigation…isn't it?*

10

2 PM, FRIDAY 29 JANUARY

"I'm really sorry, but I think we're out of options." Detective Chief Inspector Richard Fitzwilliam looked down at the blue cotton tablecloth and wiped an invisible crumb away from in front of him. "If Street won't, er…help us, then I can't do much more."

Sitting opposite, Lady Beatrice, her hand resting on the head of her little terrier curled up beside her, saw a muscle in the side of his jaw twitch and noticed the way the shadows in the corners of his eyes deepened. *He's obviously feeling bad about his lack of progress.*

She couldn't help but feel a little sorry for him, though she doubted he would welcome her sympathy. She twisted the rings on her right hand and let out a deep breath. Her clenched stomach relaxed. Although the disappointment was real, deep down she'd known all along they were clutching at straws. It had been fifteen years since James's car accident. No one was going to sanction reopening the investigation into his death even if they'd found out new information about his relationship with Gill Sterling.

She took a sip of her coffee and scanned the room. The

senior staff dining room at Gollingham Palace was bright and cheerful, with large windows overlooking the gardens. The pale yellow walls added a subtle splash of colour to frame the fine works of art from the royal collection displayed on them. Mahogany tables of various sizes, some occupied, others not, were set around the room, with chairs upholstered in a deep-blue fabric. Over by the far wall, a large sideboard ran the length of the room, with cups, saucers, cutlery, and plates piled at one end and coffee, tea, milk, and sugar at the other. In between were serving platters laden with scones, cakes, and biscuits.

Three deep-red velvet couches were arranged around a wooden table in front of a wood-burning stove on the far side of the room. Two grey-haired men, glasses of brandy in hand, sat on one sofa, their heads together, deep in a discussion. Bea suppressed a smile. It was well known within the family that the serious work that kept the monarchy running like a well-oiled machine was done in this very room.

She turned back to Fitzwilliam, who was now drinking his coffee. Bea cleared her throat. "I think deep down I wasn't holding out much hope anyone could do anything after such a long time," she said, trying to keep the disappointment out of her voice. "I just hate not knowing..." She hesitated. *What is it I really want to know?* It wasn't about why James had gone home that night when he had been due to be in London or what had been bothering him in Miami. In truth, she wanted to know if a clever woman had manipulated James into leaving her and their life together or if he'd simply fallen in love. She swallowed and took another sip of her coffee.

Fitzwilliam looked up at her, his dark eyes scanning her face, then he leaned forward, his piercing gaze fixed on her.

"You're wondering if James was conned into leaving by Gill Sterling."

Bea's eyebrows shot up. She'd never seen Fitzwilliam as the perceptive type, especially when it came to feelings, but he seemed to have hit the nail on the head. Heat rose in her cheeks, and she looked away. "I don't know," she answered honestly, her voice barely above a whisper as she buried her fingers in the wiry fur of Daisy's back. "I just... I don't understand why I didn't notice he was so unhappy. I thought we wanted the same things…"

Fitzwilliam sighed and leaned back in his chair. He ran a hand through his hair, and she could tell he was choosing his words carefully. "It happens," he said hesitantly. "I didn't know my wife was having an affair until it was too late."

Bea's heart skipped a beat. Her gaze met Fitzwilliam's, and he gave her a reassuring smile. She grabbed her coffee and took a large gulp. She hadn't expected him to open up like that, especially not when he was so distant and unemotional most of the time. *Well, except for when he was telling me off for interfering in his cases…*

"My wife left me for another man," Fitzwilliam continued quietly, almost as if he were talking to himself now rather than conversing with Bea. "I didn't know she was unhappy. I was so wrapped up in my work, trying to progress my career. I never really paid enough attention to how she felt, even though now I can look back and see that she tried to tell me." He sighed and shook his head. "I was in shock for a while. My entire world crashed down around me, and I didn't see it coming. But as I picked up the pieces and moved on, I was able to admit I'd been so focussed on making a future for us, I'd forgotten about living in the present."

Bea moved her jaw from side it side. Her fingers were curled around her warm mug of coffee like a lifeline. Who was this man sitting across from her, sharing his personal story in an attempt to…what? Make her feel better about not seeing that her marriage was unravelling or to show that he, too, had been blindsided by the end of a relationship? Either way, she appreciated his effort, even if it was a little clumsy. He was seeming to imply that maybe things hadn't been as great with James as she'd remembered.

She stifled a groan. Had the signs been there, and she'd simply missed them? She glanced over at Fitzwilliam, now engrossed in his coffee cup again. *What happened to his wife and the man she ran off with? It would be rude to ask, wouldn't it? Yes!* She sat back and let the silence, thick like fog, curl around them like a veil of understanding.

Fitzwilliam shifted in his chair and cleared his throat, as if suddenly embarrassed by what he'd shared. He gave her a forced smile and said lightly, "Anyway, it was a long time ago now." He shrugged. "And life goes on. I'd like to think I've learnt my lesson and changed because of it, but I bet if you asked Elise, she'd say I'm just as work obsessed as ever." He grinned sheepishly. Bea grinned back. She'd met Fitzwilliam's sister last year and could imagine Elise wouldn't hold her punches with her older brother.

Just then, Daisy stretched beside her and sat up, looking towards the doorway. Bea followed her little dog's gaze as Detective Sergeant Tina Spicer walked into the room. Daisy gave a low *woof* and jumped down as Bea smiled. It had been a few months since she'd last seen Fitzwilliam's right-hand woman. She'd missed her presence during their last case in Scotland even though Spicer had been at the other end of the phone to support Fitzwilliam. Seeing Daisy, Spicer stopped and bent down to greet the little terrier before looking up and spotting Bea. The DS nodded, then quickened her pace, her long blonde bob swishing around her shoulders as she made her way across the room, Daisy at her heels. It was only then Bea noticed a woman with long straight black hair following behind Spicer. She wore a business suit — a sleek black number with a crisp white shirt and was looking around the room like she was unsure if she should be here or not. *I wonder who that is…*

Spicer had a broad smile on her face as she approached Bea. She held out her hand. "It's good to see you again, Lady Beatrice," she said warmly.

"Likewise," Bea responded as she stood and shook it. "We missed not having you with us at Drew Castle."

"Thank you, my lady. Although you did a pretty good job without me there."

Fitzwilliam cleared his throat, and Spicer glanced at him before gesturing to the woman behind her. "Sir, this is DS Arabella Hardwick from Intelligence, who I mentioned to you this morning."

Fitzwilliam rose and held his hand out to the sergeant. "Good to meet you, DS Hardwick. I'm sure Spicer here will look after you well."

"Thank you, sir. I'm very grateful she's taking the time to help me," Hardwick said, the trace of a London accent just perceptible.

Spicer turned to Bea. "My lady, can I introduce Detective Sergeant Arabella Hardwick? She's taking part in a mentoring program I'm involved in and will shadow me for the next few weeks." Bea stood as Spicer turned to the DS. "Bella, this is Lady Beatrice, the Countess of Rossex."

Hardwick's eyes widened, and she froze on the spot as if she hadn't expected to meet the very people her organisation was sworn to protect. Bea smiled to herself. The DS quickly recovered and offered Bea a hesitant handshake.

Bea smiled warmly at Hardwick, taking in the woman's

obvious discomfort. "It's nice to meet you, Detective Sergeant Hardwick," she said kindly as they shook hands. "And this bundle of trouble," Bea added, looking at Daisy, who was now sitting by Fitzwilliam's leg, "is Daisy." Hardwick glanced at the little dog and smiled. Bea turned to Spicer. "Are you joining us, sergeant?"

Spicer glanced at Fitzwilliam, who gave a curt nod. "Yes, my lady," she said with a smile as she walked around him and took the seat opposite Bea.

"Indeed. Excellent," Bea said as she sat down and quickly brushed the chair beside her. "Please sit down, sergeant."

Hardwick seemed slightly taken aback by Bea's offer but quickly nodded. "Thank you, my lady."

Fitzwilliam moved to the front of the table. "I'll get drinks. Tea, Spicer?" he asked.

"Yes, please, sir."

"Hardwick, tea or coffee?"

"Tea, please, sir."

"More coffee, Lady Beatrice?"

Bea smiled at him gratefully and nodded. "That would be lovely. Thank you, Fitzwilliam." Bea watched Fitzwilliam move across the room towards the sideboard with Daisy trotting beside him, then turned to the woman sitting next to her. "So what does this mentoring program involve, sergeant?"

"Well, it's part of my career development in PaIRS, my lady. I get assigned a mentor. In my case, it's Chief Superintendent Street. He advises and provides guidance to help me through my career. We meet up once a month to review my progress. I'm given tasks and challenges to understand investigation and protection and to improve my skills. The program also involves shadowing experienced officers so I can learn from them on the job."

Hardwick paused as Fitzwilliam returned with the drinks

and distributed them around the table before taking his seat. Daisy curled up by his feet. The DS continued as she picked up her cup of tea. "I'm enjoying it immensely."

Bea smiled in response, taking a sip of her coffee. She was impressed with how professional and organised the scheme appeared. "Well, it sounds like an excellent scheme, Sergeant Hardwick. It seems a very effective way of ensuring you are well prepared for whatever tasks you may face in your career." She darted a look at Fitzwilliam, who was about to take a sip of his coffee. "And how do you find CS Street?" Fitzwilliam gave her a puzzled look as he lowered his cup.

Hardwick hesitated, spots of red appearing in her cheeks. "Er, he's been...well, you know, quite supportive so far." It seemed to Bea the woman was struggling to find the right words. "But you know he's super busy all the time. It's a much more frantic environment than I'm used to in Intelligence," she said with a wry smile. "His EA Ruth has been a real help though. In fact, I'm working on a report for the CS at the moment." She pulled a face, then gave a nervous laugh. "I have to present it to him and two DCI's next week. I'm bricking it, if I'm honest."

Fitzwilliam smiled knowingly. "You don't need to be nervous. They won't bite. I'm sure it will go well." He caught Bea's eye and winked.

Ah, so he's one of them...

They chatted amicably for a short while, with Fitzwilliam telling Hardwick what a shock it had been for him when he'd first moved from Intelligence to Investigation and Protection. He assured her it would be a good experience, especially if she ever wanted to move from one to the other. After a short while, Spicer looked at her phone and rose. "Right, we really need to get on. I'm showing Bella where we store evidence."

Fitzwilliam rose. "I'll see you back in the office later."

Bea nodded and smiled at the two women as they left, then turned to face Fitzwilliam as he sat back down. "I really need to be going—"

"Why did you ask Hardwick about Street?"

She hesitated, realising how it must have sounded to him. "I was just interested to hear what she thought of him. The way you reported on your meeting with him, I got the impression you don't quite trust him."

"No, that's not true," he said firmly but not unkindly. "Why do you think I don't trust him?"

Have I upset him? No, she didn't think so. She could tell from his tone, he wasn't angry, more curious. She ran her hand through her long auburn hair and shrugged. "Just a feeling I had..." She let out a deep sigh before looking back at Fitzwilliam. "You know how sometimes my woman's intuition kicks in, and I don't know when to keep my mouth shut..."

Fitzwilliam chuckled. He'd teased her before about her woman's intuition, although these days, he was less inclined to dismiss it as he had been when they'd first met.

Bea continued, "I'm sorry; it's really none of my business."

Fitzwilliam gave her a small nod of understanding before leaning back in his chair and folding his arms across his chest. After a moment, he said, "Well, I can assure you it's nothing like that."

She rose. "Indeed... Good... Well, I need to find Perry. Thank you for everything."

He stood and bowed his head slightly. "You're welcome. It was a pleasure talking with you, as always."

She looked at his face to see if he was being sarcastic, but he was openly smiling at her. She still wasn't used to this new and improved Fitzwilliam. Bea smiled at the compliment before turning to her little dog. "Come on, Daisy," she said as the terrier got up and did a little shake.

As she walked away, Fitzwilliam spoke again. "Although I still don't know how much I believe in this woman's intuition of yours…"

Bea turned back and gave him a mischievous smirk as she replied, "Oh, I think there have been plenty of occasions when it's been spot on. Like the time—"

He raised his hand, laughing. "Okay, okay. I believe you. See you later, my lady."

With a grin plastered on her face, she walked across the room and out the door.

Stepping out into the corridor, she couldn't help but feel a little proud of herself; she thought she'd handled that encounter well. Things certainly seemed to be getting easier between them. She sighed. She still thought there was something odd about Street though. *Maybe I can engineer a meeting with him and make up my own mind?*

11

MORNING, SATURDAY 30 JANUARY

"I told you he'd be up for it, Bea." Perry Juke sounded smug on the other end of the phone. "So when will you move in?"

Bea swapped her mobile phone to her other hand and wiped her palm down the side of her jeans. She leaned back against the bannisters in the cavernous hallway of The Dower House and sighed. "I don't know. We're here now, and there's a lot to do…"

Taking a deep breath, she looked around in awe. The grand foyer was huge and lofty, with an intricately carved ceiling and walls lined with paneling. A wide staircase swept up ahead of her to the other floors of the house. Even in its current state, there were still hints of how lavish this place had been when she and James had lived here. Fifteen years ago, after she'd moved out and it had become clear she wasn't coming back, the place had been emptied of all her and James's personal effects. The more expensive items of furniture had been put in storage and replaced with more basic and less valuable items from the estate. The house had been rented out, mainly to families of those who'd been getting married in the famous Francis Court orangery or to friends of her parents who'd wanted a few days away in the country. "It's got a distinctly shabby country look to it at the moment," she told him as her eyes fell on the peeling paint-work on the skirting board and moved up to the faded wall-paper hanging above the panelling. "It's looking neglected, you know — scuffed walls, dusty furniture, and carpets in need of replacing."

"But it's all easily fixable, I assume?" Perry asked.

"Indeed. It just needs some TLC. Nothing structural from what I can see, although I'll get the estate surveyor to check it out just to be on the safe side."

"And the kitchen?"

"Sam's down there now with Mrs Fraser. I imagine he wants everything replaced with state-of-the-art appliances and marble worktops! Mrs Fraser will hopefully tone down his requirements a bit, and we'll agree on a compromise that doesn't cost a fortune." She smiled, wishing more than anything that Perry was here to see this place with her. They could discuss the options together and make a plan. He had an eye for detail, and it would be wonderful to hear his suggestions about what needed doing. "I hope you can come and see it soon. I need help."

She ambled down the hallway and entered a large drawing room. Tall windows dominated the place and framed the wintery landscape outside. Bea had always loved this room with its bright, airy atmosphere. She'd spent countless hours in here reading or talking to James about upcoming public duties or just enjoying the peace and quiet together. Now it was rather bare, with only a few pieces of furniture scattered around. She closed her eyes and could still picture how beautiful it had been when they'd been living here.

"I'm sorry I couldn't make it back home this weekend. With Simon's book signing being just down the road from here tonight and his reading event tomorrow in Central London, I would have missed him completely if I'd gone back to Fenshire."

"I know." Bea was pleased Simon Lattimore's nationwide promotional book tour for his recently released ninth crime novel was going well. She also knew how much Perry missed his fiancé when he was away. She missed Simon too. "Is he still buzzing from it all?" she asked as she stepped through the connecting door, into the dining room. Memories came flooding back just as strongly. This was where she and James had hosted lavish dinners for family members and friends alike, where they'd celebrated special occasions. A place full of laughter and love. The emptiness in the middle of the room filled her heart with profound sadness. She shook her head. *Come on, Bea. It's time to make fresh memories.* As soon as they redid this room, she and Sam would host Perry and Simon for a slap-up meal.

"You can say that again!" Perry said, dragging her back to the present. "He's had queues of readers lined up at his book signings, and the reviews have been great so far."

"Are you going to the signing he's doing this afternoon?" she asked.

"Yes, I'm going to sit next to him and hand him books to sign. It's ages since I've been involved with his book stuff, and I'm quite excited. Then after that, we're going over to Em and Izzy's for a late supper."

Really? Bea's heart sank. Perry was going to the book signing, then meeting up with Adler and Izzy for supper? That all sounded fabulous. She stifled a huff. They were all having fun without her... "Oh, that sounds nice," she said, her voice flat. There was a strange feeling in her stomach, something she hadn't quite experienced before. Perry and Adler had been exchanging funny text messages during the last week, *and* they had been huddled together over dinner on Wednesday. Did Perry prefer spending time with Adler over spending time with her? Bea tried to push the thought out of her head and focus on what Perry was saying, but the feeling was growing stronger.

Am I jealous? If so, it was certainly a new feeling for her. Was she going to lose her best friend to these new people? The thought terrified her, so she dismissed it quickly from her mind and stood in the bare room, listening to Perry talk about his upcoming plans with Simon over the weekend.

Suddenly, he stopped babbling. "What's wrong, Bea? You've gone quiet."

She let out an inaudible sigh. "It sounds fun. I just wish I was there too."

"So do I. It's not the same without you here…"

Bea felt the warmth of Perry's words, and immediately, all of her doubts and fears melted away. How silly she'd been to think Perry would replace her. She should know better than to feel insecure like this.

He continued, "And I'm desperate to get my hands on that house of yours too!"

She smiled, looking around her. "I'll tell you what. I'll send you a video of some of the rooms downstairs. You can see what you think."

"Perfect!" he replied.

Just then, there was a muffled voice from below. Bea glanced towards the stairs leading to the basement. "Sam's calling. I better go down and see what ridiculous demands he has for its improvement. Have a lovely afternoon and evening. Say hi to everyone from me."

After Perry said goodbye, she walked along the corridor and through the open door leading to the basement. The wide stairs made of a mahogany-coloured wood were worn from years of use. Half-way down, a large landing was illuminated by a small cluster of ceiling lights, and as she descended further, she ran her hands along a groove in the aged walls where the stone had softened and was now shiny. At the bottom of the stairs was a small alcove that led to the different rooms in the basement. To her left was a corridor that went to the butler's pantry, housekeeper's office, laundry room, and wine cellar. On the right was the kitchen and a small staff dining area. As Bea entered the kitchen, Sam and Mrs Fraser were standing around a large cast iron range, discussing ideas of how to modernise the room. They greeted Bea warmly, both clearly excited about the changes they were proposing, and she listened as they explained their plans.

She couldn't help but smile at the pair. Her fourteen-year-old son, now at just over five foot ten, stood at least eight inches above the plump white-haired woman beside him. Maggie Fraser and her husband William had run The Dower House for her and James ever since they had moved in here immediately after their marriage. When James had died and Bea had withdrawn to Francis Court, the Frasers had gone to work for Bea's sister Lady Sarah Rosdale. But once Sarah's family had grown up, Maggie had gone to work with Mrs Ward in the kitchens at Francis Court, and William had become the head footman. They had been ever since. Now they were looking to semi-retire, and Bea was hoping she could persuade the couple to come and live in the annex at The Dower House and look after the house and gardens, as well as her and Sam.

Bea grinned as the unlikely pair argued over the large black cooking range that took up most of one wall. Sam was keen to replace it with an induction hob and two electric ovens, but Maggie Fraser was having none of it. "I've cooked for twenty people on this range. I can tell you now, Master

Sam, you won't be able to do that with your fancy hobs and pokey little ovens." Sam looked over at Bea and pulled a face. She shrugged at him. He could fight his own battles with the determined cook. They both knew who would win in the end. She grinned. It was wonderful to see them buzzing with enthusiasm over the project, and Maggie's steadfast resolve that the range was only being removed "over my dead body", gave Bea hope that the Frasers were onboard with coming back to The Dower House.

Bea left the two of them to it and went back up the stairs, her hand lingering on the stone as she ascended. Arriving in the hallway, she took out her mobile phone and began filming. As she went, she took in all the details of the house she had once called her own. Her heart lightened at the thought of restoring it to a family home again. The winter sun streamed through the windows, into the long hallway, stippling the walls with light and shadow along its length. In one corner sat an enormous grandfather clock ticking away with a steady beat, its pendulum swinging in time with each chime of its bell. A thick red carpet runner ran down from under it, stretching over the tiled floor towards her feet like an offering from ancient royalty.

After she finished in the drawing room and the dining room, she moved on to the study — the room that had been James's domain. She felt a lump rise in her throat at the thought of him and the many hours he'd spent here. She surveyed the room, taking in all its little details. The walls were lined with a deep-navy wallpaper that had faded slightly. An oak desk stood against one wall, its surface cleared. *James's desk.* She paused the video, laid her phone on the top, and pulled out the large leather-bound chair tucked up under the desk. The seat still retained some of its original shine, as if waiting expectantly for James to return once more. She ran her fingers over the deep-red leather inset on the table's top, then moving her hand down to the front of the desk, she slowly tugged on one of the two ornate metal drawer handles, and the drawer slid open. *Empty.* Her stomach clenched. *Of course it's empty, silly.* All James's things had been removed after she'd moved out. She pressed her lips together tightly, trying her best to hold back the tears that threatened to spill. *Pull yourself together, Bea!* She took a deep breath. She could ask Fraser to uncover James's things from storage. *Yes, that's what I'll do. Just for my own purposes...*

Bea turned around and faced the opposite wall where a large painting of The Dower House's grounds James had commissioned shortly before his death hung, and she found herself lost in its beauty for several moments before turning away from it, her heart heavy but also filled with joy at being back in this place again. She took a deep breath and turned her attention to all the improvements she could make now she was back here — rearranging furniture and restoring some pieces she remembered being here, as well as replacing carpets. Maybe she would give this room to Sam to study in. With his exams coming up soon, he'd need somewhere tranquil to work when he was back home from boarding school at the weekends. James would have been so proud of Sam and the way he'd grown into such a responsible young man; she was sure he would have wanted this room to be part of Sam's journey. With a smile on her lips, she retrieved her phone from the top of the desk and pressed the record button as she moved around the room, occasionally making a comment for Perry about her ideas.

12

9 AM, MONDAY 1 FEBRUARY

"Your first appointment is at ten-thirty with a Detective Inspector Carmichael from City Police, sir."

CS Street's heart sped up. "From the Organised Crime Unit?"

Ruth Ness nodded. "Yes, sir."

So the DI had made an appointment already, had she? *That's quick.* He'd rather hoped it wouldn't be until next week at the earliest. He'd replied to Carmichael's email on Friday, saying he was very busy at the moment but would try to find time to see her in the next few weeks...

When he didn't reply straight away, Ruth continued, "She rang yesterday afternoon and was most insistent she see you as soon as possible. I asked her what it was regarding, but all she would say was that it was urgent." Her eyes narrowed. "I assumed you knew about it."

A wave of anxiety washed over him. Just a routine inquiry... *Hopefully.* She'd found out he and Preece had worked together in the past and probably just wanted some background on the man. He glanced up at Ruth, who was studying him intently. He didn't want to alarm her. *Pull yourself together. It's nothing.*

"Yes, yes, I remember. It just slipped my mind for a minute."

"Do you want me to ring her and put her off, sir?"

He clenched his jaw. *That's so tempting...* He smiled at Ruth. "No, no, it's fine. She probably wants some background on the inspector who died the other day. Preece. I knew him from way back, during my early days at City. And after that?"

"You'll need to leave for your lunch meeting with the Secretary of Defence, sir. I've booked you a car to take you to the House of Commons. You're eating there."

Street suppressed a sigh. He remembered the days when lunch with a government minister had meant slowly dining at their club, followed by a lazy afternoon drinking brandy and putting the world to rights. Now it was all business over a quick bite in the House of Commons' buffet restaurant with sparkling water and no dessert.

"Just to remind you, you need to have DCI Bird's appraisal form submitted by the end of the day." Her eyes moved to the almost completed handwritten assessment on his desk. Bird was a pain. Always asking questions, sticking his nose in. It had got even worse since he'd moved next door. *Should I give him a bad report and get him moved sideways, away from here, or a good one and get him promoted out of my hair?* "Yes. I'll make it my next job."

"Then later this afternoon..." Ruth continued to scroll. "You're meeting with Superintendent..."

Street let her words wash over him as his mind was pulled back to his meeting with DI Carmichael in an hour and a half. He'd been trying to ignore the sense of dread building within him since Ruth had told him about the appointment, but it was to no avail. How much did Carmichael know about Preece? *Could she have found out the real connection between us?* He would see if he could find out anything from Bird. He might be a pain, but sometimes he could be a useful source of information. Bird liaised with City a lot; he might know what she wanted.

"…and then a car will take you home and wait for you to get changed. The presentation starts at seven. You'll be expected to stay for at least an hour." Ruth took a breath and closed the lid of her tablet. "And that's it for today, sir. Oh, and I've emailed you the list of guests who stayed at Drew Castle that you asked for."

"Thank you, Ruth. Is Bird in today?"

"He's in his office now, sir. Do you want me to get him?"

He needed a few minutes to think. He didn't want to rouse Bird's interest by demanding to meet him now. "No, it's alright. It's nothing urgent. I'll catch up with him later. Oh, one thing, Ruth. I have George Rockcliffe coming in at about ten."

His assistant's eyes flew open wide. He stifled a snigger. Ruth hated it when he made plans on his own and didn't tell her until the last minute.

"George Rockcliffe?" Her voice had risen, and there was a scowl on her face.

Oops, I really have riled her up this time.

"Yes, you know, the approved contractor who's been selected to manage the rebuild of the offices." She said nothing, her silence unnerving him. *Maybe I can make her laugh.* "You know, the chubby guy with the enormous nose? Looks like Cyrano de Bergerac as played by that French actor chap."

"I know who you mean, sir," she said in an icy tone. "What I don't understand is why you needed to see him today *and* without running it by me first."

He felt like a naughty schoolboy being told off by the headmistress. *Enough now.* He didn't need her permission. *I'm the boss here.* He raised his chin. "Look, it's not a big deal, Ruth. I just want to see the final designs before they start work."

"But, sir, you have DI Carmichael coming in at—"

"I know, and he'll be gone by then, don't worry. It will take twenty minutes tops."

She stared at him for what seemed like an age, her steely green eyes piercing his, her mouth holding a slight pout. He suppressed a shiver. *She's not happy at all.* He sighed. He didn't have time for a stroppy assistant today. What with Carmichael snooping around and with the Preece thing being such a mess. He needed to get Carmichael off his back and then think of a strategy to deal with the fallout. *They* were getting jittery. He couldn't have that. "Look, I'm sorry, Ruth. I should have told you. I won't do it again, I promise." He gave her a hopeful smile. Ruth didn't return it; instead she nodded briskly and silently left the room.

Street let out a puff of air and frowned. He leaned back in his chair and rubbed his forehead, an endless loop of questions and worries whirling in his head. *Am I being paranoid?* Ever since Preece's death, he'd been unable to shake the feeling that it was all about to come crashing down around him. *But what can I do?* He had to keep his cool and act as if everything was under control. He needed to assure them he had all the loose ends tied up even if he wasn't sure that was true anymore. *Maybe I should just....*

He reached down and pulled at the handle of his bottom desk drawer. It didn't open. He looked down, expecting to see a bunch of keys sticking out of one of the drawers, but they weren't there. He frowned. *When did I last have them? Ah, yesterday...* That's right, he'd found them in his coat pocket when he'd got home. He couldn't remember how they'd got there, but he'd taken them out and hung them up by his car keys so he'd remember to bring them back in today. But of course he'd forgotten all about them when he'd left this morning. He swore under his breath. He'd need to pop back to his flat on his way to Westminster and pick them up just in case...

He huffed, then leaning forward, he tapped his mouse, and his screen came alive. One thing he *could* find out now was who Fitzwilliam's informant was and how likely it was that they knew more than Fitzwilliam was letting on. He clicked on the attachment in the email Ruth had sent him and opened it. His eyes scanned the Drew Castle guest list. Hector McLean, Fergus McLean, Edward Berry, and Rose Berry — he discarded each of them. He knew they'd only been invited to act as a smokescreen for the real purpose of Lord Frederick Astley's little gathering. Ben Rhodes and Max Rhodes — he dismissed them. They were no longer relevant. Eve Morrison — he nodded. The MI6 recruiter. Of course she'd been there to assess —

Street stopped as his eye came to the last name on the list, a name he hadn't expected to see. Brett Goodman. He frowned. What was a CIA agent doing at Drew Castle? Surely Goodman hadn't been there in an official capacity, or Street would have been told. He scrolled down through his old emails and found one from the beginning of January titled 'Shooting Party Guests — Drew Castle'. He opened it and read the note. Sure enough, there was no mention of the CIA or Brett Goodman. He closed it and sat back in his chair, letting out a deep sigh. Was this another thing he had to worry about, or was there some logical explanation?

Street chewed his lip as he reached for his mouse again. He clicked on the search bar in his email and typed in 'Brett

Goodman'. After a few seconds, an email popped up with 'fwd: Additional guest at Drew Castle' on the subject line. Street's shoulders relaxed as he read the contents of the message. It had been forwarded by Intelligence from Lord Frederick Astley's private secretary, informing PaIRS that Lord Frederick had invited a friend, Brett Goodman, who was in the UK on holiday, to join him at the shooting party. A note stating 'Vetted and approved' had been written above the original message. Street let out a sigh of relief. *I'm getting paranoid! I must have simply missed it...*

So the two most likely candidates to have known James Wiltshire fifteen years ago were Eve Morrison and Brett Goodman. Street opened a new tab and searched for Eve Morrison in the PaIRS database. Her record was labelled 'restricted', but it had a photo and some basic information. He nodded. As he'd thought, Eve was only in her late thirties and had joined MI6 at aged twenty-five. She wouldn't have been around when James had been involved with the national security organisation. He closed the record and searched for Brett Goodman. Again, there was limited information, but it confirmed Brett been the CIA-MI6 liaison sixteen years ago. That would have been about the time James had been recruited. Street slammed his hand down on his desk. *I've got it! Brett Goodman is Fitzwilliam's source of information.*

Street chuckled to himself in satisfaction. Fitzwilliam had been so reluctant to reveal his source earlier. *Fitzwilliam underestimated me!* Now the big question was — had Fitzwilliam told him everything, or did Goodman know more about Miami and what James had found out there? He'd have to do some more digging.

He glanced at his watch and jumped up from his chair. Finding out what Carmichael wanted to talk to him about was more pressing right this minute. *I need to talk to Bird.* He leaned over his desk and quickly logged out of the PaIRS database. He closed his laptop and headed for the door.

Ruth Ness was on the phone when he entered the outer office. She stopped talking immediately, politely telling her caller to, "Hold please." She raised an eyebrow at her boss. "Yes, sir?"

"Ruth, is Bird still in his office?"

She smiled and nodded, pointing to the door further down the hall. "I warned him you might need a word," she said. "I think he's waiting for you."

Street thanked her, then headed towards DCI Bird's office. He paused before entering. Taking a deep breath, he pushed the door open.

13

11:30 AM, MONDAY 1 FEBRUARY

In his corner office, Detective Chief Inspector Richard Fitzwilliam gazed out the window at the palace gardens below. He wished he was down there right now instead of stuck here with a mountain of paperwork. His mind meandered off to the conversation he'd had with Lady Beatrice on Friday. He still couldn't quite believe he'd told her about the breakdown of his marriage. He never really spoke of it to anyone. And yet there he'd been, blurting out that his wife had run off with another man.

He huffed. Lady Beatrice had clearly been slightly shocked at his confession. Had she also thought to herself, *I'm not surprised*? Maybe. He knew from their clashes in the past that her opinion of him was that he was high-handed and ungrateful for her help. And yet...he'd thought he'd seen a flash of sadness in her eyes. Had that been for him or for herself? He'd had an urge to reach out and take her hand to comfort her, but he couldn't have done that, of course; it was his job to protect her, not make a grab for her.

He rubbed the back of his head. She looked hurt and lost whenever James's betrayal with Gill Sterling was mentioned.

He wished he could help her find closure, but with Street unwilling to pursue their new leads, it was unlikely he could do any more. Her sad green eyes flashed before him, and he sighed. Should he tackle Street again? Be more insistent about the new information needing investigating? The office phone on his desk beeped, and a button lit up green.

Fitzwilliam shook his head to clear it and returned to the present. He leaned over his desk and grabbed the handset. "Yes, Carol?"

"Chief inspector, I have Superintendent Blake on the phone." She lowered her voice to an almost whisper. "And he doesn't sound happy."

That's just want I need — an unhappy boss. What was it now? Had he or one of his team upset his exacting superior? Or had Lady Beatrice stumbled over a dead body while she was here at Gollingham Palace? He wouldn't put it past her. After all, it wouldn't be the first time. *She really is a trouble magnet...*

He suppressed a sigh. "Thanks, Carol. Please put him through."

The line clicked, and the deep voice of Superintendent Blake filled Richard's ears. "Richard, I have some extraordinary news," Blake said in a sombre tone. "Detective Chief Superintendent Tim Street is dead."

14

DCI Richard Fitzwilliam recoiled as if someone had punched him in the stomach. *Chief Superintendent Tim Street is dead?* "What!" he managed to say, feeling light-headed and totally unable to comprehend the news.

"He was found dead in his office a short while ago," his boss, Superintendent Nigel Blake, told him.

Fitzwilliam's mind raced as he tried to process the news. He'd seen Street only three days ago. He'd looked tired, but he hadn't looked unwell. "That's terrible, sir," he finally said, his voice low and heavy with emotion. "What happened?"

"We're not one hundred percent sure," Blake replied. "But it appears he dropped dead in between meetings. The scene is being secured, and the witnesses have been detained. This is going to be your case, Richard, and I don't need to tell you how high-profile this investigation will be."

Fitzwilliam's stomach sank. It was an enormous responsibility. Street was a very senior officer and a respected public figure. He stretched his neck from side to side. *Hopefully it will be straightforward.* "I assume he died of natural causes, sir?" A heart attack most likely. *How old is Street? Late fifties maybe... Too young to die, but it isn't unheard of at that age.* Especially with someone who'd had a highly pressurised job like Street...

"We don't know yet, Fitzwilliam. That's why I need you to go now."

Rats! "Yes, sir, of course. I'm on my way."

"And Richard?"

"Yes, sir?"

"Keep me posted, alright?"

"Of course, sir."

Fitzwilliam slammed down the telephone receiver and jumped up from his chair, adrenaline pumping through his limbs as he realised the gravity of this assignment.

Rushing out of his office, he yelled across the room, "Carol, find DS Spicer, please, and ask her to meet me at the Special Projects Department as soon as she can." Without waiting for an answer, he pulled open the heavy outer office door and plunged into the dingy corridor beyond.

15

11:50 PM, MONDAY 1 FEBRUARY

DCI Richard Fitzwilliam's footsteps echoed around the corridor of the security sector at Gollingham Palace as he rounded the corner and came to a stop. His breath laboured, he paused to allow his heart rate to reduce, then he opened the door and stepped into the chief superintendent's outer office. Taking in the scene before him, his eyes darted around the room, memorising every detail.

A police constable from the Royal Household Police (a division of City Police) was standing in the far corner of the room next to the balding Detective Chief Inspector Henry Bird and a slim woman with a short thick black bob dressed in a navy-blue suit. Attached to her lapel was a visitor's pass, along with an ID badge. City Police maybe? Fitzwilliam nodded at Bird and turned his attention to the two constables standing guard by Street's office door. They seemed on edge, their attention shifting uneasily between him and the closed door. Turning around, he spotted an officer sitting with Ruth Ness on one of the red leather sofas over by the wall. Slumped forward, Ruth's face was hidden behind a curtain of fine blonde hair. In front of her was an empty glass, and in her hands was an untouched cup of tea. The PC next to her was speaking softly in comforting tones, her hand resting lightly on Ruth's arm while she nodded slowly.

Fitzwilliam cleared his throat and watched as Ruth's head slowly rose, her eyes meeting his with an expression of relief at his presence. He paused for a moment and offered her a gentle smile in response as he walked over. "I'm so sorry, Ruth. Are you okay? Can I get you anything?" Fitzwilliam asked softly.

Ruth managed a small, hesitant smile that didn't quite reach her green eyes before she shook her head.

At that moment, the woman in the navy-blue suit stepped towards him. "Ah, Detective Chief Inspector Fitzwilliam, I presume? I'm Detective Inspector Madeline Carmichael from City Police." She glanced quickly at Ruth, who had bowed her head and raised her tea to her lips, before continuing in a low voice. "I found the chief superintendent."

Fitzwilliam acknowledged her with a polite smile before turning back towards Ruth and briefly placing his hand on her shoulder. "I'll talk to you shortly, Ruth," he assured her before indicating to DI Carmichael to follow him. As they moved towards the centre of the room, Bird joined them. "I still can't believe it," Bird said in a quiet voice as they all looked at the closed door.

Fitzwilliam nodded. He'd not worked for Street, but he had admired the man since they'd worked on the investigation into the Earl of Rossex's death together. Indeed, it had been Street who had encouraged him to consider the move from Intelligence to Investigation and Protection at the end of the case. The shock at Street's sudden death was great, yet he felt strangely disconnected. He glanced over at Bird, who seemed similarly lost in his own thoughts. Bird had been more familiar with Street than he'd been, although

Fitzwilliam had the impression their relationship had had its challenges. Was Bird sorry as well as dumbfounded by the unexpectedness of it all?

Carmichael broke the silence with a single word: "Shocking."

Fitzwilliam nodded in agreement. "I'll speak to you when I'm done in here if you wouldn't mind waiting," he told her, gesturing towards Street's office. She tilted her head in acknowledgement as he reached for the door handle. Footsteps outside made him pause. DS Tina Spicer rushed into the outer office with DS Bella Hardwick on her tail. They halted just beyond the doorway, both a little out of breath.

Spicer took a lungful of air. "Sir, I got your message. What's—" She scanned the room, stopping when she saw Ruth Ness huddled in the corner with the police officer. She scooted over to Fitzwilliam and said in a low voice, "What's happened?"

Fitzwilliam tilted his head towards the door of Street's office as he opened it. "Come with me," he whispered. He glanced back to see a look of confusion flicker across Spicer's face before she nodded, and the two sergeants followed him in.

The office was brightly lit and silent save for the soft ticking of a clock on one wall. As Fitzwilliam's eyes adjusted to the brightness, he started to make out Street slumped over his desk, his head resting on the tabletop.

Spicer gasped, and Fitzwilliam turned to look at her. "It's most likely natural causes," he said softly. "But we won't know for sure until after the doctor arrives and has a look."

Next to Spicer, Hardwick stood motionless, her mouth slightly agape as she stared at Street's lifeless body. Fitzwilliam addressed her, "I'm sorry, Hardwick. I know he was your mentor. If you want to sit this one out, Spicer and I can handle things here."

Hardwick shook her head and blinked. "No, sir," she replied, her voice barely a whisper. "I want to stay and observe, please." She pulled on the gloves Spicer handed her and grabbed an evidence bag.

"Okay, then I'll examine the body. You two look around the room and see if there's anything unusual," Fitzwilliam said as he took the pair of gloves and handful of bags Spicer held out to him. He pulled his pocketbook from his jacket and flipped it open.

Spicer, looking down at his hands, took her mobile phone out of her pocket and turned to Hardwick. "We use a bespoke PaIRS investigation app to make notes, record details of suspects and witnesses, and take photos, et cetera. Everything gets uploaded directly to the system in real time." She looked back at Fitzwilliam. "It's a real time-saver, isn't it, sir?"

Her steely blue eyes met his, and with a huff, he put the notebook away, then took his phone from the back pocket of his dark-blue trousers and opened the app.

———

"See here." The doctor moved around Fitzwilliam in Street's office and pointed to the side of Street's neck. "I'm not sure what this is."

Fitzwilliam leaned in. There was a small indented red mark the size of a pea on the right side of Street's neck, just under his ear. "An injection site?" Fitzwilliam suggested.

Dominic Elmes shook his head. "I can't see a break in the skin, so unlikely." He straightened up. "It could just be a spot, of course. I won't know until I do the autopsy." He stood back and removed his mask, revealing a weathered face with piercing blue eyes. "But apart from that, there's nothing obvious to suggest he died from anything other than natural causes. Most likely a heart attack."

Fitzwilliam stifled a sigh of relief. It was a straightforward death and *not* murder. *Thank goodness.*

The doctor packed away his tools, talking as he did so. "Of course, a heart attack can happen to anyone. Even a fit and healthy person like Mr Street. Tragic…" He shook his head and closed his bag.

"Any guess on time of death?" Fitzwilliam asked. He was sure once he interviewed Ruth Ness and DI Carmichael, he would be able to pinpoint when Street had last been seen alive, but it was always good to get a medical view.

He leaned in and looked at Street, whose head was now resting on the back of his chair, his eyes closed, his face relaxed. *As if he's taking a nap.* "He's a bit cold, but there's no rigor in the face yet." He looked down at his watch. "So I would say within the last two hours or so."

"So after ten this morning?" Fitzwilliam clarified.

"Give or take," the older man replied.

Fitzwilliam nodded. He knew from experience that getting a straight answer from a pathologist was like trying to get blood from a stone. "How long before you can perform the postmortem, doctor?"

Dominic Elmes shrugged. "I should be able to start it later today or tomorrow morning. But, of course, it might not be conclusive. We may have to wait for test results."

Fitzwilliam frowned. *But that could take days.* He needed to be sure sooner than that. "But—"

The pathologist held up his hand. "I know your boss is keen to have a definitive cause of death as soon as possible, but depending on how busy the lab is, it could be two or three days before I have the full picture." He reached out and patted Fitzwilliam's arm. "I'll do my best, chief inspector."

Fitzwilliam nodded and thanked the doctor before exiting the room and leaving the doctor's team to remove Street's body.

16

12:30 PM, MONDAY 1 FEBRUARY

DCI Richard Fitzwilliam scanned the outer office. *Where is everyone?* At first the entire office seemed empty until his eyes fell on DS Tina Spicer and DS Bella Hardwick sitting on one of the red sofas in the far corner. Spicer was typing something on her mobile phone while Hardwick looked over Spicer's shoulder. *Probably updating the PaIRS investigation app*, he thought as he walked towards them. He had to confess (although he wouldn't admit it to Spicer), the new app *did* make life much easier. He'd dictated everything he'd seen in Street's office into the app and had supported it with photos. Even his conversation with the pathologist had been recorded. He knew it was all on the central system already, key words identified and organised. No more hours spent typing up observations, notes of conversations, and interviews. No more irate calls from his boss or the admin team chasing up paperwork. But as efficient and effective as this new streamlined system was, he still missed the feel of his pocketbook in one hand and a pencil in the other. *Proper policing.* He suppressed a sigh. *I sound like an old stick-in-the-mud.*

Spicer spotted him approaching, and the women stood. "How did it go, sir?" she asked.

"The doctor is fairly sure the chief superintendent died of natural causes and places the time of death within the last two hours." He looked around. "Where's everyone?"

"Ruth Ness has been taken to another office while they —" She stopped as Street's office door opened and two men pushing a trolley with a black body bag on top trundled out of the room and across the outer office to the exit. Behind them, the pathologist raised his hand to Fitzwilliam as he followed the men out. The metallic *clang* of the trolley wheels bouncing off the floor sounded as they pushed it through the exit and down the hallway. The door slowly closed behind them, and a solemnness hung in the air like a heavy fog. No one spoke for a few minutes, then Spicer broke the silence. "Well, for that reason, really…"

Fitzwilliam nodded. Poor Ruth. *This must be especially hard on her.*

"And the DI from City who found him?" he asked.

"DCI Bird took her to the canteen, sir. They should be back any minute."

As if summoned by the sound of his name, the door swung open and the lanky detective chief inspector stepped through, trailed by the sharply dressed Detective Inspector Madeline Carmichael.

"I assume that was…" Bird, his black glasses in one hand, waved his other hand towards the corridor.

Fitzwilliam nodded. "Sorry to have kept you waiting, DI Carmichael. Maybe now would be a good time to talk?"

The woman smiled, her white teeth standing out against her dark skin. "Yes, of course, chief inspector." She turned to Bird. "Thanks for keeping me company, Henry."

Bird smiled at her, then turned to Fitzwilliam. "If you need me, Fitzwilliam, I'll be in my office."

Fitzwilliam dipped his chin as Bird headed off, then gestured towards the red sofa. "Please take a seat, Detective Inspector Carmichael."

Carmichael adjusted her navy suit as she stepped closer to the red velvet upholstered sofa and sat down gracefully on the corner, her long legs stretched out in front of her. Fitzwilliam perched on the side of the chair opposite her while Spicer and Hardwick hovered behind him. He took out his phone. "I'll be recording the interview if that's okay with you?"

She nodded and laid her hands on her lap.

"This is DS Tina Spicer from my team," he said. Spicer nodded, and Carmichael tipped her head in acknowledge-ment. "And this is DS Hardwick. She's here on attachment as an observer. I understand you found Chief Superintendent Street's body when you arrived for a meeting with him earlier this morning. Can you talk me through what happened, please?"

Carmichael began briskly. "Yes, of course. I had an appointment to meet him at ten forty-five," she said, then paused. "Actually my original appointment was at ten-thirty, but it got moved back fifteen minutes. Anyway, I arrived a few minutes early. CS Street's assistant was on the phone, so I waited for a short while, then she paused her call and told me to go straight through." She took a deep breath and continued, "I knew something was wrong immediately. Street was slumped over his desk. I hurried forward and checked for a pulse, but I couldn't find one. I shouted out for his EA to call an ambulance, I don't think she heard me the first time. I ran to the door and hollered at her. She came running in but just froze, so I picked up the phone on his desk and made the call myself. DCI Bird must have heard me shout as he rushed in soon after. The EA was crying by this time, so he told me to take her outside. I led her out of the office, got her a glass of water, and sat down with her to wait for the royal police."

"Thank you. Was anyone else in the outer office when you arrived?"

Carmichael shook her head. "No, just Street's assistant."

"And can I ask you what your meeting with CS Street was regarding?"

Carmichael hesitated, her eyes darting away from Fitzwilliam's gaze. She shifted in her seat and paused before finally replying, "Our meeting was about…an ongoing investigation I'm leading." Her voice trailed off, and she seemed reluctant to elaborate. *Intriguing…* About to probe further, he caught Carmichael's eye. She raised her chin. He checked himself. This wasn't a suspicious death. He really had no business asking for more details. And from the look on the DI's face, she would be unlikely to share them with him even if he did. "Did you know CS Street well?" he asked instead.

She shook her head. "I've never met him."

And now never will…

"But you know DCI Bird, ma'am?" Spicer asked from behind him.

"Yes, sergeant. We've worked together on several joint projects."

Again, she seemed reluctant to elaborate. He could ask Bird if need be, but again, it wasn't really relevant. He stood. "Well, thank you for your cooperation, detective inspector. I think that's it for now."

Carmichael seemed relieved as she rose. "So you're treating CS Street's death as a natural one then?"

Fitzwilliam frowned and stared at Carmichael for a moment, searching her face for any signs she might know something he didn't. "Is there any reason you think it might not be?"

Carmichael shook her head, her face reddening slightly. "No, no...of course not," she stammered.

Fitzwilliam gave her a tight-lipped smile and nodded. "We'll be doing an autopsy to confirm the cause of death, of course. But it appears as though Chief Superintendent Street's death was due to natural causes."

"Good, good," she said as they moved towards the door. She handed Fitzwilliam her card. "Give me a shout if you need anything else."

As she left, Fitzwilliam looked down at the card she'd given him. What had City's Organised Crime Unit wanted to talk to Street about? He frowned. Bird had alluded to Preece being on their radar, and Street and Preece had worked together back in the day. Was it just a coincidence? Fitzwilliam licked his lips, then put Carmichael's card in his pocket. He didn't like coincidences...

"Sir?" Spicer stopped by his side. "What now?"

Fitzwilliam glanced at his watch. "Let's grab a quick lunch and then we'll interview Ruth Ness."

———

The canteen was bustling with activity as lunch was in full swing. The noise and chatter filled the air, along with the smell of fresh food cooking. Fitzwilliam, Hardwick, and Spicer joined the queue of police and security officers taking a brief respite from their duties. Fitzwilliam heard whispered mentions of Street's name. The news about the chief superintendent's death had clearly spread quickly among them, creating an atmosphere of shock and disbelief.

Fitzwilliam and Hardwick ordered sandwiches and Spicer

a salad before they moved through the busy canteen, scanning the room for a free table until eventually they found one near the back wall.

The three of them sat in silence for a few minutes until Bella Hardwick cleared her throat. "I was on the phone to Ruth when his body was found," she said, her voice low as her eyes darted between him and Spicer. "Of course, I didn't know that at the time. I just heard a shout in the background at the other end, and Ruth suddenly said she had to go."

Fitzwilliam took a bite of his sandwich. He doubted the information was important, but the sergeant clearly wanted to talk, so he nodded and asked, "How long were you on the phone with Ruth?"

Hardwick raised her eyes to the ceiling. "Um, quite a long time. Maybe forty-five minutes?" She looked back at him and shrugged. "She was helping me with the information I needed for my presentation. Street asked her to…" Her voice trailed off, then her eyes widened, and she gasped. "I was probably talking to Ruth when he died, wasn't I?" She looked down at the sandwich on the plate in front of her and pushed it away.

Could've been. "Did you hear her talk to him during that time?" Maybe she could help him narrow down the time of death.

She wrinkled her petite nose. "No, I don't think so. She broke off to say goodbye to the first visitor—"

So there had been someone there before Carmichael? He'd have to ask Ruth who that had been and what time they'd left. Street must have died in between them leaving and Carmichael arriving. *Did he look ill to his first visitor?* Fitzwilliam wondered.

"But she stayed on the line. And again when the inspector from City arrived, Ruth paused while she told her to go in. But we were on the phone the whole time."

"How long was the gap between the first visitor leaving and Carmichael arriving, do you think?" Spicer asked, putting down her knife and fork on the empty plate before her.

A section of long straight hair fell across Hardwick's face as she tilted her head to one side. "Ten…maybe fifteen minutes? We were going through some numbers on a spreadsheet at the time. I'm sure Ruth will know exactly. She's terribly efficient."

Fitzwilliam popped the final piece of his sandwich into his mouth and nodded. In his experience, Ruth was the perfect assistant — cool, calm, and efficient. It had been a bit of a shock to see her so emotional earlier. As the two women chatted about the presentation Hardwick was working on, Fitzwilliam's mind turned again to the possible link between Street and Preece. *Adler!* He should tell Adler about Street's death. He picked up his phone and texted her the news. It surprised him when she replied almost immediately, saying she'd already had a call from one of her team.

Adler: *Was it really a heart attack?*

Fitzwilliam: *Looks like it, although there will be an autopsy because it was so unexpected.*

Adler: *Don't you think it's strange that both Preece and Street have died of a heart attack within a week of each other?*

Fitzwilliam blinked at Adler's message. He hadn't. Not until now…

. . .

Fitzwilliam: *Surely it's just a coincidence?*

Adler: *We hate coincidences, don't we? And stop calling me Shirley!*

He chuckled at their standing joke (they could both quote big chunks from the *Airplane* series of films), then quickly rearranged his face to one of concern when Spicer and Hardwick stared at him. "Adler thinks it's odd both Preece and Street have died of heart attacks so close together," he said.

"Who's Preece?" Hardwick's brown eyes searched his.

"He's a DI from City who was shot during the unsuccessful kidnapping of the Duke of Kingswich at the end of last year," Spicer explained. "He was in hospital but due to make a full recovery when he died of a heart attack last week." She frowned. "Did they know each other, sir?"

Fitzwilliam nodded. "Yes, from when Street worked for City Police and…" He was about to say that they'd both worked on the Earl of Rossex's accident investigation but stopped. He wanted to keep that between himself and Adler at the moment. He had a feeling it could be relevant to something. He just didn't know what.

"And what, sir?" Hardwick asked.

"Oh, er, he recommended Preece for a bravery award back in the day."

Hardwick looked confused. "Is it really that surprising they knew each other? After all, most PaIRS officers transferred in from City."

She was right, of course. But even so…

Fitzwilliam: *See what else you can find about Street and Preece from when they worked together. Also, see if your City contact knows of Madeline Carmichael. She's a DI on the OCU. She found the body.*

Adler: *Since when did I become your lackey?*

Fitzwilliam: *Since you're supposed to be off work and resting!*

He looked at his watch and rose. "Let's talk to Ruth Ness now, shall we?"

As they crossed the canteen, Fitzwilliam's phone vibrated in his pocket. He stopped mid-stride and quickly opened the text.

Adler: *Have you told Lady Beatrice about Street's death yet?*

Fitzwilliam rubbed his hand over his forehead. Street's death was the final nail in the coffin of getting the earl's accident investigated any further. Only Street had had all the information and contacts that were needed… His stomach felt heavy. Lady Beatrice would realise all this the minute he told her of Street's death. He glanced at his watch again. He really needed to get on. *I'll do it later, when I have the time to word a message properly. Or maybe I'll ring her? Yes, that would be best. I'll ring her later.* He returned his phone to his pocket and hurried to catch up with Spicer and Hardwick, who had just disappeared through the door.

17

2 PM, MONDAY 1 FEBRUARY

"I'll try to keep this as brief as possible, Ruth, and then you can go home." DCI Richard Fitzwilliam smiled at Ruth Ness, who sat opposite him on one of the red sofas in the outer office. Perched on the edge of the couch, her knees together with her legs slightly tilted away from her and her hands resting on her lap, she looked completely composed and fully in control of her emotions, only the slight redness around her eyes giving her away. She didn't return his smile; instead her eyes flickered towards the closed door of Street's office. "But there's so much to do. I'll need to clear—"

"Not today, Ruth." Fitzwilliam shook his head. "You've had a tremendous shock and—"

"I'm fine, chief inspector," she snapped as she raised her chin and met his eyes, giving him a steely green-eyed look.

Fitzwilliam's smile faded. This was much more like the efficient assistant he'd dealt with in the past. Her no-nonsense manner combined with her height (*she must be at least two inches taller than Lady Beatrice*) must have made her a good gatekeeper for someone as in demand as Street.

"Even so," he said gently. "Until the autopsy is

completed, the chief superintendent's office will remain a crime scene, I'm afraid. That means no cleaning or clearing any of his things away until the investigation is concluded."

Ruth's eyes widened as her mouth dropped open slightly. "A crime scene? But I thought... He had a heart attack, didn't he?"

Fitzwilliam nodded solemnly. "Yes, it appears he did, but we can't take any chances. It's standard procedure in this kind of situation, so until the pathologist has made an official ruling, we have to be cautious."

Ruth swallowed as she clasped her hands together. A look of something passed over her face. *Fear? But why?*

She nodded slowly. "Of course," she said, giving him what looked like a forced smile.

Her job! She must be worried about what will happen to her now. Would she be reassigned to Street's replacement or moved somewhere else? Fitzwilliam had no idea how these things worked.

"It also means, I'm afraid, we'll need to ask you for your copy of the key to his office."

Ruth nodded, and getting up, she walked over to her desk and fished a set of keys out from one of the small top drawers. She wrestled a key from the keyring and threw the remaining bunch back before walking over and handing it to Spicer, who sat on his right.

"Does anyone else have keys?" the DS asked.

"As far as I know, it was just me and the chief superintendent. Oh, and the Palace Facilities Department has the master," Ruth replied as she resumed her place on the sofa.

Fitzwilliam nodded at Spicer. He knew they had Street's key already as it had been retrieved from his jacket hanging up on the coat stand in is office and used to lock the door after Forensics had finished. "Thank you, Ruth. Can I now ask you to talk me through today, please? I'm interested to know CS Street's movements up until his death."

Ruth nodded and grabbed the tablet resting beside her on the sofa. After she opened it up, her fingers flew across the surface of the screen, entering commands into what Fitzwilliam assumed was a diary program.

"He came in at his normal time, around eight forty-five. At nine we had our usual brief meeting to go through his diary for the day, and his first appointment was with George Rockcliffe at ten."

"And he is?"

"The building contractor working on the rebuild of the offices. You know, the ones that collapsed." She briefly glanced over at DCI Bird's office in the corner.

"Can you email his details to Spicer, please?"

She tapped on the screen and typed something, then continued, "His next appointment after that was at ten forty-five with DI Carmichael. And then, well…you know…" She closed the tablet and placed it beside her.

"Thank you, Ruth. And how did CS Street seem to you earlier today?"

She hesitated for a few seconds, then straightened up. "Perfectly normal, chief inspector."

"Did Mr Rockcliffe arrive on time?"

She gave a clipped nod.

"And what time did he leave?"

Ruth Ness's eyes moved to settle on DS Bella Hardwick, standing behind the sofa opposite her. "I can't be exactly sure as I was on the phone to DS Hardwick here, but it was about fifteen minutes before DI Carmichael arrived, so I'd say just before ten-thirty."

Fitzwilliam looked over his shoulder at Hardwick, and she nodded in agreement.

"And did you see or hear the chief superintendent after Mr Rockcliffe left?"

"No. I was still on the phone."

"And you were still on the phone when DI Carmichael arrived?"

"Yes, sir. She was expected, so I told her to go straight on in." She looked down at her hands and wiggled her fingers.

"Okay, so just to be clear, when was the last time you actually spoke to your boss?" Fitzwilliam wanted to get it right, although it seemed clear to him that Street must have died between Mr Rockcliffe leaving Street's office at ten-thirty and DI Carmichael going in around fifteen minutes later.

Ruth frowned. "Just after Mr Rockcliffe arrived, I suppose. I followed him into the office with a cup of tea for the chief superintendent and offered Mr Rockcliffe a drink. He refused, and I left them together." She paused, then whispered, "That was the last time I saw him alive."

For a moment, she seemed lost in her own world. *Perhaps she's thinking of what might have been if she hadn't been on the phone at that critical moment?* If she'd entered the office after Rockcliffe had left, then perhaps she would have noticed if Street had been ill and been able to summon help in time to save him. But of course there was no way of knowing, and he hoped she wouldn't torture herself about it for long. He wished there was something he could say to make her feel better, but as if sensing his pity, her face suddenly cleared, her mouth holding a line of determination as she locked eyes with him for a moment. "So I imagine that would have been about five past ten."

Sensing she'd had enough, Fitzwilliam leaned forward and stopped the phone recording. "Well, thank you, Ruth. I think that's just about it. Would you like me to arrange for someone to take you home?" he asked as he stood.

Ruth shook her head, rising. "No," she said firmly. "I'll walk to the station. The fresh air will do me good." She walked over to her desk and dragged an oversize bag out from under it.

"Can you get hold of this George Rockcliffe, Spicer, and arrange for us to see him, please?" Fitzwilliam said as he watched Ruth Ness shrug off her navy-blue jacket and hang it over the back of her office chair. *Will she be alright?* She'd been Street's assistant for how long? He tried to recall as she unbuttoned the rolled up sleeves of her cream blouse and plucked a grey hoodie out of her bag with 'Train like a beast…' and a picture of a bear standing on its hind legs, its mouth open, its arms outstretched as if letting out a mighty roar on the front of it. It must be at least five years. She pulled the hoodie down over her head and kicked off her blue pumps, then reached under her desk and retrieved a pair of trainers.

How did she feel about Street's death? They'd worked together day in, day out for several years. Had she liked him or merely tolerated him? Had the pair had banter like he and Carol did (well, that's what she called it; he called what she said to him bordering on abuse), or had their relationship been purely professional and businesslike? She bent down and straightened her shoes by her chair, then rising, she chucked the bag over her shoulder and walked to the coat stand. Removing a black full-length puffer coat, she slung it over her arm, and with a last glance at Street's office, she smiled sadly and walked out of the room.

"Sir?" He turned and looked down at Spicer, who had now been joined by Hardwick on the sofa. "I can't get any answer from Mr Rockcliffe's phone," Spicer said as she cut the call on her mobile phone. "I've left a message."

"Okay, thanks." Fitzwilliam sighed. There wasn't much else he could do now other than wait for the autopsy report. It all seemed straightforward at the moment. *I should have it wrapped up by this time tomorrow.* "You two can go back to the office. Let me know if Mr Rockcliffe gets in contact—"

"Fitzwilliam?" DCI Henry Bird poked his head around his office door. Fitzwilliam strode over to him while Spicer and Hardwick left the room.

"All sorted?" Bird asked as Fitzwilliam stopped in front of him.

"I think so. I'm waiting for the postmortem, but…" Fitzwilliam shrugged.

"So he died of natural causes then?" Bird asked, leaning against the door frame.

"It seems so..." First Carmichael had asked him and now Bird. *Do they know something?* "Any reason you think it wouldn't be?"

There was a look of surprise on Bird's face as if he hadn't been expecting such a direct question. He quickly recovered and shook his head. "No. No reason."

Really? Hadn't Bird asked him about Preece earlier? Should he share Adler's concerns about two seemingly healthy people dying of natural causes in such rapid succession? *Is there something else at play here?*

He opened his mouth to say what was on his mind, but Bird had already shifted his weight away from the door frame and was now stepping back inside his office. "See you later," he said, waving off Fitzwilliam's unspoken question with a dismissive gesture, then shut the door behind him without another word.

18

FIRST THING, TUESDAY 2 FEBRUARY

The Society Page online article:

<u>*Senior Royal Police Officer Dies Aged 57*</u>

Detective Chief Superintendent Timothy Street from the Protection and Investigations (Royal) Services died unexpectedly yesterday. He was 57. No cause of death has been released at this time. He served in policing for over thirty years and has been described in tributes as a greatly respected man with a strong commitment to public service.

Superintendent Nigel Blake from PaIRS said, "It is hard to put into words how devastating this news is for the entire organisation who liked and respected Tim. He was the epitome of a great leader whose commitment to public service was unswerving. Our hearts go out to his family at this difficult time, and we will support them as much as we can. We want to respect their privacy and the coroner's process and would ask that the public and media do so too."

Superintendent Frances Copson, also from PaIRS, posted

on social media: 'I am shocked and extremely saddened to hear this tragic news. Tim's death will be a great loss to many of the people he worked with. All we can do is pull together and mourn the loss of a well respected man.'

Timothy Street grew up in Wimbledon and was educated at the private boys' school, Chartwell College, in Chessington, then attended university at the London School of Economics before joining the City Police on the Graduate Entry Scheme. He later moved to the Protection and Investigations (Royal) Services as a detective inspector, where he started in Intelligence, moving to the Investigations and Protection side of the organisation when he became a superintendent.

Tim was also described as a keen runner chairing the PaIRS Sports and Leisure Committee and City Police Benevolent Fund. Eight years ago, he was made an Honorary Doctor in Criminology and Policing at Cambridge University. Tim was awarded the King's Police Medal on the King's New Year's Honours List five years ago, and last year he was awarded the Sir Robert Peel Sword by the Institute of Criminology at Oxford University for Outstanding Leadership in Specialist Policing.

Tim was divorced and leaves behind two children and one grandchild. His eldest son, Jonathan Street (36), issued the following statement on behalf of the family: 'It is with great sadness we confirm DCS Timothy Street KPM has passed away unexpectedly earlier today. My father devoted his life to serving his King and country, and he will be greatly missed by his friends, family, and colleagues. We ask that you respect our privacy as we come to terms with this loss.'

———

"Did you see this?" Perry Juke waved his mobile phone in front of Lady Beatrice's face as they stood in one of the guest suites they'd yet to start at Gollingham Palace. "Isn't this the guy who Fitzwilliam was talking about?"

What guy? Bea grabbed his arm as it swooped by and brought it to a stop. "Let me see," she said as she prised the phone from his hand and read. *Detective Chief Superintendent Timothy Street from the Protection and Investigations (Royal) Services died unexpectedly yesterday.* She gasped. That's the man Fitzwilliam had gone to see about the investigation into James's death. The one who had refused to reopen the case.

"Well, is it?" Perry asked, holding out his hand for his phone.

No cause of death has been released at this time. Had he died of natural causes? He was very young to just drop dead. *We want to respect…the coroner's process…* Was that code for a suspicious death? *Was Street murdered?*

"Bea?" There was a trace of impatience in Perry's voice as he stood, hand on hip, and stared at her.

"Indeed."

"So was he murdered, do you think?" Perry whispered, his eyes wide.

Bea laughed, shaking her head. "Not all deaths are murder, you know," she said with a grin.

He raised an eyebrow as he placed his hand on his chest. "Don't tell me you didn't think the same thing."

Busted! She blushed. "Well, then we're as bad as each other. I'm sure it's nothing untoward."

"You're probably right. Should I ring Adler and see what I can find out?"

A thought struck Bea. She pulled her phone from the back pocket of her black jeans. "Wait. I have an even better idea."

. . .

Lady Beatrice: *I have just read about DCS Street's death. I'm so sorry for your loss.*

"Oh, yes?" Perry's eyes sparked with excitement.

"Fitzwilliam," Bea said with a flourish. "He knew Street well. Let's see what he has to say."

"Genius!" Perry clapped his hands together.

"In the meantime, what are we going to do with this room?" Bea waved her arms around and sighed. "The shape is all wrong for the Louis XVI green beechwood armchairs *and* the rosewood desk. We need to rethink the—" Her phone beeped.

Fitzwilliam: *Thank you. Sorry, I intended to ring and let you know before it became public, but I'm preparing the report for the coroner and time has run away with me.*

"Is that Fitzwilliam?" Perry said, leaning towards her and peering over her arm.

"Indeed. Looks like he's in charge of the investigation into Street's death," she said typing.

Lady Beatrice: *Please, no need to apologise. He was very young to die. I hope it's all straightforward?*

. . .

She and Perry watched her screen, waiting for a reply.

Fitzwilliam: *It seems to be. I'm still waiting for the autopsy report, but it looks like he had a heart attack.*

They let out an audible, "Oh…"

"Well, that's that then," Perry said, sounding disappointed.

"So it seems," Bea said, sighing. Then she checked herself. *I should be glad the poor man didn't die a brutal death at the hands of a killer.* She and Perry had been around murder too much recently and appeared to be getting a taste for it. *That can't be good…* "Well, that's excellent then," she said with forced brightness. "I mean…it's sad that's he died so young, but it's good he wasn't murdered."

"Yes, definitely," Perry replied, wandering over to a vase, absentmindedly picking it up and studying the bottom.

Lady Beatrice: *That's very sad. Please let me know if there is anything I can do.*

She pressed send and returned the phone to her pocket, then turning to Perry said, "Right. Let's get—"

Her phone rang. *Is it Fitzwilliam?* She'd said, "if there is anything I can do", but that was just something people said. *No one actually takes you up on it…* She retrieved her mobile from her pocket. The name 'Fraser' flashed on the screen. She frowned, then hit accept, "Fraser?"

"My lady. Sorry to trouble you, but I just wanted to let you know I've found the earl's business papers."

Her pulse quickened. "Really? Is there much?"

"There are a couple of boxes of loose notes and six bound notebooks. I just wanted you to know, my lady."

"That's great, Fraser. Thank you for that. Can you take them to the study in The Dower House, and I will go through them there? I'll make arrangements to come back in the next day or so."

"Yes, my lady. I'll get that done right away."

She stared at her phone screen as the call disappeared. *James's papers!*

Eagle-eared Perry hurried over. "Where are you going?"

She smiled. "Back to Francis Court. Just for twenty-four hours. Fraser has found some of James's papers, and I want to have a look through them."

She hadn't allowed herself to hope too much that she would find anything significant, not after all this time. But just on a whim, she'd contacted Rory Glover, who had been her and James's private secretary at the time James had died, and he'd told her he'd boxed up the earl's papers and had left them at The Dower House. That's when the glimmer of hope had poked through the dark. Maybe there would be something in there about Miami?

"Do you think you'll find anything pertinent to James's death?" Perry asked.

She bit her lip. "I don't know. Maybe," she said, trying hard to keep her voice light but knowing now it could be a waste of time. Street had been the one person who could've helped answer all the questions she had. Now he was gone, what hope did she have of finding out what had really happened? She took a deep breath and shook off the heaviness in her shoulders. If there really was something in James's papers, then she'd rather know. And maybe with the help of her friends, they could figure it out. "Anyway, I'm going to have a look."

"Can I come too? It seems like ages since I was home, and I want to have a proper look at The Dower House as well."

She looked around the room they were in. There was more work needed in here than she'd expected. One of them really should stay behind and get started. In fact, it wasn't great timing for either of them to be away right now. *Should I wait and go later?* But then she caught the hopeful look in Perry's eyes. It would be good to get away for a while, and they were ahead of schedule on the overall project. They could afford to take a brief trip back home. Maybe a change of environment would help give them both some much needed perspective on how to tackle this room when they got back.

"Indeed," she said with a smile. "We can leave right away and return tomorrow morning. Hopefully, we'll come back with fresh eyes and bursting with ideas about what to do in here."

Perry grinned widely and clapped his hands together. "I'll ring Simon and tell him we're coming home," he said, turning towards the door. "If we're lucky, he'll cook something special for dinner tonight if I give him enough warning."

Bea licked her lips. The thought of one of Simon's dinners sealed the deal for her. "Come on, Daisy," she said, turning to her little dog. As Daisy rose from under the window, Bea's eyes were drawn once again to the view; it really was special. *Of course!* She raised her hand to her forehead and tapped it. The solution to making the best of this awkward shaped room was literally staring her in the face. "Window seats!" she cried triumphantly. "This room needs window seats."

19

AFTERNOON, TUESDAY 2 FEBRUARY

Detective Chief Inspector Richard Fitzwilliam drained his coffee cup, then drummed his fingers on the desk in his office. "Well, can you chase him up please, Carol?"

"I can, sir. But it has only been just over twenty-four hours, so…" He glanced up at his assistant's face as her voice trailed off. The look she was giving him clearly said, 'are you *really* sure you want me to do this silly thing that you've asked me to do?'

He huffed. It seemed like it had been a lot longer than that since CS Tim Street had been found dead. Was he being unreasonable to expect the pathologist to have completed the autopsy by now? Carol clearly thought so. He just wanted to get this wrapped up and get the report off to the coroner as soon as possible. *Then I can get back to my day job.* He needed to review the security arrangements for the Duke and Duchess of Kingswich's trip to India in May in light of the attempted kidnapping of the duke just before Christmas. He must also—

"Sir?"

"Alright, Carol, I take your point. Leave it until towards

the end of the day and then call for a status update. Is that better?"

He could detect a smile in her voice as she said, "Yes, sir. Anything else?"

"Have we got hold of George Rockcliffe yet?" They had been unable to contact him using the number Ruth had given them. His wife had said he was in Spain on business for a few days with a poor signal.

She shook her head. "No, sir. I rang his wife again, but all she could add was that he was staying with a business contact. She didn't know the address or the contact's name. She claims to not even know the name of the town he's in." It was obvious Carol didn't believe her. "All she *could* tell me is his flight went into Malaga. Spicer is checking the passenger lists of all the flights into Malaga on Monday right now."

Just as well this isn't a murder inquiry, or George Rockcliffe would be the number one suspect at this point!

"Okay, thanks, Carol. Keep me posted."

Carol reached over and plucked his used cup from his desk. "Yes, sir."

As he watched her leave his office, Fitzwilliam let out a deep sigh. *It doesn't really matter anyway.* His requirement to talk to Rockcliffe to confirm when he'd last seen Street alive was a tick in the box he needed for the coroner's report. He didn't care about Rockcliffe's plans, just wanted no loose ends for the inquest.

A *ping* alerted him to a new email, and he opened up his inbox to find an update from Spicer about Rockcliffe's flight. She confirmed Rockcliffe had flown out of London Gatwick to Malaga on Monday morning — just hours after Street had been found dead. Fitzwilliam's brow furrowed as he read over the details one more time and then closed the email with a huff. He'd just have to wait for Rockcliffe to respond to their messages.

He picked up a security report and leafed through it when his mobile rang. The name 'Adler' flashed up on the screen.

"Howdy Hop-A-Long," he answered, doing a terrible impression of a southern drawl.

"Like that's the first time someone's called me that," she responded, sounding bored.

"Ah, but did they do the accent at the same time?"

"No, you've got me there. Just wait while I engage my funny bone."

"Don't bother! What can I do for you?"

"Are you free for dinner tomorrow night? Izzy's just bought a tagine and has gone all Moroccan on me. She says she wants to try it out on someone who appreciates good food, which I thought was rude."

"But true."

She snorted. "Okay, yes. I suppose. So will you come over and take the pressure off me?"

Fitzwilliam chuckled. "Yes. I'd love to."

"Great. Seven o'clock then. I have my hospital appointment tomorrow morning, so hopefully we'll be able to celebrate me being cast-free too."

He smiled. It would be good to have Adler back in the office.

"How's it going with the Street thing? Have you had the autopsy report yet?"

"No. As Carol pointed out in her subtle but not so subtle way, it has only been twenty-four hours."

"Is that all? It feels a lot longer. But even so, I'd have thought they would've rushed it through considering his seniority."

"Maybe if they suspected it was anything other than a

natural death. Anyway, I'm sure it will be sometime today." He mentally crossed his fingers. "Have you found out anything more about Preece?"

"I'm still digging. But I'll tell you what — he didn't live like most DIs I know. Both his kids are at boarding school. And it's not one at the cheaper end of the spectrum either. They had at least two holidays abroad every year, their last one being two weeks at Disney World in Florida, and his wife drives a brand new Range Rover Sport. Seven years ago he bought an old Victorian house in Islington and had loads of work done on it. It's worth about three and a half million now. According to a mate at City, his wife came into some money ten years back, and they've been living it up ever since."

"Nice for some." Fitzwilliam frowned. "I'm surprised he carried on working in the circumstances." He knew from experience that life for a City CID police officer was hard work. He'd been glad to transfer to PaIRS as soon as he'd had the chance.

"He used to say he went to work to get away from his wife, apparently. No one was really sure if he was joking or not."

He knew officers like that in PaIRS. They'd had the chance to take early retirement but had refused, having said that if they stayed home, they would only be given a long list of jobs to be done by their other half. As one colleague had explained, "My wife's a much more exacting taskmaster than any superintendent I've ever worked for. I'm not even allowed a coffee break at home." Fitzwilliam smiled.

"I'm trying to verify it at the moment," Adler added. "But the consensus is he was an unambitious, ordinary kind of officer who got on with the job, didn't argue but never did more than the basic that was required of him."

"Was he popular?"

"It seems so. He had quite a few mates on the force. One of them is on holiday this week, but I'll give him a call when he gets back and see if he's got anything to add. I've found nothing so far to explain why he would be deliberately targeted."

"By the way, did Henry Bird ring you? He was asking me if I knew anything about Preece a few days ago. I suggested he ring you."

Adler's pitch rose. "No, but that's interesting. I'll give him a ring. Okay, well, I'll let you get on. I'll see you tomorrow night."

"You will. And good luck at the hospital tomorrow."

"Thanks, Fitz. I can't wait to be able to scratch my ankle…"

20

EVENING, TUESDAY 2 FEBRUARY

"So Detective Chief Superintendent Tim Street is dead," Simon said, putting his knife and fork down and picking up his napkin. He wiped his mouth. "I thought you'd come storming in here like Starsky and Hutch demanding we investigate immediately."

Bea almost choked on her last mouthful of chicken cacciatore. Perry snorted out a spray of red wine, some of which landed on a sleeping Daisy, and the little dog jumped up, startled. *Are we really that bad?* She looked over at Perry, now simultaneously wiping himself down with his napkin and trying to resettle a confused looking little dog. She ignored the voice in her head saying, *Yes.* Alright, so it might have been true that in the past, she and Perry had been keener than Simon to investigate unexpected deaths. But then they'd had a compelling reason on each occasion to get involved. *This is different.*

She cocked her head to one side and gave Simon a look. "Well, sorry to disappoint you, but it's not murder. He died of a suspected heart attack." Simon raised an eyebrow. She pushed her empty plate away and continued, "And even if it was a suspicious death, we didn't know the man and have no actual connection to him, so why would we?"

"Fitzwilliam is in charge of the investigation," Perry told him.

"And he thinks it's a natural death, does he?"

Why's Simon asking? Had he heard something to the contrary from his ex-CID colleagues in Fenshire? Or was his crime writer's brain searching for a more exciting explanation than just the tragic death of someone so young? "Yes. Why do you ask?"

Simon shrugged. "He was a fairly young and, from all accounts, healthy guy who exercised regularly—"

"I've always said exercise was bad for you," Perry piped up smugly. His very vocal dislike of exercise was well known to anyone who knew him. He was lucky he had a naturally slim frame that allowed him to eat what he wanted without having to spend hours in the gym working off the calories. It was a source of irritation to both Bea, who ran most days, and Simon, who reluctantly worked out three times a week and regularly played five-a-side football with his ex-workmates at Fenshire Police.

"—but, more importantly, he was the second officer to die unexpectedly from a heart attack within a week," he continued, ignoring Perry's jibe.

Bea's eyes shot open wide. "Really?"

Perry gasped. "What?"

Simon frowned. "Didn't you see it in the news?"

Bea looked over at Perry. She had shut off her news alerts last year after her relationship with a famous chef had been widely publicised. Now she relied on Perry to keep her up to date.

Perry shrugged. "I don't remember seeing it."

"A detective inspector from City Police called Preece died in hospital last Sunday. He was about Street's age too."

Bea frowned. "But he was City Police. Street was PaIRS. Why would the two be connected?"

"Em told me about it when we were over there for dinner on Saturday. Preece was shot during the failed attempt to kidnap your uncle before Christmas. The same incident where she broke her leg. Preece was still in hospital recovering from his injury and suddenly had a heart attack."

"But what's that got to do with Street?" Perry asked.

"According to her, they worked together at City before Street transferred to PaIRS, and they both worked on the investigation into the earl's accident. She wanted to know if I'd met either of them during the inquiry."

"And did you?" Bea asked.

"I was at Francis Court the day Street visited, but I wasn't included in the briefing he gave about James working with MI6. It was way above my pay grade then. But actually, I did come across Preece when I was collating all the evidence we had just before the inquest. He was a DS then, and it was him and his team who went to your flat in Knightsbridge Court where your husband had been due to stay the night he died."

Bea's heart jumped. Preece had been to their grace-and-favour flat in Knightsbridge? Was he the one who had taken James's overnight bag containing the letter addressed to her that had been subsequently found nine years later? She took a deep breath. *It's all just a strange coincidence, surely?* "Is there any question Preece's death wasn't a heart attack?"

"I don't know. But I had the conversation with Em before Street died. Maybe now they'll review it…" His voice trailed off as he stood up and gathered the plates and cutlery. "Coffee?"

Bea nodded. "Indeed. And that chicken dish was delicious, by the way."

Simon smiled. "I want to do a bit more experimenting, but I'm happy with it as a first attempt." He walked across the open-plan kitchen and deposited the plates on the island before continuing on to the coffee machine.

Bea looked across the large wooden table at Perry, who was sitting opposite her. "You're very quiet. What do you think?"

"I thought it was super tasty, but you know what he's like. He's—"

"Not the food, doofus! What do you think about the fact Preece and Street both died of heart attacks within days of each other?"

Perry sighed. "I don't know. It seems like just one of those strange coincidences to me."

"I don't like coincidences," Simon said, plonking a large pot of coffee and three mugs down on the table. "And neither will Fitzwilliam."

21

AFTERNOON, WEDNESDAY 3 FEBRUARY

"You mean he was murdered?" Detective Chief Inspector Richard Fitzwilliam's eyebrows shot up as he stared disbelievingly at Detective Sergeant Tina Spicer.

"Well, my contact didn't actually say that, sir." She tapped her phone screen. "What he said was they're now treating Detective Inspector Ethan Preece's death as suspicious," she clarified, tucking her blonde hair behind her ear.

"It's the same thing," Fitzwilliam mumbled as he leaned back in his office chair and crossed his arms.

Spicer looked up and turned to DS Bella Hardwick sitting next to her. *What was the look Spicer just gave her?* He wasn't sure he liked having Hardwick still here, trailing after Spicer like a devoted puppy dog. He felt outnumbered!

"It's not the same thing, sir. It could be an accidental death or manslaughter."

Fitzwilliam uncrossed his arms and held his hands out. "And that's what they think, is it?"

"They don't know just yet, sir. The toxicology results have only just come back." She looked back down at her phone screen. "Okay, here we go. They found high levels of metanephrine and normetanephrine in Preece's cardiac blood, significantly higher than those normally measured with cardiac deaths. The urine analysis revealed extremely high levels of catecholamines, metanephrines, and 3-methoxytyramine compared to concentrations normally measured in cardiac fatalities." She met his eyes with a look of triumph.

Like that explains anything! "Which means what in English?"

"It means the results are consistent with him being given a high dose of adrenaline that caused him to have a heart attack."

"And that could have been deliberately or accidentally given," Hardwick added.

Yes, thank you. I worked that out for myself. "So what now?" he asked Spicer.

"According to my contact at City, they're working with the hospital on an extensive review of the hours leading up to Preece's death to see if he was given a dose of adrenaline by someone there."

"Is that likely?" he asked.

Spicer shrugged. "It's a drug that's used in the hospital regularly, and it has to be accounted for. They should be able to give a definite yes or no once they've checked their records."

Fitzwilliam sighed. "Okay. Well, thanks for that, Spicer. Let's keep a watching brief on it."

"There's one more thing, sir." Spicer leaned forward. "They're keeping it all very low key at the moment, but the person heading the investigation into Preece's death is Detective Inspector Madeline Carmichael."

Fitzwilliam leaned forward, resting one elbow on the top of his desk and cupping his chin. "Now that *is* interesting. Do you know when the autopsy results on Preece came in?"

Spicer shook her head. "No, sir. But I can find out."

"Please do." He repositioned his hand and stroked his chin. "I wonder if that's what she wanted to talk to Street about?"

If Adler was right and someone had deliberately tried to shoot Preece during the bungled kidnapping of the Duke of Kingswich, then did that mean they had tried again while he'd been in hospital and been successful? Maybe Adler should talk to Carmichael. It might help her if it turned out to be murder. He'd talk to her tonight at dinner.

"That reminds me, Spicer. Where are we with getting the results of the postmortem on Street?" It had been forty-eight hours since Street had died.

"The latest update was that they had made a start yesterday afternoon. We should have something later today, sir."

He huffed. "I hope so."

"So do you think the possible murder of DI Preece is just a coincidence, sir?" Hardwick asked, her eyes shining.

He met Spicer's gaze. Spicer broke the contact, turned to Hardwick, and smiled wryly. "The chief inspector doesn't like coincidences."

22

5:15 PM, WEDNESDAY 3 FEBRUARY

Richard Fitzwilliam checked his email one last time. Still nothing from the pathologist. He sighed as he closed his laptop screen and unplugged the power supply, then he slipped his laptop into his bag. There was nothing more to be done today. He may as well quickly pop home and get changed before going to Adler's for dinner. As he rose, the phone on his desk flashed. He sat back down again and picked up the handset. "Fitzwilliam," he said briskly.

"Good afternoon, chief inspector," said a friendly female voice. "I'm so glad I caught you. I'm ringing from Pathology on behalf of Dr Elmes. He asks if you could possibly come to his office if you're available."

Fitzwilliam's pulse quickened. "Now?"

"Yes. If that's convenient."

Why would Elmes need to see him in person? *It has to be something to do with Street's death… Something unusual…* He swallowed the lump in his throat and took a deep breath. "Yes, of course. Please tell him I'm on my way."

Grabbing his laptop bag and shrugging on his jacket, he hurried out of the room. Scanning the outer office, he saw

Spicer's blonde head poking up above the privacy screens around the section where his team worked. "Spicer!" he hollered, and she turned her head, then stood up to face him over the screen.

"Sir?"

"I've been called to a meeting with Dr Elmes," he said. "I don't know what it's about, but I think we can assume it has something to do with Street's autopsy results. I'll ring you as soon as I'm done. Okay?"

"Yes, sir."

He nodded, then turned and rushed out of the room.

———

"Thank you for coming so promptly, chief inspector," Dominic Elmes said. "I know it's getting late, but I thought you'd like to hear the results of my findings as soon as possible."

"Absolutely," Fitzwilliam responded, following the older man into his office.

Elmes sat behind his desk and gestured for Fitzwilliam to sit opposite. He reached out and switched on his computer screen. "I'm sorry it's taken so long, but as I warned you on Monday, sometimes it takes a few days to get a full picture."

Fitzwilliam nodded, resisting the urge to ask the doctor to get on with it. *Did Street die of natural causes, or was he murdered?*

Elmes tapped on his keyboard, and the image of a report flashed up on the screen. He turned it so Fitzwilliam could see it. "It's been an interesting case. I've had to run a few extra tests and take samples from the body. From those results, I can tell you I believe my initial assumption that he died of a heart attack was misleading."

Fitzwilliam leaned forward. *So what—*

The doctor continued, "I've found no evidence of any pre-existing condition, congenital defect, or any other sign his heart was weak." He leaned back in his chair and looked at Fitzwilliam with an expression of satisfaction. "In fact, his heart and lungs were in perfect working order, the arteries free of blockage, and his cholesterol levels within healthy limits. I'm afraid I can find nothing wrong with Street's heart that would have caused him to suffer a heart attack. There is nothing to explain why his heart stopped, although stop it did."

Fitzwilliam stared at the doctor. If Street had not died of a heart attack, then what was Elmes saying? "So he didn't die of a heart attack?"

Elmes's expression grew serious, and he leaned in closer to Fitzwilliam. "His heart simply stopped beating, as if shut off or disrupted by something."

"Like what?"

"And that's the million dollar question, chief inspector," he said, crossing his arms.

Fitzwilliam's heart sped up. Adrenaline! He must have been killed the same way as Preece had — a heart attack brought on by an overdose of adrenaline. "What about the adrenaline results?"

Elmes nodded thoughtfully. "It was quick thinking of your sergeant, on your instructions, no doubt, to get in contact earlier this afternoon with the information that a possible related death had been deemed an adrenaline overdose. I was able to contact the lab straight away and ask them to do the additional tests from the samples they already had. It saved a lot of time."

Fitzwilliam's breath quickened. *And? Come on, man, out with it!*

"They did a full and thorough test of his blood and urine but found nothing unusual. No traces of metanephrines or anything that would indicate any kind of drug in his system."

Fitzwilliam sagged back in his chair, his body feeling heavy. So there was no direct link to Preece's death.

"But" —the pathologist held up his hand— "don't despair, chief inspector. There are a few other things I found."

Fitzwilliam's fingers tingled. He took a deep breath.

Elmes picked up a mug with, 'Pathologist (noun) 1. Like a normal doctor, only much cooler', on the side that looked half full and took a sip. "I'm sorry, Fitzwilliam. I didn't offer you one," he said as he placed the tea back on his desk. "Would you—"

Fitzwilliam clenched his hand tight. "No, no, doctor. I'm fine. Please continue."

"Okay, if you're sure?"

Fitzwilliam bit his tongue and nodded.

"Very well. So there were a few things I noticed on the body as I did my initial examination. I noted the victim's eyes were slightly bloodshot, and there was some congestion and oedema — that's where tissues fill with fluid, over the mucous membrane that covers the front of the eye and lines the inside of the eyelids. I wondered if the chief superintendent had been suffering from a mild bout of conjunctivitis. There was also a little bluishness around the lips. Neither of these things in themselves were especially noteworthy. As I was looking for signs of a heart attack, they didn't seem important at the time. But of course, when I couldn't find anything wrong with the heart, I went back and reconsidered them." He paused and took another sip of tea.

Fitzwilliam grimaced and gripped his jaw tight.

"I've seen these signs in other cases, generally with strangulation or choking, but they would normally be much more pronounced and widespread and accompanied with external signals like bruising and redness around the neck, maybe even finger marks. There would be signs of a struggle and, most likely, a broken hyoid bone in the throat, a telltale sign of trauma. I found nothing like that." He gave a clipped nod. "There was, you may remember, a small red blemish on the neck, but when I examined it further, there was no puncture wound or anything obvious to explain it. On further examination, it wasn't a spot but an indentation in the skin with a tiny amount of lividity. That's a bluish-purple discolouration of skin where blood pools after death, and that was all." Elmes raised an eyebrow. "There's one more thing I'm struggling to account for. I found bruises on the top of Street's legs and some on his knees."

Fitzwilliam frowned. *What does that mean?*

The doctor continued, "They're consistent with his legs being forced up against the underside of his desk."

"Caused by what?"

The pathologist leaned back in his chair and looked directly at him. "It's not my job to speculate, Fitzwilliam. I can only tell you what I've found."

With a headache now threatening, Fitzwilliam wished he'd asked for a drink earlier. He moved his jaw from side to side to release the tension. "So your conclusion is?" he asked.

"Death will be noted as due to myocardial infarction, which is the medical term for a heart attack, but the cause will be recorded as unknown and passed to the coroner to open an inquest. I'm sorry, chief inspector, but I think you need to look at who may have had a motive to kill Chief Superintendent Street."

23

EVENING, WEDNESDAY 3 FEBRUARY

"Do you think there's a connection between Preece's death and Street's?" Simon Lattimore asked Richard Fitzwilliam from across the table in the dining room at Adler and Izzy's house in Clapham.

A possible double murder? Lady Beatrice shivered as if someone had opened a window behind her and let in the cold night air. Fitzwilliam had told them over dinner about the possibility of Preece's death being deliberate and the result of his meeting with Elmes. He'd made it clear what he was telling them was highly confidential and needed to be kept between them only. Deep down, she'd suspected he was more interested in Simon's take on things. In the past, he'd always been more readily accepting of Simon's input over hers and Perry's, no doubt because of his police background. But even so, she still felt a warm glow over Fitzwilliam having taken them into his confidence. *Last year it would have been unheard of for him to openly discuss a case with us…*

Fitzwilliam shrugged. "It's impossible to say for certain, but I can't help but feel there's something linking them. To have two people who knew each other and worked together in the past both die within a week seems too much of a coincidence to me. Especially as we know Preece's death was most likely murder, and now I suspect Street's is too. But with no physical evidence to link them together, it's hard to see what the connection is."

James? Bea's heart skipped a beat. Preece and Street had both been involved in the investigation into James's accident. Was that another coincidence? She didn't like coincidences. And something was telling her that it was all linked somehow. About to open her mouth and tell them her thoughts, she hesitated. She glanced over at Fitzwilliam, who was raking his fingers through his short brown hair, brushing the greying temples with his fingers. He'd told her that there was nothing more they could do, and she'd agreed. How would he react if she brought James's death up again? *Will he think I'm someone who can only live in the past?*

"Well, whatever it is, it must be something big if it's resulted in both of them being killed," Simon pointed out.

And Street and Preece were not just two people who had been killed. They were two *police officers*. From everything she'd read or seen on television, that was a very risky thing for someone to do. So who was willing to take that risk? Someone who wasn't afraid of the law? Her stomach dropped. What did she know about these things? *I'm out of my league.* Best leave this to Fitzwilliam and Adler. *This is their world.*

"Now I'm officially back," Adler said, waving her now cast-free leg by the side of her, "I can get in on the action."

Fitzwilliam cocked his head at Izzy. "Didn't the hospital tell you she still needed to take it easy for at least three weeks while she has physio?"

"Yes!" Izzy cried, the frustration coming through loud

and clear in her voice. "But she's interpreted it as she can go back to work tomorrow."

"Hey! I am here, you know."

Fitzwilliam turned to face her. "Adler, you need to make your physio a priority. I know you want to get back in the office as soon as you can, but—"

"Okay, okay. I get it!" Adler huffed. "But surely I can do something?"

Fitzwilliam smiled. "Yes. Keep looking into Preece's background. I'm going to talk to Madeline Carmichael again now Spicer has confirmed she knew about the results of Preece's autopsy before her meeting with Street on Monday. I think there's a good chance it's relevant to why she was seeing him. If she confirms that, then she might be interested in your theory that someone tried to shoot Preece during the kidnapping."

What? Bea's ears pricked up. Adler thought the shooting of Preece had been deliberate? She looked over at Perry, frowning. He looked back, a guilty look on his face, and mouthed, "Sorry," at her. So he'd known! Her stomach hardened. *Probably another thing I missed on Saturday at their cosy dinner without me.*

"I'm not sure," Adler said tentatively.

Fitzwilliam frowned. "Why?"

"Well, they're only rumours, but some of the guys at City think she's, let's say… unreliable. They think she's been in the OCU too long and knows too many of the wrong people."

What's OCU? Bea caught Simon's eye and raised an eyebrow.

"How long has she been in the Organised Crime Unit?" Simon asked.

Thanks! She smiled at him.

*"*Ten years. It's quite unusual for someone to be there that long," Adler answered.

"So they think she's bent?" Simon asked, then looking at Bea and Perry, added, "She's on the take? Being paid by the bad guys to keep the heat off them?"

Bea stifled a giggle. *Why's Simon talking like a bad cop show?*

Adler, a slightly confused look on her face, replied, "Er, yes. Well, that's the rumour, anyway. I'm not saying it's true, but I think you need to be wary of her, Fitz. If she's on the wrong side of this, then she could even be your murderer."

Fitzwilliam's mouth downturned, and he frowned. "That's a good point. We only have her word Street was dead when she went into his office." He twisted around to Bea. "What do you think?"

Oh no, what do I say? "Er, I didn't know either of the men, so…" She caught Fitzwilliam's gaze, his brown eyes searching hers. *Come on, Bea, think!* She quickly reviewed what everyone had said over dinner. "I agree it's unlikely two people who knew each other would be murdered so close together and their deaths are not connected." *Is this the right time to mention James? I'll be subtle.* "Maybe it's to do with a case they both worked on in the past?" Fitzwilliam's eyebrows rose. *He'll think I'm obsessed.* "Er, you know. You hear of people who come out of prison and seek revenge on the people who put them there years ago." *Chicken!*

Fitzwilliam nodded, and Adler said, "That's a thought," then started telling the others about a case back when she'd been in City Police, and a son had tried to kill a police officer who'd arrested his father. The father had died prematurely in prison before his case was heard, and the son believed he had been innocent and that his incarceration waiting to go to trial had been what had killed him. "I'll do some cross checking on cases and see if there's a link there," she concluded.

"So the doctor had no theory as to how Street could have been killed?" Izzy asked.

Fitzwilliam shook his head. "From how he described it, it was as if he'd been strangled or choked but in a way that didn't leave the usual marks or break any bones."

Perry, who'd been sipping his wine while listening to them, returned his wineglass to the table with a *thud*, his eyes wide. "Simon!"

His partner spun around. "What?"

"What was that murder method you were going to use in one of your books a few years ago, but your editor made you change it because he said it was too niche? Wasn't that some sort of choking?"

Simon nodded, smiling back at Perry. "I can't believe you remembered that; it must have been two years ago."

"I do listen to you, you know," Perry said, raising a hand to his chest.

This is all very cute, but… "So what was it" Bea asked, giving Perry a look.

"I can't remember the details. You tell them, love."

Simon leaned back in his chair and gave them all a wry smile. "What do you know about martial arts?"

What? Bea frowned and leaned forward.

Fitzwilliam said, "Er, nothing."

"Neither did I until a few years ago. But while researching for one of my books, I came across a pathology article about a death that had happened during an MMA competition in Poland."

"MMA?" Adler asked.

"Oh sorry. Mixed martial arts. Anyway, the article was about a competitor who died during a round or bout, I believe they call it. His opponent had used a technique known as a blood choke on him. A blood choke can cause unconsciousness in eight to twelve seconds, then the hold is released, and the recipient wakes up. There's normally no external bruising or redness and it's generally considered harmless. However, an overzealous application of such a manoeuvre can injure a person, and extremely vicious use can kill. The police were trying to establish if the death was accidental or was, in fact, murder, and they looked to the pathologist to help them. Anyway, I won't bore you with all the details. In the end, the post mortem was inconclusive as to the intended use of force, although the police did eventually charge one of the competitors with murder when they found out in this particular instance the two men knew each other and had a great rivalry over the same girl, so they were able to prove motive."

"So," Perry said, looking rather smug. "It sounds like that's what could have happened to your CS Street."

It certainly seems possible, Bea thought as she sipped her wine.

Adler frowned. "I get how you could use it to make someone unconscious, but won't it require a lot more pressure to kill them and that would show up in the autopsy?"

Simon shook his head. "I don't think so. I'd have to check my notes, but from what I can remember, it was about eight seconds to render someone unconscious. Then if you maintained the hold using the same pressure, it takes something like another four minutes before oxygen to the lungs and heart are cut off and the blood flow to the brain stops. In the article I read it resulted in a cardiac arrest."

Bea looked at Fitzwilliam. His brows were creased, and he was rubbing his chin. *Is he considering it as a possibility?* It did seem to fit with what he'd told them about the autopsy results.

"What do you think, Fitz?" Adler prompted.

"If someone gave him this blood choke until he lost consciousness, then held the position for up to four minutes so he would die, why wouldn't he try and stop them?" Fitzwilliam said thoughtfully.

One, two, three, four, five, six, seven, eight. It wasn't very long if it was unexpected, and you were losing consciousness. "I don't think eight seconds is that long if you're distracted or busy doing something, especially if you're taken from behind—"

"By someone you know!" Perry jumped in.

And maybe he did struggle. "Didn't you say there was bruising in his upper legs and knees?" Bea asked. Fitzwilliam nodded. "Well then, wouldn't that suggest he hit them on the underside of the desk as he fought losing consciousness?"

"Possibly, I suppose." Then Fitzwilliam shook his head. "I don't know. It seems a great method for a book. But for real life, it still seems a bit fantastical."

"You're right," Simon said. "The person who did it would have to hold their nerve and not be tempted to put too much pressure on the neck. They would have to know what they were doing. It's why my editor rejected the idea in the end. He said it would require someone with martial arts skills and, in that particular novel that was set in a small village in the Shetland Islands, it would have felt too contrived." He leaned forward and picked up his wineglass. "Now I think about it, it was quite a good murder method though. I might try and use it again sometime."

Bea sighed. When they put it like that, it did seem unlikely.

"I'll ring Elmes in the morning and run the scenario past him." Fitzwilliam said, taking a sip of wine. "You never know."

24

LATER, WEDNESDAY 3 FEBRUARY

Lady Beatrice pulled the tie of her silk dressing gown tight over her pyjamas, then sat down on the green sofa in her rooms at Gollingham Palace. She tucked one foot under her and stared at the boxes and notebooks on the low glass coffee table in front of her. It was getting late, and she hadn't intended to do this now, but she'd lain in bed for the best part of twenty minutes, and sleep was eluding her. She missed Daisy, whose warm furry body tucked into her back normally relaxed her. She was already regretting leaving the little dog behind at Francis Court.

Staring at a pile of papers, she felt slightly sick. *Come on, Bea. It's just a bunch of papers. They can't hurt you.*

Taking a deep breath, she picked up the first leather-bound notebook, its spine worn and faded. She opened it cautiously, her heart lurching as she saw James's handwriting. She ran her finger over the first few sentences, and her chest tightened as tears welled up in her eyes. Flipping through the pages slowly and carefully, she took in every word he'd written as tears tickled her cheeks. Memories of James flooded back to her — his smile, their laughter, and the warmth of his arms around her.

As she worked her way through the bound books, she marvelled at his ability to capture their life together. Told through a mixture of funny anecdotes and short stories, he'd faithfully recorded many of their more colourful royal trips. He'd even included rough sketches of people they'd encountered along the way. She grinned through her tears. She came across entries from when he'd been away on solo trips. Her heart skipped a beat as she read his open declarations about how much he missed her. She lingered on each page filled with her husband's words. They were confirmation that he'd truly loved her when he'd written them. She sighed. *When had that all changed for him?*

As she closed the last book, she wiped her face. She smiled to herself. She was grateful she'd found them. And now she could reread them whenever she wanted to, or she could even share them with Sam someday. She glanced at the clock above the marble mantelpiece. It was *very* late now. She really should go to bed. But although she was glad she'd taken the plunge and read the notebooks, she was disappointed none of them contained anything about his trip to Miami. She stared at the two boxes and stifled a yawn. *I'll just take a quick look at them…*

———

An hour and a half later, just as Bea was beginning to feel a deep sense of anti-climax when she'd found nothing of importance, her eyes caught sight of a large envelope tucked away in the bottom of the second box. She pulled it out and set the box aside. Her heart skipped a beat as she stared at the word 'Miami' in James's handwriting on the front of it. *Could this be it?* With trembling fingers, she opened the envelope and grabbed the papers inside. Laying the pile down, she fanned the pages out in front of her. They were all typed papers containing agendas, itineraries, attendee lists, notes, and profiles. On each one were comments in James's handwriting. She sighed. She wanted to make sense of it all, but her tired mind wasn't cooperating. Even worse, the papers didn't seem to be in any particular order.

Bea quickly scanned the sheets before her, and a familiar name jumped out at her — Rudy Trotman. James had circled it on an attendee list, and next to it, he'd written 'dodgy!' On another page by Rudy's name, he'd written 'Link to Grazzi F?' She frowned. Rudy Trotman was the wealthy American father-in-law of her friend, Sybil, who'd married Trotman's elder son Otis at a lavish wedding at Francis Court last year. When the Trotman's cook had been murdered a few weeks before the nuptials, Bea had become involved in the PaIRS investigation, much to Fitzwilliam's consternation, and they'd caught the killer in time for the wedding to go ahead as planned. Rudy Trotman had told her over dinner he'd met James in Miami a few months before he'd died, so seeing his name wasn't a surprise. But why had James written the word 'dodgy' by his name? Was it a joke? She remembered James having used the phrase 'dodgy geezer' a few times after a Cockney had taught it to him during a royal visit to a youth boxing project in the east end of London. Had James *really* thought Rudy Trotman had been up to no good in Miami? She shook her head. Her brain was scrambled. She should call it a day…or rather, a morning.

Gathering up the papers, she shuffled them into a pile when her eye caught another name she was familiar with. Suddenly, she had difficulty swallowing as she stared at James's note. 'Meeting — Tim Street Mon 19 Dec'.

25

8 AM, THURSDAY 4 FEBRUARY

Lady Beatrice yawned as she took a sip of her coffee. Perry Juke, sitting opposite her, took a large bite out of a bacon roll while Simon Lattimore, sitting next to him, devoured a full English breakfast. A wave of nausea washed over her. *How can they eat like that when they had such a huge dinner last night?* As she took another gulp of the strong black liquid, she closed her eyes, letting the heat trail down the back of her throat. The bitterness revived her a little. She opened her eyes in time to see the outline of Detective Chief Inspector Richard Fitzwilliam standing in the doorway of the senior staff dining room at Gollingham Palace, his head moving as he scanned the room. Putting one hand up to shield her eyes from the low sun beaming through the tall windows, she waved at him with the other. He raised his hand, then strolled across the wooden floor to their table.

"Good morning, my lady," he greeted as he stopped beside them. "Perry. Lattimore." He nodded at the men, and they nodded in return.

She smiled. "Fitzwilliam, thank you so much for coming."

"I'm intrigued," he said, sitting down next to her. "Your text just said you found something strange when you went through the earl's papers." He raised an expectant eyebrow.

Perry wiped his mouth with a napkin and pushed his plate to one side. "She hasn't even told us yet," he told Fitzwilliam and pulled a face, then waggled his fingers by the side of his head. "It's all very mysterious."

"It seemed easier just to tell you all together," she said defensively. She looked at Simon, who nodded and took his final mouthful. "Okay, so I was going through James's paper-work last night, and I found this…" She took a piece of paper from the back pocket of her jeans, unfolded it, and laid it out on the table so they could all see it. She smoothed the paper flat and pointed to the note James had written in the margin.

"Oh my giddy aunt!" Perry slumped back in his chair and raised his hand to his mouth.

Simon leaned in to take a closer look as if he didn't quite believe what he'd read the first time.

Bea twisted to face Fitzwilliam. His head was cocked to one side, and he was blinking rapidly. *What is he thinking? Does he think it's as significant as I do?*

Fitzwilliam slowly shook his head. "It didn't even occur to me they might've known each other. But I suppose it makes sense they did." He frowned. "But when I mentioned the earl had concerns about Miami, Street didn't mention he'd spoken to him…" He rubbed his forehead.

"Miami?" Simon leaned forward.

"What concerns?" Perry frowned.

Rats! She'd forgotten Perry and Simon didn't know about their conversation with Brett Goodman when they had been in Scotland. *It seems Fitzwilliam has forgotten too.*

A pained expression crossed Fitzwilliam's face as he turned to look at her. *Don't worry; I'll fix it.* "I remembered recently that James was a bit distracted when he came back from Miami." *Actually, that's true.* She suddenly recalled he'd been worried about some notes he hadn't been able to find. "And he was looking for some notes he'd made about the trip. Something about it was clearly bothering him. He seemed worried."

Next to her, Fitzwilliam let out a slow breath. *Did we get away with it?*

Simon spoke first. "Do you know what he was worried about?" Bea shook her head. "Just so I'm clear then, are we now thinking the earl spoke to Street about these concerns following his trip to Miami two weeks before he died?"

Bea and Fitzwilliam nodded. "But I don't know why Street didn't say anything," Fitzwilliam said.

"Maybe they didn't have the meeting," Perry suggested. "The earl could have cancelled it maybe, or Street might have."

Fitzwilliam nodded slowly. "It's possible."

"Or maybe it was secret squirrel stuff, and Street couldn't talk about it to you," Perry added.

"I think if that was the case, he still would have told me. Is there more?" Fitzwilliam asked Bea.

"There's a pile of printed papers James wrote notes on. I didn't have time to go through them all, but this is what jumped out at me. Also, he wrote something beside the name Rudy Trotman. Do you remember him from our case at Fawstead Manor last year?"

They all nodded. "Well, James wrote the word 'dodgy' with an explanation mark by his name, then later 'Link to Grazzi F' with a question mark."

"Dodgy as in suspect?" Simon asked.

"I think so." Bea turned to Fitzwilliam. "Who is or are Grazzi F?" Fitzwilliam shrugged.

"Oh, oh, I've got something here," Perry said excitedly, holding up his phone. "It's about a suspected organised... Oh my..." His eyes sprung open wide.

What? "Organised what?" Bea's voice rose in tone.

"...crime family in Florida and New York called the Grazzi Family." Perry raised his hand to his lips, staring wildly about the room. "Do you think that's them?" he leaned in and whispered.

"Let me see." Simon gently took the mobile phone from Perry and read.

Bea's heart pounded. *Could it be true?* Was Sybil's father-in-law really connected to a crime family? She thought about the times she'd been with Rudy and his wife last year. It was true, Sheri Trotman's dress sense was questionable, but apart from that, they'd seemed perfectly respectable. Rudy Trotman had said nice things to her about having met James. Could it be possible he was leading a double life? The fact that James had written something against his name made her question her impression of the man. James had had good instincts.

"There's not really much substance to this article," Simon said. "It's a blog that's not had any activity on it for over five years. It claims that the death of some guy in Miami was down to someone called Silvo Grazzi, rumoured to be the son of Aldo Grazzi, who in turn, is rumoured to run protection rackets in the two states." He continued to the end of the article. "It's not much to go on..."

"But Rudy Trotman is based in Miami, isn't he? So it could be related," Perry insisted.

They were silent for a few minutes.

"I need a coffee," Fitzwilliam said rising from his chair. "Anyone else?"

Bea nodded. "Yes please." Perry and Simon declined.

When he returned, he sat beside her. Picking up her cup, he filled it up from the pot. "My lady," he said, handing a cup of steaming black coffee to her.

That's thoughtful. She smiled. "Thank you."

"So what do we do now?" Perry interjected.

"Your brother Fred might be able to help us. If you give him a copy of the papers, tell him what we know and see what he makes of it," Fitzwilliam said.

Bea nodded. That was a good idea. Her brother had contacts....

"Do you think Street's and Preece's deaths could be linked to the earl's accident?" Simon asked in a low voice.

Bea's heart skipped a beat. *Simon, I love you!* She wasn't the only one who thought it was a possibility. She checked herself. *Will Fitzwilliam think it's ridiculous?* She held her breath.

"I really don't know," he said, shaking his head.

She stifled her disappointment. *Well, at least he didn't dismiss it entirely out of hand.*

"It's true that so far the only link Adler has found between Preece and Street is that they were both involved in the investigation into the earl's death." He sighed. "But my priority right now is investigating Street's death. If there's a connection, then it may become clearer as I do so." He turned to Simon. "Do you still have contacts at Fenshire Police?"

Simon nodded sheepishly. Bea suppressed a grin. It was Simon's friend, Steve, in Fenshire CID who had helped them on past cases. But Fitzwilliam didn't know that.

"Great. I want to know more about how Preece knew about the letter the earl had addressed to Lady Beatrice." Fitzwilliam told them what Adler had found on the memo Preece had sent Fenshire CID.

Bea's limbs were heavy. She thought she, Fitzwilliam,

Street, and the Fenshire police archivist were the only ones who knew about the letter. And now Preece. She swallowed, then licked her dry lips. "How did he know about the letter?"

"Exactly!" Fitzwilliam said. "That's what I want to know. It's possible Street told him, but that would have been nine years later, so how did it end up on an archived memo?"

"Maybe he saw it at the time and then wondered where it went?" Simon said.

"But then why not say? It would have been important evidence in terms of the investigation. That's why maybe someone at Fenshire Police knows something."

Simon nodded. "I'll see what I can do."

"What about us?" Perry asked Fitzwilliam, eagerly pointing to himself and Bea.

Fitzwilliam sighed. "I suppose it would be pointless to ask you not to do anything…"

Perry cocked his head to one side and smirked. "Totally."

"Okay," he said, sounding resigned. "Maybe you two can find out if the earl spoke to anyone about Miami. It's not something we were aware of at the time of the investigation, so it's possible—"

"Rory!" Bea cried. "Of course. Rory went with him. He might know something."

They all stared at her.

"Rory Glover. He was our private secretary. I've only just remembered he went on the trip too."

"I recognise the name now," Fitzwilliam said. "Adler interviewed him during the investigation about the earl's movements in the days leading up to his death."

"Yes. He kept James's diary." A thought occurred to her. "He may even be able to confirm if James met with Street in December or, indeed, any other time."

"Great. So if you and Perry can talk to him, that would be helpful."

"Of course."

Fitzwilliam glanced at his watch and jumped up. "Right, I need to get on. I have a missing witness to find." He paused, his face suddenly serious. "Without wishing to sound over-dramatic, but if any of this *is* linked, then it could be danger-ous. It's hard to know who we can trust." His voice was low. He held Bea's gaze for a second. A shiver passed down her spine. "Please try not to confront a possible killer." He shifted his gaze to Perry and back. "Either of you."

Bea bristled. It wasn't their fault that in previous cases they had ended up in a face-off with a murderer. It had just happened that way... She raised her chin and looked up at Fitzwilliam. "We don't deliberately get—"

Fitzwilliam raised his hand. "I know." He smiled. "But I'm not getting any younger, and I'm not sure I'll survive the worry of one of you being threatened by a murderer again." His voiced softened. "Please, my lady, just be careful."

Their eyes met. She nodded. "Okay, I'll try."

26

9:30 AM, THURSDAY 4 FEBRUARY

"No, sir, I'm afraid we still can't get hold of him." Detective Sergeant Tina Spicer shook her head, then tucked a strand of blonde hair that had fallen across her face behind her ear.

"Well, now we need to find him urgently." Detective Chief Inspector Richard Fitzwilliam was perched on the top of his desk in his office with his arms crossed, facing Spicer and her shadow, Detective Sergeant Bella Hardwick. "George Rockcliffe has, excuse the pun, rocketed to the top of our suspects list. He was either the last witness to see Street alive, or he's the one who killed him."

He'd already briefed the two sergeants on the results of the pathologist's report and informed them he was now treating Street's death as suspicious. Spicer had quickly recovered from the shock and was now alert, her eyes wide open and her hand on her phone. *I bet she's recording this briefing on that pesky app.* Hardwick on the other hand, her head down and her eyes focussed on the cheap laminate floor, seemed to be struggling with the news that someone had most likely killed her mentor. "We know he flew to Malaga from

Gatwick after he left here. See if we can find out if he hired a car and if so, where he was going. Maybe he was travelling with someone else on the flight? If so, check them out too."

Spicer, typing into her phone, nodded. "I'll go and see the wife, sir. She told Carol again first thing this morning that she's not heard anything from him, but I find that hard to believe. It's been almost three days. Maybe she'll find it harder to lie to my face."

"Yes. And put some pressure on her if you need to. Tell her that her husband will be in serious trouble if he doesn't make contact with us within the next twelve hours. If we don't hear from him then, I'll be issuing a warrant for his arrest and sending it out via Europol." Fitzwilliam stifled a groan. He really didn't want to have to go down that route. The paperwork alone would bury him for half a day. But he couldn't ignore that Rockcliffe might have fled the country after having killed Street. The longer they left it, the longer he would have to go deep into hiding and the more time he'd have to cover his tracks if he really was a murderer.

Spicer stood. "Yes, sir. I'm on it." She scrolled on her phone. "The fingerprint analysis of the room has come back, sir, and it's interesting."

Fitzwilliam sat up straight. "Tell me."

"They have identified fingerprints found in the office belonging to DCI Bird, Ruth Ness, DI Carmichael, the cleaner, and one set of unidentified prints. They're not getting a hit on the system. They're probably George Rockcliffe's, but obviously, we'll need to verify that when we finally get hold of him. But here's the interesting thing, sir. The report says the desk drawer handles were wiped clean. Not even Street's fingerprints were on them..."

Fitzwilliam lifted an eyebrow. So someone had been in

Street's drawers, looking for something after he'd died. *Did they take anything?* "Thank you, sergeant. That *is* interesting."

"And, sir. I think that supports the notion Street was murdered."

"Yes, most likely. And it may also give us a motive if we can find out what they were looking for. That's why we need those drawer keys. Any luck with getting a set?" Despite a thorough search of Street's belongings, they'd been unable to find the keys that unlocked the two bottom drawers. It was possible someone had taken them. *Maybe the person who searched the drawers?*

"I'm waiting on a call, sir."

"Okay. Well, in the meantime, I need to call the pathologist. Then I've got Detective Inspector Carmichael coming in. I want to get to the bottom of why she was meeting with Street." And of course, she was also his other chief suspect. She could've killed Street when she'd arrived and just pretended she'd found him dead. The time between her entering the office and raising the alarm was still unclear. Her statement said it had been less than two minutes, but neither Ruth Ness, Street's EA, nor DS Hardwick, who had been on the phone with Ruth at the time, were able to confirm how long the DI had been alone in Street's office. What had Lattimore said? It would take about four minutes of holding the blood choke position to cause death. Four minutes was a long time, but it was possible.

Hardwick rose and stood next to Spicer. Her heavy makeup couldn't hide the paleness of her skin beneath it. "Are you okay, Hardwick?" he asked. "In the circumstances, I don't think anyone will mind if you'd prefer to return to Intelligence until this investigation is over."

She raised her brown eyes, surrounded by exceptionally large thick lashes (*they must be false*, he thought), and stared at him in alarm. "No," she said sharply, then her voice softened. "I mean, I'd like to stay, sir, and see it through to the end." Some colour started creeping back into her face.

He smiled at her to hide his disappointment. He could well do without an extra body hanging around and slowing Spicer down while they completed this investigation. *Should I insist?* He glanced at Spicer, and she nodded slowly. *Okay.* It was Spicer, after all, who would need to babysit her. "Very well," he said.

The phone on his desk beeped as the green light flashed. He dismissed Spicer and Hardwick with a nod and then leaned over his desk to pull the phone towards him. "Yes, Carol?

"I have a message from the head of the Facilities Department, sir. He said to tell you he has found the master keys to CS Street's desk."

"Thank you, Carol. Can you pick them up for me when you have a chance, please?"

"Yes, sir. And I have Dr Elmes, the pathologist, on the line returning your call."

"Great, put him through, please."

———

"So do you think it's possible?"

Fitzwilliam had expected Elmes to dismiss Perry and Lattimore's theory almost immediately, but as Fitzwilliam had repeated what Lattimore had told them last night, the pathologist had been silent. *As if he's seriously considering the option.*

"Well, it's definitely an out-of-the-box theory. But not out of the realm of possibility, I don't think."

"Really? But it would be so risky."

"I agree. But if successfully accomplished, there would have been a very high likelihood they would have got away with it as his death would've been ruled a heart attack."

Fitzwilliam grimaced. "But *you* spotted something was up, doctor."

"Ah, but I think in this case, the killer, if there is one, was very unlucky. At Street's age, I would have expected to find some signs of cardiac strain, some enlarging of the heart, some blocking of the arteries, anything that would have supported the conclusion he'd had a heart attack. But his heart was in fantastic condition, and that's unusual for someone of his age." He paused. "Of course, it's possible it could be what we call SADS or sudden arrhythmic death syndrome. That's where we can't tell post death if the person had a problem with their heart."

Fitzwilliam raised an eyebrow. "So Street could have died of SADS?"

"It's possible, but..." He trailed off and took a deep breath. "I think the other signs, however small, suggest it was murder."

"And the red mark on his neck?"

"Well, if we go with your new scenario, then I think when he was being held in a chokehold, something got caught between the killer's arm and Street's neck and caused an indentation."

"Like what, doctor?"

Elmes sighed. "I'm afraid I don't know, Fitzwilliam. Something small and round but not sharp is all I can suggest."

"Well, thanks doc, that was very helpful."

Fitzwilliam placed the phone receiver in its cradle, and it immediately beeped. "Yes, Carol?"

"DI Carmichael is here to see you, sir."

"Send her in then, please."

He put the receiver down again, and as he did so, there was a faint knock on the door. "Come in," he hollered, and the slim DI dressed in a navy-blue suit with a fitted white shirt underneath entered his office.

She smiled as she held out her hand, and her large mouth revealed straight teeth that stood out almost blindingly white against the dark tone of her skin. "DCI Fitzwilliam," she said as she shook his hand. "I wasn't expecting to see you again so soon. Has there been a new development in the investigation into CS Street's death?"

Fitzwilliam studied the woman's face as he shook her hand. *Is it possible she doesn't know the pathologist's report indicates a suspicious death?* He doubted it. Carmichael struck him as someone who very much had her finger on the pulse. "Let's just say it's inconclusive at this time." He dropped her hand and indicated for her to sit down in the chair Spicer had recently vacated. He took his usual position perched on the side of his desk. "I'm therefore having to look at the investigation with a fresh pair of eyes."

Her nostrils flared as she inhaled deeply, then she crossed her arms and leaned back in the chair. Fitzwilliam studied her closely, trying to determine if the rumours of her being on the take were true or just a misunderstanding. He took note of the sharp creases that were prominent in her neatly tailored suit and how she maintained a straight posture, not too stiff but still professional. Her facial features revealed nothing more than what one would expect from an ambitious officer, no signs of guilt or deceit. Fitzwilliam had to admit he was impressed; she certainly appeared to be the epitome of a dedicated detective inspector. *But appearances can be deceiving*, he reminded himself as he allowed his gaze to linger on Carmichael's face for a few moments longer. Her dark eyes seemed to search him for clues, yet at the same time revealed nothing of what she might be thinking or feeling. Her calm and collected nature gave no suggestion of an ulterior motive, yet something seemed off about her. Fitzwilliam couldn't put his finger on what.

"Why did you arrange to see Street on Monday morning?" he asked, getting straight down to business.

She uncrossed her arms, and leaning forwards slightly, she rested her hands in her lap. "Like I said, it was about an ongoing investigation I've been leading." Her voice was smooth and confident, but Fitzwilliam could detect a slight undertone of false bravado in it — something that made him suspicious of her true intentions. He noticed how carefully she avoided full eye contact, as if she was looking at his nose or mouth.

"I'm sorry, but I need more details than that." He raised an eyebrow in expectation, but he kept his gaze level and steady. He wanted her to know he was serious about getting answers. "What were you investigating?"

Maddie Carmichael looked away for a moment before slowly meeting his gaze again. She hesitated for a few seconds before finally responding. "I can't go into too much detail at this point, sir. It's a highly confidential investigation," she replied as if choosing her words carefully.

"I'm afraid I'll need something more specific than that," he told her firmly. *Why is she being so cagey?* He would have to rattle her tree a bit. "This is a possible murder investigation, detective inspector, and you were the one who found the body. So this is not the time to play games with me. If you're unable to give me more than that, then I will speak to your boss."

Maddie's confident expression crumbled. She shifted uncomfortably in her chair. With a deep sigh, she finally spoke again. "My investigation was focused on DI Preece and his possible links to an organised crime syndicate called THC."

27

10 AM, THURSDAY 4 FEBRUARY

Fitzwilliam's eyebrows shot up. *THC?*

"So you've heard of them?" she asked.

Fitzwilliam nodded. He'd arrested a member of the gang, Jacky Prince, just a few weeks ago, although Jacky had been at Drew Castle under the name of Clive Tozzi. "The Hack Crew?"

Carmichael nodded. "They're prevalent in London and all over Europe."

"And you think Preece worked for THC?"

"We've suspected for a while someone within City was feeding them information. Every time we seemed to get close, we hit a brick wall. Businesses disappeared overnight. Records were destroyed. People disappeared. Evidence was 'lost'. We only recently considered the mole could be Preece when a new officer in Preece's section got suspicious and reported it to a colleague of mine in OCU. We started to look into Preece's background and came across some inconsistencies in some of the cases he'd been involved with. Anyway, I won't bore you with the details; suffice to say we felt we were onto something. I wanted to speak to CS Street because he worked with Preece during his early days in the force. I hoped he would be willing to fill in some gaps for me."

She let out a deep sigh. "Preece died before I had a chance to interview him, and I'm struggling to get hold of his records. There's a natural suspicion around the OCU in City. They all assume we're on the take, so when we ask for internal paperwork, it takes weeks, sometimes months, for them to 'find' it." She air quoted the word 'find', then leaned back and crossed her legs.

Fitzwilliam was taken aback by her frankness. She appeared to be speaking honestly and without reservation, which made him feel increasingly sure he could trust her. He nodded in understanding. He knew all too well the mentality of protecting one's own within City Police, regardless of what they might have done. "What do you think about Preece's death? Do you think it could be related to this possible connection with THC?" he asked.

Maddie paused for a few moments before answering. She seemed to be considering her words carefully as she looked off into the distance. "I don't know for sure," she said slowly. "But it seems unlikely to be a coincidence. Are you aware he died of an adrenaline overdose?"

Fitzwilliam nodded.

"They're still checking the hospital records, but I'm fairly convinced it wasn't a medical error. I think he was murdered. And if that is the case, then unless his wife stands to inherit a fortune on his death — and don't worry, we're looking into that — then the most likely scenario is he was killed by the criminals he worked for."

"For what reason?"

She shrugged. "He outgrew his use. He was becoming unreliable. He wanted out. He tried to blackmail them. It could be a number of reasons. Either way, it suggests they wanted him out of the way pretty quickly, and that makes me think maybe he was going to expose them."

Fitzwilliam paused for a moment, then leaned back, resting his hands on the desk behind him before speaking again. "Did you tell Street that's what you wanted to see him about?"

Maddie Carmichael gave a small smile. "No. I simply said I had a routine inquiry about DI Preece following his death."

Fitzwilliam remembered how cosy she and DCI Bird had seemed on Monday. "So how does Bird fit into this?"

Maddie looked away, her discomfort palpable. She seemed to be struggling with how much she should say before finally taking a deep breath and responding, "DCI Bird is my PaIRS contact over this. We think there may be a connection between Preece and the attempted kidnapping of the Duke of Kingswich."

Fitzwilliam's eyes widened. He'd not heard any talk of the kidnapping being connected to organised crime. *I shouldn't be surprised. Who else has the money to pull off a stunt like that?* He glanced at his phone to check it was still recording the conversation. He would need to listen to it again to make sense of it all.

Carmichael continued, "We believed someone was providing inside information on the duke's comings and goings, but we didn't know who or why. Then we got intelligence about an attempt to kidnap the duke when he was due to attend a Christmas dinner for military veterans. They knew exactly where to go and when. There was no guesswork involved at all. Rather than cancel the event, we decided to go ahead using a decoy."

Fitzwilliam nodded. "To capture the attempted kidnappers," he said.

Maddie Carmichael smiled. "Well, yes, that was the plan, of course," she said. "But that wasn't the only strategy. We set it up so none of the City officers knew it wasn't the real duke until the decoy stepped out of the car. We briefed them at that point that the plan was to capture the would-be kidnappers. By then it was too late for them to tip anyone off. All we needed to do was see how they reacted when we caught them."

The plan had gone wrong though. Fitzwilliam could see it in her eyes. "So…?"

She took a deep breath and continued, her voice quieter than before. "Unfortunately the team from City who were supposed to be there were involved in an accident on the way to the venue. We were about to abort the whole thing when the kidnappers turned up. There was a lot of confusion. Those on the ground said once the men realised it wasn't the real duke, they started to flee. One of the PaIRS officers got in the way and was attacked with a metal bar, then suddenly one of them pulled a gun. Preece got shot in the process."

Should he tell her Adler's theory about Preece being deliberately shot? "So do you think they tried to kill him deliberately?"

Carmichael shook her head sadly. "I'll be honest. Not at the time, no. If we had, we would've had protection for him while he was in hospital. In fact, we thought maybe we'd got it all wrong, and Preece wasn't the informant after all because why would they shoot one of their own? We interviewed him in hospital, but he said he couldn't remember much about it. We started to look into the other City officer who was also under suspicion, but there was no evidence against him.

"Then about two weeks ago, just a few days before Preece was killed, we picked up a man called Dean Foxley. We know he works for THC on a regular basis, but we never had anything we could charge him with. Then we had a tip-off from an informant that he was one of the kidnappers. We brought him in, but unfortunately, we had to let him go two hours later when he lawyered up, and we didn't have enough evidence tying him to the scene to keep him. But before his lawyer arrived, Bird and I interviewed him and ran some names by him to see how he would react. He ignored us as we mentioned the names of well-known members of THC. They're taught how to keep a straight face and not say anything, you know. But when Bird threw in Preece's name, we got something. We both saw it. He knew who Preece was. Now bear in mind that we never released the names of the injured officers after the aborted kidnapping, and we have no record of Foxley or any of his team having ever been arrested by Preece. So you see, it gave us a connection we wanted to explore."

Maddie paused. Her frustration was tangible. Fitzwilliam could feel it in the air like a wave of heat emanating from her. She ran her hands through her hair and sighed deeply as her eyes searched his. "I really hoped Street could throw some light on it all…"

Fitzwilliam nodded slowly. His head was buzzing with all this new information, unsure how or even if it was in any way connected to Street's death. He needed time to mull it over. He looked at the woman in front of him, who was now staring out of the window at the wet gardens below. *Is she Street's killer? Is this all a smokescreen to throw me off the scent? Is she using Preece as some kind of fall guy when, in fact, she's the corrupt one? Did Street know, and that's why she had to kill him?* Her posture was now loose as she sat quietly, her hands folded in her lap. His instincts were telling him she was being sincere. "One last question. Did you search Street's desk drawers when you were in his office?"

Carmichael's eyes widened. "No, of course not."

That seems genuine. He rose. "Well, thank you, detective inspector. I appreciate your candour. Please keep me in the loop about Preece's death."

She stood. "Do you think the two deaths are linked?"

Fitzwilliam paused for a moment. He didn't want to say too much, but at the same time, he felt they could probably help each other. "It certainly seems possible," he said slowly. "It would be too much of a coincidence if they weren't all related somehow."

28

10.45 AM, THURSDAY 4 FEBRUARY

DCI Richard Fitzwilliam strode into the outer area of the late Chief Superintendent Street's office and spotted DS Tina Spicer and DS Bella Hardwick sitting on one of the small red sofas. Waving the two sergeants over, he stood back to allow Spicer to unlock the door. He let the women go ahead into the room, then he closed the door behind them. "Any luck with Rockcliffe yet?" he asked Spicer as he headed to Street's desk on the other side of the room.

She handed him a pair of blue gloves. "Mrs Rockcliffe wasn't at home, sir. I've left a uniformed officer at the house. He'll let me know as soon as she returns."

Blast! He looked at his watch. "I'll give her until two, and if she doesn't turn up, then we'll find him ourselves." *I hope!*

He shoved his hands in the gloves and pulled the keys Carol had given him from his pocket and inserted one of them into the bottom drawer lock. It opened with a soft *click*. He peered in, then pulled out a worn black rigid briefcase.

His muscles tensed as he saw a biometric fingerprint security panel. *Blast!* He turned to Spicer. "Do we have anyone who can get it open by bypassing the biometric fingerprint security panel?" he asked as he ran his fingers along the leather of the briefcase, looking for an alternative unlocking mechanism.

Spicer nodded. "I know someone. I'll give him a call."

Fitzwilliam put the briefcase down on Street's desk as Spicer took out her phone and started dialling. Focusing his attention back to the desk, he turned to the other drawer. It was locked with a small keyhole. He inserted the key he hadn't used yet into it. The drawer opened, and Fitzwilliam glanced inside. It appeared empty, no papers or anything else that might be useful. About to close it, he paused for a moment. *Why is an empty drawer locked?* He pulled it wider and peered in. Still nothing. He sighed. *Maybe it was just locked out of habit? Unless...* He put his blue-gloved hand in the drawer and began to feel around. *Bingo!* He carefully unpicked the tape that was attaching a small object to the back of the drawer. It came away easily. He withdrew his fist and, opening up his fingers, stared down at a small key. It wasn't a drawer key; it was too small for that. It would have to go to Forensics to see what they made of it.

He straightened up to find DS Hardwick by his side, leaning over and gazing into the drawer. She jumped back to avoid him hitting her in the face. "Is there anything in there?" she asked, tucking her hair behind her ear and looking flustered.

Fitzwilliam tried to hide his annoyance at having her on his shoulder. "Just a key," he said sharply as he dropped it into an evidence bag. She withdrew to the side of the desk, where she shoved her hands in her pockets and looked over at Spicer. Fitzwilliam suppressed a grimace. He hoped she wouldn't be here much longer. He wanted to go back to just him and Spicer.

"Why weren't his drawers unlocked when he died, sir?"

He swung around to look at the sergeant from Intelligance. She held his gaze and lifted her chin slightly. "Ruth Ness said in her statement that when he was in the office, he tended to leave the keys in the locks, but when he was out, he locked the drawers and took the keys with him."

Fitzwilliam frowned. *She has a point.* Had someone locked the drawers after searching them and got rid of the keys? But then why wouldn't they have take the briefcase? Unless they were only looking for one thing that had been in the now empty bottom drawer? Or maybe it was more straightforward than that? "Perhaps Street didn't have them on him on Monday?"

She took her hands out of her pockets and straightened up. "Do you want me to ask Ruth Ness?"

He shook his head. "No, let's leave her for the moment. We'll know when the local police search Street's flat if they're there or not."

Her shoulders slumped, and she returned her hands to her pocket. There was a thickness in Fitzwilliam's throat. *She's just trying to help.* "But it's a good spot, sergeant. If they're missing then yes, we'll need to find out what happened to them." He smiled at her in what he hoped was a reassuring way. She gave a short nod.

Spicer hurried towards them. "He says if I take the case over to him now, he'll have a go and see if he can open it. Is that okay, sir?" Spicer asked, her mobile held out in front of her, the call still connected.

"Yes. But make sure opening it doesn't mean blowing it up. We don't want anything inside getting damaged. It could be evidence."

Spicer nodded and returned to her call.

Fitzwilliam sighed. *No Rockcliffe. No access to the*

contents of the briefcase. And a small key. He could feel his blood pressure rising. He was getting nowhere.

————

Sitting at his desk twenty minutes later, scrolling through the items logged against the investigation on the system, he opened the folder titled 'security footage'. Inside were thumbnails of footage from different sources of various durations and a text file dated Monday called 'Summary of movements'. He clicked it open. The file contained a list of camera locations, times, and names. Fitzwilliam studied the extensive list, scanning each item. The camera located in the corridor leading to Street's office had logged Ruth Ness as arriving at eight-fifteen, followed by Street at eight-forty-four. DCI Bird had arrived at nine-twenty. George Rockcliffe had been next to arrive at nine fifty-six, and he was logged as leaving at ten twenty-six. DI Madeline Carmichael had gone in at ten forty-two. Fitzwilliam paused. The next line said 'Carmichael stepped into corridor, looked around, and went back in' at ten-fifty. Presumably looking for the paramedics. The royal police had arrived at ten fifty-three and then it had got busy when the paramedics had arrived a minute later, followed by himself, Spicer, and Hardwick, then the Forensics team… Fitzwilliam frowned. So if Carmichael had arrived at forty-two minutes past ten, waited a minute or two before she'd gone in, then it would've already been forty-four minutes past. She'd popped her head around the door six minutes later.

He sighed and leaned back. Six minutes to distract Street enough she could sneak behind without him turning around or getting up, render him unconscious, then hold the choke position for at least four minutes before raising the alarm and calming down Ruth Ness? He shook his head. *It doesn't seem feasible.*

He quickly jotted the times down on a notepad, then closed the file and searched for DCI Bird's formal statement taken that afternoon by Spicer. Opening it, he scanned the details. Bird had said he'd arrived at just after nine. Fitzwilliam smiled. Bird was known for his poor time-keeping. Made a pot of coffee... worked in his office...blah, blah, another pot of coffee at quarter past ten... blah, blah.... Ruth had been on the phone. *Ah, here we go.* He'd heard a cry at quarter to eleven coming from Street's office. He'd rushed in and found Carmichael by Street's body in the chair and Ruth Ness standing in the doorway, crying hysterically. He'd suggested Carmichael take Ruth out of the office to calm her down. He'd taken Street's pulse, realised he was dead, and waited with the body until the Royal Police arrived. He hadn't touched anything. Fitzwilliam nodded and closed the document.

Next, he opened the write-up of the interview Spicer had had with Ruth Ness the day after Street's death. She'd fairly much repeated what she'd told him on Monday. She'd still been a bit vague about the times, although they broadly agreed with everyone else's. Finally, he opened Carmichael's formal statement. He began to read...

The phone on his desk flashed green and started to beep. "Yes, Carol?"

"Sir, I have DI Carmichael on the phone."

Really? What are the chances of that? He closed her statement down, oddly embarrassed, as if she'd caught him doing something he shouldn't.

"Put her through, please." The line clicked. "DI Carmichael, what can I do for you?"

"I think it's more what I can do for *you*, sir," she replied.

Her voice was strong and clear, yet held an undercurrent of excitement. "I promised I would keep you in the loop, so I'm letting you know we believe we've identified the man who killed Preece."

Fitzwilliam's mouth dropped open. *That was quick!* "That's great news. I thought it was going to take days for them to even figure out if it was an accidental overdose or–"

"Actually, sir," Carmichael butted in. "The hospital has now completed their review and have confirmed the adrenaline didn't come from their stocks. But while we've been waiting, we've been running our own investigation in parallel with theirs. We've just got hold of the CCTV footage from the corridor outside Preece's room the afternoon he was killed. One of my team has been reviewing it and has come across a doctor whose face and build doesn't match that of any of the doctors working in the department. He went into Preece's room just after three in the afternoon and left three minutes later. It coincides with time of death. We got an enhanced digital mockup of his face and ran it through our systems. We got a match."

29

12:15 AM, THURSDAY 4 FEBRUARY

"That was lucky," Richard Fitzwilliam said, stifling a sigh. Had Maddie Carmichael just phoned to gloat or was she going to tell him something useful?

"Well, yes and no." She sounded less sure of herself now. "We have identified the man as Joseph Peck. Does the name mean anything to you?"

"No. Should it?"

"I didn't know if you'd come across his name during your days in Intelligence."

Fitzwilliam racked his brains. *Hold on… Peck, as in the family?* "Is he one of the Peck Family?"

There was a smile in her voice when she said, "Ah, so you do know of them, sir?"

"I knew of the family back fifteen odd years ago. Leo, Logan, and Charlie if I remember rightly. Brothers. They were an East End gang selling ecstasy in the mid-nineties at massive raves. They made an absolute killing, then moved on to cocaine. One of them, I think it was Leo, had a son, Harry, who managed to get into Harrow and ended up supplying most of the upper class kids." He remembered the trouble it had caused when the king's cousin's son had overdosed at a party in Mayfair. It had been hushed up at the time. Thankfully the press had never got a sniff. "Harry disappeared, didn't he? Just before you guys were due to raid his flat in Chelsea?"

"Yes. We never did catch him. They know how to hide, and they know how to clean up after themselves. Well, since then they've got bigger and smarter. They merged with other crime families, one in France and one in Holland, and rebranded themselves as The Hack Crew about ten years ago.

Ah, so that's where THC originates from. No wonder Jacky Prince had been too scared to talk back at Drew Castle, preferring to risk a jail sentence instead.

"They're now into everything — drugs, human trafficking, arms dealing. If it's illegal and lucrative, then they're all over it. They also have strong links with the gangs in Sicily, Italy, Russia, and are rumoured to collaborate with some nasty people in the US too. Leo's and Logan's sons and Charlie's daughter run it these days. Charlie died a few years ago. Cancer, I think. The other two brothers shuffle between Mexico and Spain where they have huge villas and no one can touch them. And believe me, we've tried."

Fitzwilliam picked up the frustration in her voice. It never ceased to amaze him how these large well-known criminal families carried on, seemingly immune to prosecution. But powerful lawyers, lots of money, and a healthy dose of fear within their membership to not talk were walls the police were constantly banging their heads on. "So where does Joseph Peck come into all this?"

"He's small fry in the grand scheme of things. The son of a distant cousin of the original brothers. He's in his sixties and based mainly in Italy these days. But the day before

Preece died, he flew from Rome to London under another name, of course, then flew back the next morning."

"So he's a hitman for them?"

"We believe so, although he's been pretty quiet for the last five years. To be honest, we thought he'd retired." She let out a deep sigh. "The problem with Preece's killer being someone from THC is that we won't be able to hold Joseph Peck responsible. Even if we have unshakeable evidence, which we don't, *and* even if we could find him in Italy, the Italians won't hand him over to us in risk of feeling the might of their homegrown mafia raining down on them."

Fitzwilliam wasn't sure how any of this impacted Street's death. Unless…. *Is it possible Street knew and was silenced before he could spill the beans?* Fitzwilliam tried to get his thoughts in order. *Street found out Preece was dirty. He was going to expose him. THC killed Preece so his association with them was buried, then they killed Street to silence him?*

"Chief inspector?" Carmichael's worried voice broke through his thoughts. "Are you okay?"

"Yes, sorry." Fitzwilliam stretched his neck side to side, a satisfying *click* providing some relief to the stiffness. He suddenly recalled last night's conversation with Adler. Could he trust Carmichael? He was sure she wasn't a killer, but was she a bent copper? Even so…maybe he'd just ask her a simple question. "What do you know about the Grazzi Family?"

"Grazzi?" She sounded a little confused. "Not much. American organised crime. Mainly in Florida and up into Georgia. They're trying to break into New York state possibly. They're hard to keep track of, more MI6's thing than ours. Why do you ask?"

"Er, someone mentioned them in passing the other day. I

hadn't heard of them. It's not my area. It seems to be yours…"

"Can I ask who mentioned them, sir? Was it an official briefing or—"

Blast! I shouldn't have said anything. "No, nothing like that. Someone read an old article online or something. I was just curious. Anyway, thanks for the call. Let me know if you find out anything more."

She hesitated, then said, "Yes, sir. Thank you."

The line went dead, and Fitzwilliam let out a deep breath. A tightness around his head told him he needed a break and something to eat. He got up and headed out for some fresh air.

30

MEANWHILE, THURSDAY 4 FEBRUARY

"Beatrice, it's a pleasure to see you again so soon." Brett Goodman took Lady Beatrice's hand and smiled. A shiver went down her spine. She shook his hand briefly, then let go, muttering, "Thank you." *What is he doing here?* She turned to glare at her elder brother, but Lord Frederick Astley was studying something on his phone, so her attempt to give him the evil eye was wasted.

"Shall we?" Brett, still smiling at her, gestured towards a cluster of two small sofas and two chairs around a low coffee table. Leaving Fred where he was, she scanned the room as she followed Brett towards an ornate brass fireplace just behind the seats.

She'd never been to the foreign office building where Fred worked before, and she'd expected it to be a modern soulless place like most government buildings were in her experience. But this room was small and cosy and had an old fashioned feel to it. Like a gentleman's club. The lower half of the walls were panelled with dark mahogany, the space above painted a deep royal blue with several large portraits of important looking men dotted about. The worn brown leather sofas before them were accompanied by armchairs covered in soft velvet in shades of blues and dark reds. Plush curtains hung over a large bay window over the other side of the room, filtering out the sun and providing a comfortable amount of dimness. *Perfect for sipping tea or coffee whilst discussing secrets,* she thought. Bea smiled to herself, still finding it hard to believe her brother, nephew of the king of England, was a spy. Well sort of.

She let Brett move towards one of the armchairs before she lowered herself to perch on the sofa opposite him. She watched him sit down, then lean over and pick up a coffeepot standing on the corner of the table. "You take your coffee black, if I remember rightly?" he asked, grinning. She nodded. She'd forgotten just how charming the good-looking, coffee-coloured CIA agent was. Their last encounter back at Drew Castle the month before had ended with him asking her if he could take her out to dinner when she was back in London. She'd refused, of course. After she'd found out he'd been an old friend of her late husband's, it hadn't felt right. But she'd been sorely tempted. Feeling heat pulsing in her cheeks, she looked down at the coffee table. Her mouth watered as her eyes took in the array of delicate sandwiches, their crusts removed, a selection of cheeses and crackers, and fresh fruit cut into bite-sized pieces and arranged on a silver platter.

"Dig in," her brother said as he appeared by her side and leaned down to kiss her on the cheek. She looked up at him and smiled. With his Disney-prince good looks and his tall, lean frame, he even looked a bit like James Bond. He pulled out the vacant armchair opposite her and sat down with a *huff*, dropping his mobile phone on the table before helping himself to a few of the sandwiches. "Well," he said through a mouthful of food. "This has really set the cat among the pigeons."

She studied his face and noticed for the first time, the faint dark circles under his eyes. Was he alright? Were James's papers, which she'd passed on to him, the cause of his remark? She sipped the coffee Brett had handed to her a moment ago. *Is that why Brett's here?* She stared at Fred, willing him to explain further.

"I asked Brett to join us," he continued, "because he knows more about this than I do." He waved his hand at the round-faced American next to him. "The floor is all yours, my friend."

Brett nodded and put his plate down. "So what do you know about the Grazzi Family?" he said to her as he crossed his legs and picked up his coffee cup.

Bea shrugged. "Not much other than what Perry found in an old article online. They're some sort of crime family?"

Brett smiled wryly. "That's like saying the pope is some sort of priest."

She frowned. *There's no need to be rude!*

He cleared his throat, looking rather sheepish. "Sorry, I just meant that's a big understatement. The Grazzi Family is a huge network of organised crime spreading across the states of Florida, Georgia, and parts of New York state. They've been around in some shape or form since the mid nineteen-fifties. At that time, they were one of a number of small gangs operating illegal gambling dens, but now their activities include drug running, loansharking, corporate fraud, human trafficking, prostitution, money laundering. You name the pie, they have a finger in it." He shook his head, his expression now sombre. "The FBI have been trying for years to shut them down, but they've had little success."

"Why?" Bea asked. "If the FBI know they're doing all these things, why can't they arrest them and stop it?"

"Because the people who *really* run the show are hidden deep in the background. It's structured in such a way, each person only knows the one guy they report to. You have the guys on the street, you know, the ones who do all the dirty work. They only know their team leader. And he in turn only knows his area leader. And so on. So unless *everyone* in the tree tells, you hit a brick wall *really* quickly. We can arrest the guy on the street, and if he's prepared to cooperate, we may also get his boss. Then it stops. They have a very strict code of non-cooperation with law enforcement, which is ironic considering how many officials they have in their pockets. No one wants to cross them. It's fear based because they know your family, your friends. It's better to be arrested and charged. And if you do, then they'll look after you. They'll lawyer you up. You'll probably get away with it the first few times, then you're back doing what you were doing. Maybe in a different area. If you get caught too many times and convicted, they have the state prisons in their hands. So you'll have an easy few years inside, then you're out and back to doing what you were doing." He ran his fingers through his short brown hair. "It's the FBI's biggest frustration."

"Don't they go undercover and try to get names that way?" Fred asked, wiping his mouth and returning his empty plate to the table.

"They try, but it takes years to progress up the chain and that holds a high risk for undercover officers. If they stay deep in cover for too long, they end up having to do some-thing bad to stay in. And if they cross that line...then it's game over for them. We can only protect them from prosecu-tion to an extent. Some back out before they get to that point. Some cross the line, but by then, their loyalties are in question, so we have to take them out. Some change sides; it's a lucrative business. Others disappear."

Bea's eyes widened. "You mean they're killed?"

Brett shrugged. "Maybe. Or maybe they decide to stay and get moved to another part of the business. Some take the money and run, hoping neither us nor the family will find them."

Oh my goodness. This was a whole new world to her, and she didn't like the sound of it at all.

"So you see it's almost impossible to get to the people who matter. We close a small local unit, and within days, they have another up and running to replace it."

"So how does what I've given you help?"

Fred rubbed his hands together. "I can answer this. In one word: Rudy Trotman." He turned to Brett and nodded.

"There were rumours in Miami around the time of the Olympics that Rudy Trotman was working with the Grazzi Family, but the FBI couldn't prove anything. No one would talk. A couple of years later, Rudy began to clean up his act. He slowly dropped his involvement with some of the unions and the big building contractors. He moved instead into legitimate businesses. The trail went cold."

Fred took over. "Sir Hewitt Willoughby-Franklin did checks on the Trotmans when Sybil first met Otis. To everyone's surprise they all came up clean."

Sir Hewitt? Why was he involved, and how does Fred know? Suddenly it came to her. "Sir Hewitt is a spy too!"

Fred clamped his hand over his mouth, the tips of his ears turning bright red. *Well, that answers my question.* "You really are the worst spy ever, brother," she said to Fred, laughing.

Fred winced, then recovering, he glared at her. "For a

start, you know I'm not a spy. I'm an SO. A MI6 Special Observer. Not a spy! Do you understand?"

She nodded, still grinning. *Of course you're a spy!*

"Secondly," he continued. "I didn't say anything about Sir Hewitt being an SO. Is that clear?" *You might not have done, but your ears did.* She stifled a giggle and nodded. "However, Sir Hewitt is a well-respected figure in this country and, of course, is protective of his family. It's perfectly normal he would check his future in-laws out."

But not 'perfectly normal' you would know about it, dear brother. Bea kept her mouth closed and nodded again. Fred carried on. "However, his relationship by marriage with Rudy Trotman is fortuitous for us. He's in a unique position to talk to Trotman, and with the leverage of what James knew about Trotman's dealings in Miami, he might just be prepared to talk."

But what did James know? She'd found nothing other than James's comment that he'd thought Rudy was 'dodgy'. She frowned. "But we don't know what James knew," she said, looking from one man to the other.

"Ah, but Trotman doesn't know that, does he?" Fred pointed out.

"Oh, come on, Fred. Rudy's an astute man. Why would he start spilling the beans on dangerous and powerful people unless he really believes you have something on him?"

Brett cleared his throat. "And that's where you come in."

Me? What can I do? I hardly know Rudy Trotman...

"James was an ardent note taker. He must have written some notes about Miami and what he discovered somewhere, Beatrice."

Bea sighed. Brett was right. James had always made notes. *But...* "But I've looked through all his papers, and his notebooks are full of stories about his various visits but nothing about Miami other than his notations on the papers I've given you."

"Have you looked through *all* his things?" Brett leaned forward, his eyes searching hers.

She nodded. "As far as I know." She turned to Fred. "Rory told me he'd packed up all of James's papers, and Fraser then put them into storage. I don't think anything is missing."

Fred nodded. "How about his private stuff?"

"Ma and I went through it all a few months after he died. I kept some things for Sam — you know, books, photos, trophies, and the like, and let James's parents have the rest. There weren't any papers that I recall."

Fred let out a deep sigh. "Is it possible you or Fraser missed something?"

Did we? "I can go home and have another look if you want?"

Both Fred and Brett nodded fervently. "In the meantime, can I go through the papers and notebooks you haven't given us just in case I spot something?" Fred asked.

"Yes, of course. They're at the palace. I'll get them delivered to you. What will you do about Trotman?"

"Sir Hewitt has invited him and his wife to visit him in London. They arrive this afternoon. I think he's arranged for tickets to some big event tonight he thinks Rudy will want to be at. He'll have a chat with him and see where it goes," Fred told her. "But the sooner we have something we can give him to poke Rudy into cooperating, the better."

No pressure then…

31

2 PM, THURSDAY 4 FEBRUARY

"Sir?" Detective Sergeant Tina Spicer poked her head around the office door. Richard Fitzwilliam looked up from his computer screen, where he'd been looking at the crime scene pictures of Street's office. Something was bugging him about them, but he couldn't put his finger on what it was.

"They've got the briefcase open. Do you want to go and—"

Fitzwilliam was up from his desk and had grabbed his phone before Spicer finished her sentence.

As they marched the five minutes it took to get to the Forensics Department, Spicer brought him up to date with the other outstanding items concerning the case. Fitzwilliam barely contained his frustration when Spicer informed him Mrs Rockcliffe still wasn't home. He'd have to get the ball rolling on an international arrest warrant, something he desperately wanted to avoid. He asked Spicer to remind him to ask Carol to arrange a meeting with DCI Bird. He wanted to get Bird's take on what Maddie Carmichael had told him. He had a feeling Bird knew more than he was letting on. Hardwick, who was trotting behind them along the narrow corridor linking security to the labs, cleared her throat. "Excuse me, sir."

To be honest, he'd forgotten she was here. He stopped abruptly, then had to move to one side to avoid Hardwick bumping into him. "Yes, sergeant?" he said, giving her a look he hoped conveyed the warning she'd better not be wasting his time.

"I was re-reading the statements before we got the call about the briefcase, and I'm a bit confused about where DCI Bird was when he heard DI Carmichael shout for help," she said as they huddled together just a few metres before the corridor opened up into a foyer leading to Forensics.

Frowning, Fitzwilliam said, "He was in his office, wasn't he?"

"That's what his statement says, sir."

So what's your issue? He let out a sigh of frustration that earned him a disapproving look from Spicer.

"What's worrying you, Bella?" Spicer asked.

"Well, Carmichael's statement says she shouted for Ruth Ness to call an ambulance, but she didn't think she heard her, so she ran to the door and shouted again. Ruth then came into the office and froze. Carmichael said Bird rushed in soon after."

Yes, I know all of this… Fitzwilliam bit his tongue while Spicer nodded at the other DS encouragingly.

"Bird said he'd heard Carmichael shout and rushed in, finding her with Street's body and Ruth Ness standing in the doorway crying…" She trailed off and turned to Spicer. "So how did he get in if Ruth was standing in the doorway?"

Fitzwilliam's skin tingled. *How* did *Bird get in?* Then he realised. "The connecting door!"

Hardwick and Spicer stared at him. "What connecting door?" Spicer asked.

"In the back corner of the room," he explained. "It used to be Street's dressing room, but when Bird needed an office, they put him in there." He turned to Hardwick. "Well spotted. It hadn't occurred to me he would use it to gain access to Street's office. I'll clarify that with him when I talk to him later." He smiled at Hardwick and was relieved to see her blush. *Have I been too hard on her? Maybe she will prove to be useful after all.* "Right, let's go see what's inside this brief-case." He began to move towards the foyer, but Spicer was still fixed to the spot. He halted and looked back at her. "What?"

"If DCI Bird had access to Street's office, sir, then he could be our killer."

32

2:15 PM, THURSDAY 4 FEBRUARY

Bird? Fitzwilliam's thoughts were in turmoil as he entered the Forensics Department a few minutes later. Spicer's suggestion that Bird could be the killer was one he'd not even considered. He'd known Bird for seventeen years. Could someone he'd known and liked for so long be a murderer? But he now had to consider the possibility however unpalatable it might seem. After all, in terms of opportunity, if he ruled out Maddie Carmichael, which he was quite confident he could do, then only George Rockcliffe and Bird *could* be the murderer. He could feel a tightness around his head, as if someone had placed an elastic band around it. *One thing at a time.* He would tackle the Bird dilemma when he was done here.

"Chief inspector." A tall lanky man wearing a white coat held out his hand. "I'm Duncan Neal. Tina here" —he glanced at Spicer, a smile playing on his lips— "asked me to help you gain access to the briefcase you found at a crime scene." His handshake was limp, and his skin was a little clammy. Fitzwilliam fought the urge to drop his hand immediately and wipe it on his trousers. He'd already decided he didn't much care for the man.

And surely he wasn't Spicer's type? He looked at his sergeant, her blonde hair tucked neatly behind her ears, her face tinged with red, and realised he didn't actually know what her type was. "Duncan is my cousin, sir," Spicer explained.

Fitzwilliam nodded. Maybe he should give Spicer's cousin the benefit of the doubt. He smiled at the young man. "We appreciate your help, Mr Neal."

Neal held up his hand. "Please call me Duncan. Come with me and let me show you what I've found."

They followed him through double doors and into a work-shop, where spread out on a waist-height wooden bench was Street's now opened briefcase. Lying beside it was a plastic bag containing some papers. A second bag contained what looked to Fitzwilliam like a mobile phone, and a third bag was holding something small that was indistinguishable from this distance.

"So I won't bore you with how I managed to get in. But I will say that if I'd had this briefcase three years ago, I would have struggled with it; it would have been state-of-the-art then. Fortunately, although these types of biometric locked cases are still one of your best bets if you want to keep things safe from your regular person, improvement in cracking these types of locks means they are no longer impenetrable." He pointed to the top of the case. "So it was a combination type that worked on fingerprint recognition *and* a digital code. You need both to get in. The only fingerprints we could find on it and in it were CS Street's."

"Is this something you can buy in a regular shop, Dunk?" Spicer asked.

He smiled at her. "Good question, Tina. No. It's specialist

security equipment. Mainly used in the transport of jewellery and money. It has a titanium shell, so it's also impossible to get into by using pure brute force. I believe it is used by some government agencies to transfer classified documents, but we don't use them here in the UK as far as I know."

So where did Street get it from? From his days at MI6 maybe? He'd have to ask someone.

"So now on to what we found inside. First was this wad of papers. It looks like some sort of letter or memo. My colleagues haven't been able to make much sense of it. We think it could be some sort of code. Again the only finger-prints on it are Street's." He reached under the desk and handed Fitzwilliam a plastic wallet. "Here's a copy for you, sir." Fitzwilliam glanced quickly down at the papers as he took them. It looked like rows of number sequences. There were pages of them.

"Then we found this phone. It appears it's a standard pay-as-you-go model; however, it requires a ten digit code to gain access, which makes me believe it's anything but standard. I'll be sending it up to the guys in electronics to have a look, but I'll be honest, I suspect it's a burner phone, and it won't hold any numbers or call history. I wouldn't hold your breath."

A chill ran down Fitzwilliam's spine. Why on earth would Street have had a burner phone? Who had he been talking to? What had he been up to? He had a bad feeling about this.

"And that's it for the case." Duncan held up the last and smallest bag. Something small and silver-grey in colour laid at the bottom. *The key I found in the other drawer.* "This is the key you also gave us," he told them. "I'm not sure what it's for, but if you ask me, I would say it looks like the one my father has to open his gun case. There were no usable fingerprints on it."

Gun? The muscles in Fitzwilliam's shoulder tightened. Only specially-trained firearms officers were issued with guns in PaIRS. As far as he knew, Tim Street hadn't been one of them.

"Of course I could be wrong," he said as he handed the small bag to Fitzwilliam.

"Wait a minute, Dunk. Do you mean like a metal box with padding in?" Spicer asked.

He shrugged. "Could be."

She quickly scrolled through the photos on her phone, then stopped and tapped one. "Like this?"

Fitzwilliam leaned in as she placed her phone on the bench. The picture was of a green metal box just smaller than a sheet of A4 paper with dimpled grey eggshell foam lining inside. "Where did that come from?" he asked her.

"SOC officers found it in a locked filing cabinet in Street's office, sir. They only gained access this morning, so haven't got around to confirming what it held yet. They posted the photo on the PaIRS app an hour or so ago." She gave him a look that said 'if you used the app, then you would know these things'.

Dunk straightened up and nodded. "From looking at the lock in the photo, I would say it's very likely the key you have there will fit." He smiled. "And that's it from me. Oh, and we used a special metal detector to check there was nothing else hidden inside the briefcase, but there wasn't, sorry."

A coded letter, a burner phone, and a key that possibly unlocked a gun case. *What was Street up to?* His stomach twisted. *And where is the gun?*

He thanked Duncan Neal, having revised his opinion of the young man, and they left the workshop.

As they entered the foyer, his phone beeped.

. . .

Lady B: *Off to FC to see if I can find any more of James's papers. I might have missed something. Will be back tomorrow.*

He quickly typed a reply.

Fitzwilliam: *Okay. Let's catch up tomorrow evening. Will confirm details nearer the time.*

A thumbs up emoji appeared on the screen, and Fitzwilliam returned the phone to his pocket. Next to him, Spicer's phone rang. "DS Spicer?" she said.

She listened to the caller and nodded. "And what time does his flight land?" She smiled at Fitzwilliam as she told the caller, "Well, thank you for letting me know, Mrs Rockcliffe. And no, it won't be necessary for us to issue a warrant for his arrest now as long as he's on the flight as you say." She was still smiling as she cut the call. "George Rockcliffe has been in contact with his wife, and he's flying back to Gatwick tomorrow morning." She grinned. "And I'll be there to meet him."

33

6 PM, THURSDAY 4 FEBRUARY

Lady Beatrice watched the little white terrier pick her way across the floor of the storage room in the basement of Francis Court. "Daisy, be careful," she cried, not wanting her to get injured by any of the objects scattered across the floor. *Why didn't Ma warn me it was such a mess in here when she gave me the key?* Bea moved forward carefully, hunched over to avoid hitting her head on the beams hanging from the low ceiling. A strange musty smell seemed to cling to everything as she moved through, filling her nostrils and making her want to sneeze. She glanced over at an old rocking chair standing in one corner, covered in a delicate grey dust. Bea remembered it from when she had been down here fourteen years ago. Hadn't her mother told her it had belonged to Pa's aunt when she'd been a little girl?

She headed to the far wall where there was an array of trunks of varying heights and widths; some were shut, while others were half-opened, revealing their contents. Next to them were boxes full of old photographs from past birthdays, Christmases, and family gatherings. *How far do they go back? I must come down here sometime with Sam and go through them all.* She started as Daisy barked sharply, the sound echoing around the small room.

The little dog had run up to a large blue trunk standing in the corner and was now scratching at it. "Daisy, what is it?" Bea moved closer to investigate. When she got there, she recognised the intricate patterns carved into the wood around the edges of the chest. *James's old school trunk!* She frowned. Hadn't this gone to James's parents all those years ago? She searched her memory. Yes, she remembered now. Her and William, her father-in-law, had agreed it should go to Durrland Hall, and when he felt Sam was ready, they would explore the contents together. *So why is it still here?* She bent down, gently pushing Daisy to one side, and opened the lid. Immediately, Daisy stuck her head inside, sniffing its contents. *What's she so interested in?* As Daisy's main reason to live was food, she couldn't imagine what she would find to—

Her and Daisy saw the packet of jelly babies at the same time. Bea shoved her hand in and made a grab for them just as Daisy hurled herself up and over the side of the box, landing in it just as Bea made contact with the package. "No, Daisy. Leave!" Bea shouted. Daisy hesitated just long enough for Bea to hoist them out and straighten up, the packet held high in her hand and out of Daisy's reach. Bea studied the faded packaging. The name had almost disappeared.

How long have they been in there?

She shook her head, smiling, and placed them on a shelf to her right. She bent and plucked Daisy up and out of the trunk. "Good girl, Daisy," she said as she placed her carefully down on a clear area of floor by her side. Bea peered into the chest, the contents now slightly trampled by Daisy. This wasn't what she'd come to do. She looked over at the far wall. She was supposed to be searching for any papers they might have missed. She looked back and stared into the trunk. Unable to resist the temptation, she knelt down and leaned in. Inside the box were old battered notebooks filled to the brim with sketches, maps, and notes from James's time at school. Along with these were some of his childhood toys — a wooden train set, a model boat, and even an old telescope. She was looking into her husband's past. A wave of emotion washed over her. Her eyes stung as she ran her fingers across the items. As she wiped a tear from her cheek, her eye was caught by a hardback book propped up at the end of the trunk. She reached for it and turned it to look at the spine. *Lord of the Flies* by William Golding.

She smiled. This had been James's favourite book from school. Bea looked down at Daisy, who lay at her feet snoozing away contentedly. *I'll just have a quick peek.* She opened the book. On the title page was a stamp familiar to her. Wilton College. James's school then. Sam's school now. She turned to the first page and frowned. It was littered with letters underlined in black. She stared, her mind attempting to make sense of what she could see. She looked more closely. The 'T' of the first word 'The' had been underlined, as had the 'e'; further along, the first letter of the word 'lowered' was marked, and the sixth letter of the word 'himself'. Her eye followed the first sentence. The 'b' of 'began' was underlined, also the fifth letter of 'toward', the last letter of 'the', the first letter of 'Though', and the first letter of 'taken'. Then there was a gap with no letters underlined for a while. Then it started again. The 'g' of 'grey', the 'o' of 'to', another 'o' of 'to', further along the line, the last letter of 'forehead'. Then the last letter of 'him', the third letter of 'scar', the 'm' in 'smashed'. Bea's heart jumped. She stopped and went back, reading them all together this time. *Tell Brett Goodman...*

34

9:20 AM, FRIDAY 5 FEBRUARY

Detective Chief Inspector Richard Fitzwilliam glared down at his watch and then back to his office door. *Where is he? It's all very well being shoddy at time keeping, but—*

Carol's head appeared around the door. "Detective Chief Inspector Bird has rung to apologise, sir. He's running a few minutes late but says he'll be here within the next ten minutes."

"Thanks, Carol." He let out a deep sigh as she disappeared into the outer office. He looked down at his desk and pulled the plastic wallet Duncan Neal had given him yesterday towards him. He'd already passed a copy on to Intelligence to see if they could make any sense of it. He slid the first sheet out of the protective sleeve and studied it. It was a single A4 sheet of white paper, identical to the kind found in any office. At the top was a heading written by hand in black biro, all in capitals — LETTERS TO MARIE MONTH. It had been underlined twice. Under that was a series of number combinations. 12-5-2-3; 14-7-31-5; 15-14-50-2 and so on. There were ten number combinations on each line, and he counted thirty-two lines of them on each side of the paper.

Who on earth is Marie Month? They'd searched the PaIRS and City Police databases, but no match had been found. They'd been through Street's personal contacts on his phone and his laptop. Nothing. Spicer had suggested it was a clue of some sort, but they'd got no further than that at the moment. They were stumped.

Fitzwilliam squeezed his eyes shut, then opened them again. No. Nothing. He sighed and returned the sheet to its wallet. *Hopefully Intelligence can run it through their super computers and break the code. If that's what it is...* But then what had Street been doing that needed to be written in code? And why had it been kept in a briefcase only he could access? For that matter, why had he needed a burner phone? And then there was the gun. Or rather the lack of it...

After a quick trip to Forensics yesterday afternoon, Spicer had been able to confirm that the small key he'd found in Street's office drawer did indeed fit the metal gun case found in Street's filing cabinet. And when she'd contacted the armoury, not only did they confirm Street was firearm trained and that he'd completed his annual firearm assessment back in November, passing without any issues, but much to Fitzwilliam's surprise, they'd also confirmed that Street had been issued with a personal firearm a few months back. When he'd asked his boss, Superintendent Blake, about it, his answer of, "It's not unusual for senior officers to have a personal firearm," had been suitably vague and unhelpful.

Last night, City Police had searched his flat, but there was no gun to be found. However they had found his desk drawer keys hanging up, so at least that mystery was solved. Discreet enquires with his ex-wife confirmed that to her knowledge he'd never kept a gun at home. Fitzwilliam ran his fingers through his short brown hair and blew out air. *Is this all a wild goose chase?*

He checked his watch. He pinched his lips together. It had been more than ten minutes since Carol had told him Bird would be late. *Blast!* He stood up to get himself a refill from the coffeepot that was permanently on in his office just as his door opened and DCI Henry Bird strolled in. "So sorry I'm late, Fitzwilliam. You wouldn't believe the traffic some mornings."

Well, get out of bed a bit earlier then, you lazy—

"Is that coffee? I'm dying for one…"

Fitzwilliam clenched his jaw and grabbed an empty mug from the stack by the coffee machine. He poured black liquid into each cup, then looked over his shoulder at Bird. "Do you still take it black?"

Bird nodded, and Fitzwilliam picked up the two cups, handing one over to Bird as he gestured for him to take the chair in front of his desk.

"So," Fitzwilliam began as he sat down and placed his mug, that had 'Coffee for my sanity and your safety' emblazoned on the front in big black letters, on a coaster . *Well, that's certainly true today,* he thought as he stared at Bird. "First, I need to clarify something you said on your statement."

Bird raised an eyebrow but didn't say anything.

"You said you went into Street's office when you heard Maddie Carmichael cry out. How did you get in?"

Bird frowned for a moment, then his face cleared. "Oh, through the connecting door. Didn't I say that?"

"No, you didn't," Fitzwilliam said, trying to keep the edge out of his voice. "So the connecting door isn't locked then?"

"It was at one time, but then I think the key went missing…" Bird shrugged nonchalantly.

"So did you and Street use it often when you needed to talk to each other?"

Bird shook his head. "Never. We always went via the outer office." He gave a short laugh. "It would be more than my job's worth to barge in when he could have had someone in with him."

"So why did you use it this time?"

"I heard a woman shout, and it sounded like an emergency. I just grabbed the door and went in. It was instinctive, I guess."

Fitzwilliam remembered the picture in Bird's office partly obscuring the connecting door. Would it be instinctive to move the painting and open the door? Or would you just go out the way you normally did? He wasn't convinced.

"Did you try and search Street's drawers while you were waiting for the emergency services to arrive?"

Bird stiffened. "Why would I do that?"

So that's not a 'no'…

"I don't know. The drawers were locked. Someone wiped the handles clean, presumably after they tried to get into them."

"Well, it wasn't me," Bird said sharply. Again Fitzwilliam wasn't convinced. There had been something about the way Bird had talked about Street last week that had suggested he hadn't liked him. But was it more than that? He was beginning to consider if Bird could have a motive to want Street dead.

"You didn't like him, did you, Henry?"

Bird cocked his head to one side. "Why do you say that?" He leaned back and crossed his arms.

Fitzwilliam suppressed a sigh. Bird hadn't changed. The

minute he thought you were gunning for him, his defences went up. *I'm not going to get anywhere like this.* A change of tactic was needed. "Come on, mate. We've known each other for years. I could tell from the way you spoke about him that he wasn't your best buddy. You normally get on with everyone. Why not him?"

Bird uncrossed his arms and leaned in. "Because I didn't trust the man further than I could throw him." He grabbed his coffee cup and took a swig. "Did you know I caught him putting a gun in his drawer?"

The hairs on the back of Fitzwilliam's neck prickled. "When was this?"

Bird shrugged. "A month or so back."

"Did you say anything?"

Bird shook his head slowly. "It all happened so fast. I didn't get a good look, but I'm sure it was a gun. He saw me in the doorway and stuffed it back into his drawer and shut it quickly."

"Which drawer?"

Bird frowned. "Er, the one on his right. Why?"

That was the empty drawer that had been locked. He wouldn't have just had a gun lying around loose in there, would he? But the gun case had been found in the filing cabinet...

"Fitz?" Bird had raised his voice.

"Tell me about Street and why you didn't trust him."

Bird leaned back and stroked his chin thoughtfully. After a few moments of silence, he seemed to come to a decision. "You know City have been investigating DI Preece for a while now?"

Fitzwilliam nodded.

"Well, Street and Preece worked together when Street was at City, but when Street moved to PaIRS, as far as anyone knew, they didn't stay in contact. In fact, when someone asked Preece how Street was one time, he said he'd no idea because they'd lost contact. But that's not true. Last summer, one of the lads recognised them together out near Battersea. They were having a right ding-dong according to him. Preece was shouting, and Street was trying to reason with him. Now maybe it was nothing. Maybe they were still mates and had just kept it quiet or got back in touch. But it didn't feel right to me, not when we knew Preece was on the take. I mean—"

"But do we know Preece was dirty? Maddie Carmichael—"

"Had a wobble when Preece got shot and started to second guess herself. If you ask me, it just proves the case even more. *And* it proves to me someone here at PaIRS was involved too."

Fitzwilliam's mouth dropped open. *Someone here?*

"Look, let me lay it out for you, Fitz, and see what you think."

"Okay," Fitzwilliam said slowly. *Do I really want to hear this?*

"I think someone wanted to kill Preece the night of the kidnapping, but thanks to your pal, Adler, they failed. I spoke to Adler, by the way. She told me she thinks one of the kidnappers deliberately shot Preece. In fact, I'll go further and say I think the whole thing was a ploy to kill Preece."

"What? You mean the whole kidnapping of the duke?"

"*Failed* kidnapping, Fitz. What a great cover, heh? City Police officer gets shot in a kidnapping attempt. It's not personal. Preece is just collateral damage." He stopped and took a sip of his coffee. "You worked in Intelligence, mate. How often did we get such clear and detailed information about an attempt to take a member of the royal family?" His eyes search Fitzwilliam's.

He's right. Of the four attempts Fitzwilliam knew of, they'd known nothing about any of them in advance. Fortunately, well-trained close protection officers and, in one case, the subject themselves, had been able to stop those attempts.

"None, heh? But this time we're given very precise information about this so called kidnapping. And you know what? I can't get to the bottom of where the tip-off came from. Everybody seems to know about it, but no one can pinpoint the source."

Fitzwilliam frowned as he gulped down his coffee. *That's strange.*

"So here's what I think happened. THC wanted to stage Preece's elimination, so they find out from him about the duke's movements, then leak their strike plan to PaIRS. We go into prevention mode, whisk the duke off, and set up the decoy. They know we're going to do that. They turn up, pretend to panic about it being a decoy, appear to flee, shoot Preece, and scarper."

Fitzwilliam's head spun. He stared at Bird. "But that would be really dangerous. Too much of a risk."

"Why? You ask Adler. They barely got close enough to see it was a decoy before they turned tail and ran. And did you know the order for us was 'Don't shoot. Capture'?"

Fitzwilliam shook his head.

"They knew they weren't going to be taking much of a risk."

Fitzwilliam shook his head slowly, still trying to process everything he'd heard. It was starting to make sense, but it seemed so unbelievable. He thought back to what he knew of the tip-off they'd received. Bird was right — it had seemed too good to be true. In hindsight, maybe that was because it had been. He shook it off and tried to think logically. "But why go to such lengths to kill Preece?"

"An attempt to eliminate an inconvenient truth or loose end in someone's mind. The most obvious suspect is THC, but who knows? We're talking about organised crime, after all. That means a lot of money and influence behind them. It could even be a rival gang. The possibilities are endless."

Fitzwilliam nodded slowly, trying to take in what Bird had just said. "Carmichael suggested maybe Preece wanted out."

He nodded. "They could've killed him for that. And if you factor in his encounter with Street, maybe Street was the PaIRS mole. Maybe he was trying to dissuade Preece from leaving, but when that failed, he anonymously revealed the kidnapping plot to facilitate Preece's murder."

Street, a bent copper? Fitzwilliam's brain was struggling to accept the possibility. "Do you have any proof CS Street was bad?"

Bird huffed, then shook his head. "Honestly? No, not really. But we were on it. We were going to see how Street reacted during his meeting with Maddie. She was going to tell him about the investigation into Preece."

We were going to see how Street reacted... The penny dropped. "You were going to listen via the connecting door? That's why you went in that way. You were there already!"

Bird coloured and looked down at his knees. He didn't say anything.

"Do you think he would have been rattled by Carmichael's visit?" Fitzwilliam asked.

Bird, still looking a bit sheepish, nodded. "I know he was. He came into my office that morning and not very subtly tried to find out what she wanted. I told him Maddie was heading up the investigation into Preece's death, and she was talking to everyone who knew him. I didn't give anything away, but I could tell he was concerned."

Fitzwilliam held Bird's eye. "Did you try to go through his drawers to see if you could find proof against him?"

Bird shook his head, retaining eye contact. "No."

What a pity, Fitzwilliam thought. *Because if you had, you would've found the briefcase with the burner phone and coded letter inside.* Proof that Street had been up to something.

Bird let out a deep sigh. "Okay...I was looking for my appraisal."

What? Fitzwilliam's eyes opened wide.

Bird continued, "He was due to submit it on Monday. I knew from Ruth he hadn't finished it yet. Did you know he hand wrote all appraisals, then gave them to Ruth to type up and submit? I wanted to know what he'd written. I was convinced he was going to get me side-lined."

"Did you find it?"

Bird smiled wryly. "I glanced at the papers on his desk, then I tried the drawers, but they were locked. Then I realised I was an idiot and someone might come and do a sweep for fingerprints, so I used my handkerchief and wiped the handles clean. After, when I was waiting for the royal police, I looked over at his desk and saw it. It was almost completely covered up by another report." He paused, shuffling awkwardly in his seat, then carried on. "I uncovered it to see he'd recommended me for promotion. Can you believe it? He probably thought it would be the best way to get me out of his hair."

35

MEANWHILE, FRIDAY 5 FEBRUARY

Detective Chief Inspector Emma McKeer-Adler scrolled through the subfolders on the restored hard drive of Street's laptop. They had been lucky. Street had deleted a number of files during the week before his death, but a recent update in IT policy that had changed the daily emptying of trash folders on all laptops to a weekly process meant they hadn't *actually* been deleted yet. She stretched her arm out across the large wooden table and grabbed the cup of tea Izzy had brought in for her a few minutes ago. One of the advantages of working from home was that her wife regularly popped into the dining room and refilled her mug. She sometimes brought biscuits too. *I could get used to this.*

Suddenly she froze, her cup half-way to her mouth. The name Fitzwilliam had flashed up on the screen. *What the—* It was a subfolder. She put down her tea and looked across the screen at the additional information. The folder had been set up last May, been last accessed in January this year, and been deleted on Friday, three days before Street's death. She double clicked on it.

There were just three files inside. She clicked on the first one — a pdf called GS-BS. The screen was filled with copies of scanned bank statements. Her eyes darted to the top. There was the sort code, account number, and account name. Gill Sterling. Adler's heart jumped. *Gill Sterling?* The woman who'd been killed in the Earl of Rossex's car fifteen years ago. *What are her bank statements doing on Street's computer?* They were in date order, newest to oldest, and she scrolled through to the end. The first date was eighteen years ago when the account had been opened. The first deposit was of two thousand pounds in cash. As Adler scrolled up the statement, she saw there had been regular payments coming in. One thousand pounds cash here, another two thousand pounds cash there. She continued scrolling. By the end of the first twelve months, the balance on the account had been just under twenty thousand pounds. The next twelve months had seen over thirty thousand pounds in and ten thousand out. But then it had stopped and nothing had gone in for five months. Adler frowned. *What happened?* She remembered Fitzwilliam talking about how much money Gill Sterling had had in her bank account when she'd died. Adler had always assumed it had been money she'd acquired to compromise James Wilshire, the earl, but this money had been coming in since before he'd been married to Lady Beatrice. It didn't make any sense.

She carried on scrolling up the statements. The balance had reduced over a period of six months by ten thousand pounds or so. Then, in the October before she'd died, an amount of twenty-five thousand pounds had been paid into the account in cash, and over the next few months, more large payments had gone in too. On the day she'd died, Gill Sterling had had almost eighty thousand pounds in her bank account. About to close the file, Adler noticed she hadn't actually scrolled back up to the top. She paged up. *What the*

— A transfer out had been made on Friday, January eighth of this year for the full amount. Two days later, a notice confirmed the account had been closed.

Adler shook her head. How could someone have transferred the money out? Well, one thing was for sure. Whoever it had been, it hadn't been Gill Sterling. She closed the file, and attaching it to an email, she sent a copy to Fitzwilliam. Picking up her phone, she opened the text message app.

Adler: *Have just sent you an email. Someone cleared Gill Sterling's bank account out in January!*

She picked up her tea, took a sip, and moved down to the next file. It was a read-only word document called JL_Draft_Final. She opened it and read the first two lines.

My sweet Bea,
    There is no easy way to tell you this. I'm sorry, but I'm leaving.

Adler's heart pounded. She screwed up her eyes to refocus them. *It can't be, can it?* She read the next few lines.

I know it will sound like a cliché, but please believe me when I say it's not you, it's me.
    I will always love you, Bea. You have been my smart, beautiful, and funny best friend ever since we were children. But I'm not in love with you and I'm not sure I ever have

been. *And if you're honest with yourself, I think you'll realise that you have never been in love with me either.*

She took a gulp of tea. *Oh my! I think it is.* It was the letter James had written to his wife before he'd died. Adler had never seen the letter, of course; she'd only heard about it from Fitz and Bea. She frowned. *But why is this a typed version?* Hadn't the original letter been handwritten? She skim-read the rest.

And even though you hate being the centre of attention, you put on a smile and face the press when you know it's required. But I'm not like you, Bea... Deep down, I have always wanted more... I have tried to live up to the mantle of the future Earl of Durrland. But time and time again I have fallen short and now I'm exhausted... I don't know how long I could have carried on like this, but four months ago, something happened that changed everything for me — I met Gill Sterling... It was such a relief to talk to someone who understood. Before I was aware of what was happening, I fell in love... she eventually told me Alex had been abusing her for years... It's taken a while to persuade her to trust me, but Alex has been getting more and more controlling... We are off to Mexico... I'm so sorry, Bea, but I can't face telling you in person... I leave tomorrow morning and she is flying to join me a few days later... I hope one day you will forgive me. For once in my life, I must do what is right for me...

Adler leaned back in her chair and let out a rush of air. Her chest was tight, and there was a pain at the back of her throat.

I shouldn't have read that. Poor Bea. How devastating. She leaned forward and, grabbing her cup, necked the rest of the now lukewarm tea. Hearing footsteps in the corridor outside, she quickly leaned over and closed the file.

Izzy walked in and, shuffling around the dining room chairs, stopped beside Adler and put her hand on her arm. "How are you doing, my love?" She leaned in and kissed Adler on the cheek. "You look tired. Why don't you take a break?"

Adler closed her eyes for a second, leaning against Izzy and feeling the warmth of her wife's body next to hers. *Poor Bea. No wonder she locked herself away from the world for all those years.* A beep from her phone made her and Izzy start. She grabbed the phone and read the text.

Fitz: *WTH? I've just finished with Bird. He thinks Street was up to no good. Will send the statement off to IT and see if they can trace the transfer. Good work!*

She gave a wry smile. She was beginning to think Street had been up to no good too. Izzy squeezed her shoulder. "You really should get up, Em, and move your leg."

"Okay, I will. Just give me five minutes, then I'll take a break and do my exercises."

Izzy squeezed her shoulder, then moved towards the door. "I'll hold you to that," she said as she left the room.

Adler looked at the laptop screen again, her mind now registering the name of the file she'd just closed. JL Draft Final. James Letter Draft Final? She shook her head. But how could this be the final draft of the letter? Unless James had typed it out first? But how had it ended up on Street's laptop?

She looked over at the file creation date. Two days before James's death.

There was just one file left in the subfolder. It was another pdf file called GS_Note_TS and had been created on the same day as the previous file. Her fingers trembling slightly, Adler clicked it open.

The first thing she saw was a photo. It was of a note scrawled on a lined piece of paper. The handwriting was loopy and scruffy but legible. Adler gasped, raising her hand to her mouth as she read what it said.

Here's the file of the final draft of the letter. I've tried to make it sound like James. Also attached are samples of James's writing I've managed to gather over the last few weeks. He's been very sweet about giving me advice on who to contact about my so-called abusive husband, and most helpfully, he's been writing it all down!

Adler snatched up her phone and called Fitzwilliam.

36

FIFTEEN MINUTES LATER, FRIDAY 5
FEBRUARY

Richard Fitzwilliam ended his call with Adler, his head
spinning after what she'd told him. The letter from James to
Bea had been a fake. He couldn't believe it. He himself had
checked the letter, and he could have sworn it had matched
with the sample of James's handwriting he'd been given. His
stomach tightened. Was he the one who'd been responsible
for causing Bea all these years of heartache? Of her believing
her husband hadn't loved her and had been leaving her for
someone else? *If only I'd spotted the fake...* He covered his
face with his hands. *It's all my fault...* How would he ever
repay her for all the pain he'd put her through? He removed
his hands and rubbed his face. *How am I ever going to
tell her?*

As he stared out of the window of his office, onto the lush
greenery of the palace gardens below, the only sound was his
heart pounding in his ears. What would be the best way of
breaking the news? He knew Bea was strong, but he feared
this might push her over the edge. *Will she forgive me or
worse, hate me?* He swallowed and took a deep breath in an
attempt to calm his racing heart. More than anything else, he

wanted to go back in time and undo this terrible mistake, but he couldn't. Instead, he had no choice but to tell her the truth and beg her forgiveness.

He looked up as the door to his office opened. Spicer's head appeared around the frame. "George Rockcliffe is in interview room one when you're ready, sir." Her eyes met his for a moment. She frowned. "Are you alright, sir?"

Fitzwilliam took a deep breath and stood. "Yes, sorry. I was miles away. I'm coming now."

She gave him a tentative smile, nodded, and disappeared from view, leaving the door ajar.

Pull yourself together, man! One problem at a time… And right now he needed to find out if George Rockcliffe was a murderer.

———

"You're a hard man to find, Mr Rockcliffe," Fitzwilliam said, splaying his hands out on the table in front of him. The interview room was windowless and dank, the grey walls and fluorescent light giving it an oppressive and dreary atmosphere.

George Rockcliffe sat across from him, his hands folded neatly on the table. He had a chubby face with short black hair slicked back with gel. "As I told your sergeant, I forgot to take my phone charger with me." He shifted uneasily in his seat, moving his hands below the table. Fitzwilliam studied him intently, looking for any signs of guilt or deceit. Rockcliffe's gaze shifted away from Fitzwilliam's before he cleared his throat. "So what's this all about, chief inspector? The sergeant said Tim Street was dead."

"That's correct. He was found dead soon after you left his office." He watched carefully as Rockcliffe grimaced, his

Adam's apple bobbing up and down nervously. "We believe he was murdered."

Rockcliffe's face turned pale, and he began to tremble. "Murdered..." he croaked, his cheeks turning a sickly shade of grey.

Fitzwilliam leaned forward in his chair. "Are you alright, Mr Rockcliffe? Do you need anything?"

Rockcliffe shook his head, but it was clear he was far from okay. He seemed to be shrinking into himself, his eyes wide with fear. Fitzwilliam had seen this before with suspects who'd been terrified of being caught in a crime they'd committed...and on those who'd simply been terrified of being found guilty for a crime they hadn't committed. He sat back in his chair and waited. Rockcliffe swallowed hard, his breathing shallow. "He was alive when I...I left... I swear!" Rockcliffe stammered, the panic clear in his voice. His hands were shaking now as he clasped them together in a desperate attempt to appear calm.

Fitzwilliam poured him a glass of water, then pushed it towards him. "Drink this, and in your own time, talk me through the last time you saw Chief Superintendent Street."

Rockcliffe took a sip of the water and seemed to relax slightly. He cleared his throat and began to talk, slowly at first but gaining speed as he went along. "I arrived at ten as arranged. I had the plans with me for the rebuild of the offices that had collapsed. We went through them, and he suggested a few changes, which I agreed to. We talked about timing. He wanted us to start straight away, but I explained we needed to order the materials first, and what with the shortage of bricks and plaster at the moment, it might take a few weeks for them to be delivered. He wasn't exactly happy about it" —he shrugged in the way tradesmen do when it's not their problem— "but there was nothing I could do. It's all this European stuff that's causing—"

"And what time did you leave?" Fitzwilliam interrupted before the man could get into his stride.

"Just before ten-thirty, I guess. I can't say I noticed exactly."

"And CS Street was alive when you left?"

Rockcliffe nodded. "Yes." He looked Fitzwilliam in the eye. His eyes were dancing. His whole body seemed to be humming with energy. "I swear, chief inspector, I had nothing to do with his death."

Fitzwilliam held his gaze. Was this man telling the truth? If so, then what now? He'd already ruled out Bird and Carmichael, so where did that leave him? No, he wasn't ready to let Rockcliffe off the hook just yet. Rockcliffe was hiding something from him, but Fitzwilliam couldn't put his finger on what it was or why he felt that way. "Did you see anyone when you left the office, Mr Rockcliffe?"

"Just the lass on the desk in front of his office. I assumed she was his PA as she brought him in a cup of tea when I arrived and offered to make me one. She was on the phone when I left." He shifted in his seat again as if he was about to spring up.

That's what it is! He's too keen to get out of here, as if the longer he stays, the more likely I am to discover something he doesn't want me to know. But what is it?

There was a knock on the door, and Spicer's head appeared. "Sir, can I borrow you for a minute, please?" She looked slightly flushed, and her eyes were shining with excitement.

Fitzwilliam suppressed a sigh. He wanted to get to the bottom of what was going on with Rockcliffe, but he also knew Spicer wouldn't have interrupted him unless it was important. He picked up his phone and paused the recording app, then he stood and nodded at Spicer before turning back towards Rockcliffe, who had been watching their exchange silently.

"I'm afraid I'm needed for something, Mr Rockcliffe," Fitzwilliam said. "So please excuse me. I'll not be long."

Rockcliffe swallowed hard as a uniformed officer stepped into the room and stood along the wall.

Fitzwilliam turned and left the room, closing the door firmly behind him. Actually, this could work well for him. Leaving Rockcliffe to stew for a short while might loosen his tongue.

In the hallway outside, Spicer and Hardwick stood by the wall huddled over a print out. He joined them. "So what's so important, sergeant?" he asked Spicer.

"We've just had the intelligence background back on George Rockcliffe, sir. He's a rumoured friend of the Peck family, *and* he's a known business associate of The Hack Crew."

37

2 PM, FRIDAY 5 FEBRUARY

The Society Page online article:

__BREAKING NEWS Man Arrested in Connection With the Death of Senior Police Officer__

Details are sketchy, but it is being rumoured in the popular press that a man has been detained by the police in relation to the death of Chief Superintendent Timothy Street, who died on Monday, aged 57. CS Street from the Protection and Investigations (Royal) Services (PaIRS) was found dead in his office on Monday morning. No cause of death has yet been released by the police. However, an interview with his ex-wife two days ago implied Mr Street had died from a suspected heart attack.

The news someone has been arrested in connection with the chief superintendent's death indicates that all may not be as it seems.

The police have yet to release a formal statement, but a spokesperson for PaIRS confirmed a 45-year-old man was helping them with their inquires and reiterated that the inves-

tigation into Chief Superintendent Street's death was still ongoing.

————

DCI Richard Fitzwilliam closed his laptop with a huff. *How do they get hold of this information?* He'd only arrested George Rockcliffe two hours ago. It must have been someone on Rockcliffe's legal team. *Blast!* Whatever he did next would be recorded and scrutinised by the press. *It's the last thing I need right now!*

He picked up his coffee. The tension in his shoulders dissipated as the hot bitter liquid ran down his throat. Had he been too rash in arresting Rockcliffe? Now the man had his lawyers with him. Fitzwilliam put down his coffee cup and pinched the bridge of his nose. He had twenty-four hours, maybe a bit more if he applied for a hold, to prove the connection between Rockcliffe and Street before the whole thing blew up in his face. And Rockcliffe's lawyers were ready for a fight, he could tell. They'd already asked to perform a medical examination on their client due to 'concerns' following an early morning flight from Spain that had been delayed by two hours on the runway and his subsequent detention (their words) immediately on landing and transport to Surrey. He was not only overtired according to them, but all that lack of exercise could cause a deep vein thrombosis that could be life threatening. It was a load of rubbish, of course; they all knew that. He sighed. He'd just have to have patience while the doctors examined Rockcliffe on-site.

He looked down at the background check on his desk and reread it again. There was no question. George Rockcliffe was linked with The Hack Crew on several building projects in and around north and west London, although, the report pointed out there was no evidence that what he was doing was illegal, hence the reason why he'd not been brought in at any time. More interestingly were photos of Rockcliffe taken with Logan Peck in Spain two years ago, where, according to the report, he'd been building Logan a new villa on the Costa Brava. But the most incriminating of all was another photo, this time of George Rockcliffe and Joseph Peck taken on the morning after DI Preece's murder. The two men were eating breakfast in a cafe in East London. The picture had been taken through a window. It was a little grainy, but Fitzwilliam could clearly see it was George talking to the older dark-haired man. There was a note stuck to the photo that said it had been sent in by an off-duty operative who'd recognised Peck and had been surprised to see him in England.

Fitzwilliam took another sip of coffee. Was that why Rockcliffe had been so nervous and eager to leave? Was he worried they would make the connection between him and organised crime?

There was a sharp knock on his door. "Come in," he shouted. It opened, and Spicer walked in, closely followed by Hardwick. He looked up and gave a weak smile to the two sergeants before him as he indicated for them to sit down. "So what do we know?" he asked, getting up and refilling his coffee cup.

"Well, Rockcliffe is just finishing up with the doctor, so we'll know soon if we can interview him again," Spicer told him. "I've also spoken to Ruth Ness just to confirm the timings of Rockcliffe's visit to Street that morning. She still can't be precise about the time he arrived or left, but the CCTV footage supports the times he gave us. He was with Street alone for a total of twenty-one minutes."

"Plenty of time to kill him then?"

She nodded. "We can also now confirm they are his fingerprints in Street's office."

"Anything else?"

"Ruth did say something interesting, sir. She told me she wasn't the one who'd arranged the meeting with Rockcliffe. She said Street had. The first she knew about it was that morning when she had her daily catchup with Street first thing, and he told her Rockcliffe was coming in." Spicer gave a wry smile. "She still seems pretty annoyed about it now. Anyway, I asked her if it was usual for Street to make his own appointments, and she said no, he normally did everything through her. She did, however, admit Street was very hands on when it came to office build and refurbishment, having been the one who'd headed the push to move Security into the main palace from their previous location in the stable block, so this wasn't the first time Rockcliffe had been in to see him."

"Do you think the building plans were a cover for them to talk, sir?" Bella Hardwick piped up.

Fitzwilliam, now behind his desk, tilted his head to one side, then shrugged. "It could be, but it seems a bit risky to me that they would choose to meet here and be seen together when no doubt they could have met somewhere much less obvious."

"But isn't that the point, sir? It gives their meeting a sense of legitimacy. Like hiding in plain sight."

He raised an eyebrow. *She has a point.* "Yes, you could be right."

Spicer jumped in. "Do you think he was sent to kill him, sir? Or do you think it was a spur of the moment thing, maybe when Street refused to cooperate or threatened to tell Carmichael what he knew?"

"I don't know. Rockcliffe's a builder, not a hitman, so it

seems strange he would have been sent as an assassin. Maybe it was more a necessity due to the way the meeting went rather than preplanned. We'll have to ask him. That is if we can get anywhere near him after the doctor has finished." A thought struck him. "Can you find out if Rockcliffe does any martial arts? Either now or in the past when he was younger."

Spicer nodded as she and Hardwick rose as one. "Yes, sir. We'll get on it now."

"Oh, and Spicer? Can we find out what Rockcliffe was doing in Spain and who he was with? I'm trying to work out why he would choose to come back and face the music. I wonder if he met with one or both of the Peck brothers while he was there. Maybe he was ordered back to take the rap on the premise that the lawyers would get him off?"

She nodded, and they left the room. He gazed out of the window. The rain had just stopped, and the landscape looked bedraggled, with water dripping off leaves and adding to the puddles on the path. A beep dragged him away from the view. A green light was flashing on the office phone in front of him.

"Yes, Carol?"

"Sir, I have Dr Dominic Elmes on the line for you."

The pathologist? Does he have new information that will prove Rockcliffe killed Street? He could only hope…

"Put him through, please, Carol."

The line *clicked*. "Doctor. I hope you have good news for me?"

There was a short silence, then Elmes said apologetically. "I'm afraid not, chief inspector."

Fitzwilliam sighed. *Great!*

"I've just been with Mr Rockcliffe, who you've arrested in connection with Mr Street's death."

What on earth was the pathologist doing with a murder suspect?

"It's a bit unusual, I know, but protocol dictates that if a suspect is examined by an external doctor after arrest, then a doctor appointed by the police has to be present too." He chuckled. "I think it goes back to the days when so-called doctors would come in to examine a suspect and give them something to make them too ill to be interviewed or even worse, kill them to stop them talking. Anyway, it was lunchtime, and I was the only doctor available on-site."

He's going to tell me Rockcliffe isn't well enough to interview. Blast!

"Overall, I would say Mr Rockcliffe is perfectly well. The lawyers' doctor was trying to push that he was too tired and flight weary to know what was happening, but I strongly disagreed, and they reluctantly withdrew their position."

Fitzwilliam frowned. *So that's good news then?*

"However, during the examination, Mr Rockcliffe complained his shoulder was hurting. He has a condition called adhesive capsulitis, better known as a frozen shoulder. It involves stiffness and pain in the shoulder joint and can take years to heal. I've checked his records, and it was diagnosed three months ago. He's due to have his first corticosteroids injection next week, which should ease the symptoms a bit for him. I examined him myself, and I can confirm the diagnosis. So I'm sorry Fitzwilliam, but if your working theory is still that CS Street was killed by a blood choke, then it's my view that Mr Rockcliffe would not have been able to perform such a manoeuvre with a frozen shoulder."

38

4 PM, FRIDAY 5 FEBRUARY

"I thought I'd better let you know the package arrived alright, and I have to say, it's causing quite a stir here."

Lady Beatrice held her mobile phone out in front of her, the voice of her elder brother Lord Frederick Astley coming out of the speaker loud and clear, as she ambled towards the window in her apartment in Gollingham Palace. "That's good. When I hadn't heard from you this morning I was worried it may have gone missing or something."

She'd spent the entire journey from Francis Court to Gollingham Palace earlier this morning cradling the precious copy of *Lord of the Flies* in her lap, much to Daisy's consternation, the privilege of Bea's lap normally being reserved for her to rest her head on. As soon as Ward, the Astley family's driver, had dropped her at Gollingham Palace, she'd given him instructions to deliver the book, carefully wrapped and addressed to Lord Fred, on his way back to Fenshire. Grateful when Ward had texted her not long after he'd left to confirm the package had been left at the Foreign Office for Fred's urgent attention, she had then got increasingly concerned when Fred had failed to respond to her messages checking if he had retrieved the book from reception. Hopefully the book would give them what they needed to convince Rudy Trotman to cooperate. They couldn't afford for it to go missing.

"I'm sorry, Bea. I should have let you know sooner, but since I got the call to tell me it was here, I've been in back-to-back meetings with Sir Hewitt, the CIA, and MI6 Intelligence."

"So Sir Hewitt was there, was he?" Surely that confirmed her suspicion that the well-respected businessman and beloved TV star was also an MI6 Special Observer like her husband had been and her brother still was. Basically, a spy.

"Ha!" her brother laughed. "Don't go there, little sister," he warned. *Yes, definitely a spy!*

"So was it as useful as you hoped it would be?" After looking at the first few pages that James had marked up, which, following the message to Brett, had appeared to be a list of names, job titles, and organisations, she'd not been inclined to go through the whole book.

"Yes. Beyond helpful. Everyone involved here is really excited, including Sir Hewitt."

"So will you be able to persuade Rudy Trotman to talk?" She so wanted James's effort and foresight in leaving the message to be rewarded in something tangible that would make a difference. Like putting away corrupt and dangerous organised crime gangs.

"Already done," he exclaimed triumphantly. "He's with our lawyers now, putting the finishing touches to his statement."

Wow! Her eyes prickled. She rubbed them with her free hand. *That's fantastic news.*

"Sir Hewitt already wore him down last night, but the

information you gave us was enough to push him over the edge this morning. He's fully cooperating and, as they say, 'singing like a bird'." His voice got thicker. "We couldn't have done it without you, Bea."

"Without James," she corrected him, feeling a little shaky. She was proud of her husband.

"Yes, you're right. He was a true SO to the very end," Fred said quietly.

She took a deep breath in, then let it out slowly. *Don't cry, Bea.* "Indeed. Well, I need to go as I'm meeting Fitzwilliam in his office in half an hour."

"That sounds cosy," Fred said suggestively.

Bea huffed. "Don't go there, big brother. It will be something to do with the case he's working on."

"Boring!" Fred chuckled.

"I'm going now. Goodbye!" She cut the call, a smile tugging at the corners of her mouth. What was so desperately important that Fitzwilliam wanted to see her now rather than wait until they were all together tonight at Adler and Izzy's? *I have so much to tell him too.* She wasn't sure if she could hang on until tonight either.

———

"I was surprised to get your call," Lady Beatrice said to Richard Fitzwilliam as he stood with his back to her, facing the coffee machine on the sideboard in his office. His posture gave nothing away to satisfy her curiosity as to why he wanted to see her alone. Butterflies danced in her tummy as she waited for him to pour their coffees.

In an attempt to calm her nerves, she reached down to pat Daisy, who sat patiently by her side. Bea took a deep breath and let her eyes slowly sweep around the room. It was a far cry from the comfortable estate offices she and Perry used back at Francis Court. It was very much a man's office — nothing fancy or plush. All very functional. The large wooden desk in front of her took up the majority of the room, its surface covered in paperwork and folders. A laptop sat on one corner, its bright screen flashing messages periodically. The only personal touch she could see was a picture on the sideboard near where he stood. It was of him with a man and woman she recognised — his sister Elise and her husband Rhys, along with two young boys, who Bea presumed were Fitzwilliam's nephews. She sighed as she took in the dark-blue utility carpet and the grey walls lined with filing cabinets. Not a cushion or a splash of colour anywhere. *If only I could get my hands on it, I could make it feel cosy and more welcoming in no time.*

Fitzwilliam cleared his throat, and she looked up. He looked strained as he handed her a mug of hot black coffee, then sat down on the other side of the desk. Daisy circled the carpet beside him, then with a sigh, plonked herself down on the floor, her head resting on her paws. "I know we're meeting up with the others at Adler and Izzy's this evening, but I wanted to talk to you beforehand. Just the two of us."

Intriguing...

He paused, averting his eyes from her face as he gave a faint smile. Was it guilt or just awkwardness that was causing him to seem so apprehensive? He'd always been so confident. *What's making him so nervous?*

"I wanted you to hear it from me first...before the others," he finally said after an uncomfortable silence. Her heart rate increased in anticipation. He shifted in his seat, unable to look her in the eyes as his hands fidgeted with his mug. He took a deep breath and opened his mouth but seemed to still struggle for the right words.

Oh my goodness, what is it? "Fitzwilliam, whatever it is, I'm sure it can't be that bad," Bea said, fiddling with the rings on her right hand.

"I made a huge mistake six years ago," he blurted out, spots of colour appearing in his cheeks.

Six years ago? What happened six years ago?

"I was suppose to check the handwriting when I read the letter. And I did. I thought it was his. It turns out I was wrong."

Confusion was making her brain slow down. *Letter? Handwriting? What...* She swallowed painfully as realisation dawned. James's letter to her. Found six years ago. *Oh my....*

"The letter wasn't from James. I was fooled. It had been forged," Fitzwilliam admitted, finally looking up at her with pain and sadness in his eyes. Bea felt the colour drain from her face. *James didn't write the letter?* "What happened?" she said in a whisper, her eyes now fixed firmly on the black liquid in the mug she was holding.

Fitzwilliam explained, his words coming out in a rush about the copy of the letter and the note Adler had found on Street's computer.

Bea's head spun as she listened to him. Gill Sterling had written the letter? Someone had forged James's handwriting. *James didn't leave me for another woman...*

"I'm so sorry, Lady Beatrice. I was completely fooled."

She raised her head. Their eyes met. She felt breathless all of a sudden. Did he really think it was all his fault? "We were both fooled, Fitzwilliam," she said slowly. "I thought it was from him too, remember?"

They sat for a few moments, the silence broken only by Daisy's gentle snoring. Bea didn't know whether to cry over all the years she'd believed James had hated his life with her or laugh that he'd loved her just like she'd thought he had.

Her instincts that her husband had been happy with their life together, the ones that had been questioned and tested by the press and the public and eventually broken under the strain of it all, had been right. *James loved me.* That was all she needed to know.

39

8:30 PM, FRIDAY 5 FEBRUARY

"I have news!" Lady Beatrice blurted out to those around Adler and Izzy's dining room table.

"Really?" Perry Juke asked, slowly placing his wineglass on the table and giving her a look that said, 'Why haven't you told me already?'

"Er, sorry." She gave him a tentative smile. "I found some more of James's personal items." She hesitated. She needed to be careful not to reveal that the message had been for Brett Goodman as Fitzwilliam was the only other person around the table who knew he was CIA. "Including a list that has now been passed on to MI6 of names and responsibilities of all the people James had come into contact with in Miami and the links between them, including Rudy Trotman, the then Mayor of Miami, the local sheriff's department officials, the City of Miami Building department staff, and members of the Grazzi Family."

"Wow," Simon Lattimore said, putting down his knife and fork.

That's the reaction I wanted! She darted a sideways

glance at Fitzwilliam next to her. He had stopped eating and was staring at her. She grinned.

Perry, open mouthed, took another gulp of his wine. "What? And it was just there? A list of that stuff?"

"Well, no. Not exactly." She briefly told them about finding the book in James's old school trunk.

"So it was a code?" Adler asked as she pushed her plate away. She turned to her wife. "That smoked salmon was delicious, love." They all nodded in agreement over the starter dish, as Izzy stood and began to clear their plates. Fitzwilliam and Simon rose to help her.

"A coded message, how exciting," Perry said, his blue eyes shining. "I guess that makes sense, what with James being MI6."

"So did you find his notes too?" Fitzwilliam asked as he walked back into the room, carrying a pile of clean dinner plates, followed by Izzy, carrying a tray holding dishes of steaming vegetables, and Simon wearing oven gloves, carrying a large earthenware pot that wafted the smell of roasted chicken around the room.

Bea licked her lips as Izzy and Simon placed the food on the table, then she turned to Fitzwilliam as he handed her a plate, but she shook her head. "Rory — you know, our private secretary from back then, told me he handed all of James's diaries and the official papers that were left on his desk at the time of the earl's death to DCI Angus Reed."

"That would make sense," Adler said. "After all, he headed up the investigation into James's death. I don't remember seeing them, though, do you, Fitz?"

Fitzwilliam shook his head as he sat down. "No, I don't. I imagine he handed them on to Street that day Street visited us at Francis Court to tell us about James's involvement with

MI6. He would have wanted to check the earl's paperwork to make sure there was nothing confidential in there."

Street would have wanted to make sure James had had nothing on him that linked him to what James had discovered in Miami. A swell of pride rose inside Bea. James had been too smart to leave something that important lying around. "All I know is that Rory said he never got any of it back. But he did confirm that James's diary for the nineteenth of December had been kept clear for James to catch up on admin. So the meeting James had with Street would've been done unofficially if it happened."

"Did James take Rory into his confidence about what he'd found out in Miami?" Simon asked as he helped himself to crispy brown chicken legs from the casserole dish.

"No. I don't think he would have done anything to put Rory at risk. But Rory did recall that when they were back from the trip, James asked a lot of questions about the building contractor selection process being used for the UK bid and challenged if it was a fair and open one." She smiled. Her husband had clearly wanted to make sure everything was above board with the UK olympic bid he was spearheading.

While Bea helped herself to food, the attention turned to Adler, who told them about Gill Sterling's bank accounts and the fake letter she'd found on Street's laptop. Listening to her now, Bea was grateful Fitzwilliam had told her in advance. Over the last few hours since his revelation, she'd had time to digest the news and was beginning to come to terms with it. The overwhelming feeling now was one of relief that her husband had loved her, although it was tinged with anger at the people who had killed him. Because there was no doubt in her mind now. James had been murdered.

Perry, on hearing the news of the fake letter, jumped up

and rushed around the table to give her an enormous hug. Although initially taking her by surprise, the gesture made her heart sing. Looking over Perry's shoulder while he clung to her, she met Simon's eyes and saw concern reflected in them. When he mouthed, "Are you okay?" to her, she smiled softly and nodded.

I'll be fine. No. I am fine.

"So how did you get on with Fenshire Police, Simon?" Fitzwilliam asked as he plugged a large roast potato in his mouth.

Simon swallowed his mouthful of food. "I spoke with the original officer who handled the earl's overnight bag. He was responsible for cataloguing the contents, and he was the one who sent a copy of the list to Preece, who'd handed the bag in. After a bit of prodding, he remembered that he'd received a follow up call from Preece asking if anything had been omitted and specifically asking if a letter had been found. He never mentioned it to anyone." Simon shook his head. "I can see now how the bag was accidentally kept and the letter not found. Honestly this guy was as useful as a chocolate fireguard."

"So Preece must have been the one to plant the letter in the bag when he'd conducted the search of the earl's apartment," Adler said.

"And it was only the incompetence of the police officer in Fenshire that prevented the letter from being part of the original investigation," Perry pointed out.

Bea put down her knife and fork and took a sip of her wine. *How would I have felt if that letter had been found at the time?* Devastated, no doubt. She would have had to face not just losing her husband but also believing he'd been leaving her for someone else all at the same time. She wasn't sure how she would have survived that. A shiver went down her spine. She was glad she had been saved that for those nine years while she'd raised her young son Sam, believing him to be a product of true love. Later, finding out about the letter had been hurtful and upsetting, but at least she'd been spared that pain when she had been at her most vulnerable.

Simon Lattimore wiped his face with his napkin and laid it down by his empty plate. "That was delightful, Izzy," he said as he picked up his wineglass and raised it to Izzy McKeer-Adler sitting opposite him on the other side of the dining room table. There were nods of agreement, and Izzy blushed before suggesting they had a break before pudding.

"So," Adler said, pushing her empty plate to one side. "James was in Miami, and he found out about the corruption that had taken place during the Miami Olympics a few years before and the link to the Grazzi Family. He came back, made notes, and then a few weeks before Christmas, he had a meeting where he told Street, who was working with MI6, all about what he'd found, assuming Street would do something about it."

"But instead Street arranged to have the earl killed," Perry concluded dramatically.

Fitzwilliam and Simon shook their heads.

"It would have been such a high-risk plan that I don't believe Street would have sanctioned it," Simon said.

"I agree," Fitzwilliam said. "I think it's more likely that the Grazzi Family picked up what James was up to and took matters into their own hands, using THC to do their dirty work for them. Then Street found out when the earl was killed and was left with the job of clearing up the mess afterwards."

Perry sighed. "You could be right. Someone who lives outside the UK would have no real idea about the kind of attention the death of a working member of the royal family would receive. It's incredible that they got away with it."

Adler held up her hand. "Okay, okay. I think we can all accept that that makes more sense." She turned to Perry, and he nodded. "So now to Gill Sterling. I think she was recruited by THC when she was living and working at Drew Castle."

Considering how Bea's brother Fred had recently used a shooting party at Drew Castle as cover to disguise some MI6 business, she could imagine how having someone reporting on the comings and goings at the king's Scottish home would be useful for an organisation with nefarious intentions.

"But then when the Sterlings moved to Francis Court when Alex took up his post as estate manager, it all stopped and—"

"Hold on," Perry chimed in. "That would explain why Gill was so unhappy at Francis Court. She was always complaining about how much better Scotland was. Of course it would have been if she was being paid to spy at Drew Castle."

"Exactly," Adler agreed. "So Gill must have been over the moon when she was contacted by the same people and offered a considerable sum to get close to the earl at Francis Court. They wanted to know exactly what he knew and, more importantly, of his plans to tell anyone other than Street."

Bea had considered this scheme of Gill's ever since Fitzwilliam had told her of the fake letter. She had come to the conclusion that James hadn't been having an affair with Gill, but being the caring person he'd been, he would have tried to help her if he'd thought she was being abused by her husband. "So Gill pretended Alex was abusing her and turned to James."

Perry leaned over and patted Bea's hand. "And being the amazing man he was, he tried to help her."

Her eyes itched, and she reached up to rub them. Bea could imagine Gill asking to meet him in secret so her husband wouldn't see them and take his anger out on her.

"So Gill found out James was going to London to talk to his MI6 contact, presumably to try and find out why Street had done nothing, and she was told to get him back to Francis Court and lure him into an ambush."

Bea nodded. Gill would have played on her need to get away and asked James to help her. *Is that what happened the evening of his death?* Had Gill contacted him to say Alex was going to kill her and she needed to get away urgently? *And my kind husband got into his car and drove from London to go and rescue her.*

"Do you think she knew they were going to kill him?" Izzy asked as she began to clear the table.

"You're the only one who knew her, Perry. What do you think?" Bea asked.

Perry rubbed his clean-shaven chin. "I didn't really warm to her, but I'm not sure she was that heartless. Maybe she thought they were going to kidnap him for a ransom?"

"It's hard to imagine they told her the whole plan," Fitzwilliam said. "That would risk her getting cold feet."

"Do you really think she was that naive?" Simon asked. "She'd bought a train ticket to Scotland and had packed a suitcase, suggesting she was planning to leave afterwards and 'disappear'. I think she was smart enough to know what was going on and was happy to take the money and run."

"But she didn't get a chance, did she?" Izzy walked back into the room, carrying a tray with six large glass tumblers on it. Each one was filled with what looked like a biscuit base topped with some sort of berry compote, cream, fresh berries, and — *is that bits of meringue on the top?* "Gill was played too, don't forget. They got rid of her to clear up all the loose ends."

She has a point, I suppose. But Bea couldn't quite find any sympathy for the woman who had led her husband to his death.

40

10 PM, FRIDAY 5 FEBRUARY

As they each helped themselves to a dessert from the middle of the table, Fitzwilliam cleared his throat. "I've been giving it a fair amount of thought, and I think I have a viable theory now of what happened on the night of the earl's death after he picked up Gill Sterling."

"I know this has been bugging you for the last fifteen years, so let's hear it, Fitz," Alder said, digging her spoon into the creamy delight in front of her.

"I believe the two black cars seen on the night of the accident were the killers. With one car as a lookout, the other car forced the earl off the road."

Bea's stomach churned, and she put down the spoon that had been hovering above her glass, about to plunge into her dessert. She took a sip of water. *Come on, Bea. Chin up. I want to know what happened to James, don't I?*

Fitzwilliam stopped and turned to Bea beside him. "I'm sorry, Lady Beatrice. If you'd rather I didn't do this n—"

Bea held up her hand. "I'm fine, Fitzwilliam. Really. I'd like to hear what you think happened."

He raised an eyebrow, and she nodded. He smiled. "Okay.

Then I think as soon as the earl's car stopped, the two men went to see how bad it was. That's why the doors were so easy to open for the witnesses; maybe they even left them open a bit. They probably realised the earl was dead immediately, and then they went to check on Gill. The witness said her pulse was very faint, and he missed it the first time. I think the two men thought she was dead too. We know she had two phones. I believe they took the one she'd used to communicate with them. Then they searched her handbag and her bag in the boot to make sure there was nothing incriminating. But here's the thing. I don't think they would have planned to leave it like that. They would've wanted to leave no trace. So their plan was to do something like torch the car."

He paused, giving Bea an apologetic smile. She smiled weakly back.

He continued, "But then the lookout vehicle saw a car heading in their direction." He turned to Simon. "Do you remember the witness who was staying in a holiday home off the road? He drove past the SUV, then turned off at the next corner." Simon nodded. Fitzwilliam continued. "But they wouldn't have known he was going to turn off the road. I think they rang the other team and told them to get out of there sharpish. I bet if we ever got access to those vehicles, we would have found petrol or something similar inside, ready to be used."

The car would have been torched? With James inside... Feeling dizzy, Bea reached out with a shaky hand to grab her glass of wine and took a huge gulp.

"And Street covered up their identities by claiming they were a foreign security detail, and it would cause a diplomatic incident to question them!" Adler finished, her eyes wide.

Fitzwilliam nodded. "Street stonewalled me when I tried to dig deeper. Now I know why."

Mulling everything over while they finished their desserts, they moved on to coffee.

"So what now?" Perry addressed Fitzwilliam as he helped himself to one of the two coffeepots Izzy had just brought in and placed in the middle of the table.

"Well, we're still working on deciphering the coded document we found in Street's briefcase," Fitzwilliam said, taking his phone out and showing Perry a picture. Perry glanced at it, frowned, then returned the phone to him. Bea, glancing over Fitzwilliam's shoulder, saw a page of numbers. It meant nothing to her. At least James's code had been easy to read once she'd found it.

"And are you working on the basis that whoever killed Street did so to keep him quiet?" Simon asked.

Fitzwilliam nodded. "For want of anything better." He sighed. "I have three suspects who had opportunity. DCI Bird because he had access to Street's office via a connecting door. I have George Rockcliffe, who was in Street's office and the last person to see him alive, and I have DI Madeline Carmichael, who says she found him dead. Carmichael I can fairly much rule out as she doesn't have a motive that I can find, and the CCTV from outside the corridor shows she didn't have time to kill him. So that leaves two. Bird doesn't have a motive as far as I can tell, and Rockcliffe, I have no evidence against."

"Is there no one else who was around at the time?" Bea asked, trying to help.

"Only Street's executive assistant Ruth Ness. But she was on the phone the whole time."

"Could she have faked it?"

"I don't think so. She was on the phone with one of my

officers, going through a spreadsheet. She confirmed hearing Rockcliffe arrive and leave, as well as Carmichael arriving and later shouting for help."

"All on the one call?" Perry asked.

Fitzwilliam nodded. "It was a complicated review."

"What if Carmichael and Bird are dirty? Could they be in it together?" Simon asked, fanning his hands out.

"I suppose it's a possibility, but again, I have no evidence to support that. We'll continue to do background checks on them and see if anything comes up..." He trailed off, pressing his lips tightly together.

He looks defeated, Bea thought as she studied the deflated man sitting next to her. He seemed to be at a loss as to what to do, and her heart went out to him. He must be so frustrated with so little evidence and no definite answers. She couldn't think of anything to say that would help.

41

FIRST THING, SATURDAY 6
FEBRUARY

Lady Beatrice yawned as she took another sip of her coffee. She wished she'd not agreed to meet Perry for breakfast in the Gollingham Palace senior staff dining room this morning. She could have done with another hour in bed. Simon had left early this morning to return to Francis-next-the-Sea as he had a book signing in nearby Fawstead this afternoon. She'd told Perry she could handle the deliveries today if he wanted to go too, but he'd insisted he wanted to stay and help. He would go back later.

Daisy, who was lying by Bea's feet, popped her head up, looked towards the door, and jumped up. Bea grabbed her harness just in time to stop her running across the room. After the last time she'd brought Daisy into this dining room, and she'd gone bounding over to Spicer as she'd arrived, the manager had very discreetly and charmingly asked her if, in future, she would, "keep your little dog on a lead for the comfort of the other diners, my lady." There had clearly been complaints.

"I'm sorry, Daisy," she whispered to her. "But we're not at home, and you can't go charging around here. We need to act with decorum at all times, young lady." Daisy, straining against Bea's hold, let out a sharp bark as Perry appeared in the doorway. "Daisy!" Bea scolded as heads turned towards them and stared. She smiled to the room in general and mouthed, "Sorry," as she gently pushed Daisy under the table in front of her. "You'll get us thrown out," she hissed at the squirming terrier.

Perry halted beside the table, then leaned in and kissed Bea on the cheek. "Morning," he said brightly, then bent down and fussed over Daisy. Bea grinned. Perry always had that effect on her, no matter how tired or grumpy she was. His enthusiasm and energy were so infectious, it was impossible to stay down for long in his presence.

Without sitting, he leaned over and grabbed the coffeepot from the middle of the table, filling his cup and topping hers up. He took a sip of his coffee, then looked over at the buffet table hungrily. "My goodness," he said, his eyes widening in delight.

The buffet table was heaving with breakfast delights. A variety of hand-crafted pastries glistened invitingly on doilies arranged in perfect symmetry while platters held towers of scrambled egg, sausages, and bacon topped with freshly chopped herbs. There were copious slices of bread and rolls piled high in baskets next to a selection of fruits and steaming hot trays of porridge. Perry licked his lips appreciatively. "Can I get you anything?" he asked, inching towards the table already.

Normally she would say no, but her lack of sleep made her hungry. "A couple of pastries would be nice."

Perry nodded and hurried away. Bea sighed and took another sip of coffee, its richness permeating her senses and warming her nose. Hopefully it would keep her awake too.

Perry returned and sank into the chair opposite her with a

satisfied sigh. He handed her a plate with three different pastries on, then looking at his own plate, said, "I need this," and tucked into his full English breakfast with gusto. Nibbling on a pain au chocolat, Bea watched him devour his food, wondering, not for the first time, where on his tall, slender frame he put it all. A few moments later, Perry picked up a slice of crispy bacon and held it under the table for Daisy, who eagerly wolfed it down in one bite before pushing her head against his arm for more. Perry laughed, then seeing the scowl on Bea's face, looked sheepishly at her. "It was only one tiny bit."

"You know she's only supposed to have lean meat and vegetables." She glanced down at her chunky little dog and sighed. She just knew the vet was going to give her a hard time about Daisy's weight at her appointment next week.

"She's fine, Bea, honestly. She just needs a bit more exercise." He wiped his mouth with a napkin and took a sip of his coffee. "So how are you after yesterday's revelation about the fake letter?" he asked casually, but there was concern in his eyes.

So that was why he'd stayed to 'help' her today. He was worried about her. Her eyes prickled, and she took another mouthful of flaky pastry while the moment passed. She smiled at him brightly. "I'm surprisingly good, actually." He raised an eyebrow, and she continued, "Since James's accident, I've lived with the public and the press speculating about the state of my marriage ever since they found out about Gill being in the car. I tried to ignore it, and I did a pretty good job until I got the letter. After that I stopped believing my instincts that told me James had loved me, and I started to doubt I had ever really known him. Because running off with someone else just wasn't what the James I thought I knew would have ever done." She lifted her chin.

"So more than anything, I now know that I *did* know my husband. And he *did* love me. I can remember and be grateful for the man I knew and loved, not the stranger he'd become to me over the last six years."

Perry reached out and grabbed one of Bea's hands while fanning his eyes with his other. "I know this sounds silly in the circumstances, but I'm so happy for you."

She looked into his watery eyes and squeezed his hand. "Me too."

They sat in silence for a few moments, then Perry took his hand back and pulled his mobile phone from his jacket pocket. He tapped the screen. "So," he said, scrolling down. "I was playing around on the internet in the bath this morning, as you do, and I came across this article on Bletchley Park in Buckinghamshire and all the clever stuff they did in cracking codes during the war. That reminded me of what you were saying last night about how James left that message in his favourite book." He stopped scrolling. "So then I went down a rabbit hole of books and coded messages, and I found this." He handed her his phone.

Bea looked at the article about secret messages sent by the French resistance during the Second World War. It described one method where they'd used a four numbered code that had referred to the page number, line number, how many words in, then the position of the letter in that word. It then spelled out the message. Her mouth went dry. *Just like the code Fitzwilliam showed us yesterday.* "It's just like—"

"The code Fitzwilliam showed me yesterday!" Perry said with a flourish.

Bea's mind whirred. Could that be the solution? *It would help Fitzwilliam so much if we could crack this for him.* "But if that's the answer, then how do we know what book he was referencing?" Bea asked, handing Perry back his phone.

"I can't remember what it said, but there was a heading or title on the page he showed me. Maybe that's the clue?"

She jumped up, startling Daisy, who gave a low *woof*. "You're a genius, Perry. Let's go and find Fitzwilliam and tell him."

"Hold on, Miss Marple. Let me finish my coffee first!"

42

TWENTY MINUTES LATER, SATURDAY 6 FEBRUARY

Detective Chief Inspector Richard Fitzwilliam stared at the array of photographs and statements spread across the table in the meeting room and rubbed his stinging eyes. He reached behind him and plucked his half-full coffee cup off the sideboard. Taking a sip and attempting to clear his clouded mind, he returned his gaze to the crime scene photos.

He had been looking at these pictures for what felt like hours, but there was something still bugging him. He couldn't put his finger on what it was that seemed so off; he just knew something wasn't adding up. He sighed and continued studying the images, his eyes scanning over each one meticulously in search for something that would jump out at him.

"Are you okay, sir?" Detective Sergeant Tina Spicer asked as she picked up her drink and raised it to her mouth. Next to her, DS Bella Hardwick was sipping from a water bottle while leaning over and reading one of the statements.

"Yes. There's something, Spicer, but I just can't figure out what." He ran his fingers through his hair.

"I'm sorry we had to let Rockcliffe go, sir," Hardwick said. "Do you think he really did it?"

Fitzwilliam took another sip of his coffee and shook his head. "I don't think so. I know we can tie him to the people who killed Preece and may have wanted Street dead too, but we have no evidence to support it. Also, the man's so nervous and has a bad shoulder. I don't think they'd trust him to kill someone."

It had turned out Rockcliffe's trip to Spain had been to take his mistress on a week's break to a spa. That's why he hadn't had his phone switched on when they'd been trying to get hold of him. He'd not met with anyone from the Peck family while he'd been there as far as they could tell. When questioned, he'd admitted to meeting with Joseph Peck on the day after Preece's death, saying Joe wanted to update his villa in Italy and had asked Rockcliffe to draw up some plans. As Rockcliffe's lawyers had pointed out, it wasn't against the law to rebuild someone's house.

Fitzwilliam gave the two sergeants a wry smile. "With nothing concrete to go on and Rockcliffe's lawyers mumbling about wrongful arrest, I had no choice but to let him—"

A knock on the door stopped him, and he looked up.

"Sir, sorry to disturb you, but the Countess of Rossex and a Mr Juke are here to see you. They have a dog with them," Carol, his executive assistant said with a hint of disdain in her voice. "They say it's urgent."

Fitzwilliam raised an eyebrow at Spicer. *What's Bea doing here on a Saturday morning?* "Thank you, Carol. Please send them in." He ran a hand through his dishevelled hair as he waited for them to enter. *I must look like I've not slept for a week.*

Lady Beatrice, Perry Juke, and Daisy entered the room. Fitzwilliam immediately noticed the excited glint in Bea's eye as she said, "Hello," to them. She was wearing an over-sized V-neck dark-green jumper over a white T-shirt with tight skinny jeans and black biker boots. Her long red hair spilled over her shoulders and cascaded down her back. *My goodness, she's beautiful.* Her green eyes met his, and for a second he was transfixed. *Stop staring at her like a love-struck teenager. Pull yourself together, man!* A paw tapped on his leg, and he looked down into a white furry face. "Hello, Daisy," he said, bending down and patting the little terrier. "Have you come to give me a clue that will solve this case?"

He looked back up as Bea, smiling warmly at him, said, "Well, I'm not sure we have a clue for you, but Perry has a brilliant idea about Street's coded pages, and we hope it might help you."

"Well, we could do with all the help we can get at the moment," he said, returning her smile. While Daisy ran around the office saying hello to Spicer and Hardwick in turn, Fitzwilliam indicated the chairs around the table and invited Bea and Perry to sit. Once everyone was settled, Bea nudged Perry, and he told them about the book code he'd read about. "So we just need to work out what book he was referring to, and we should be able to decode it. Isn't there a title at the top of the page?"

Fitzwilliam turned to glance at the papers spread across the desk and hurriedly began to search through them, an excited energy coursing through him as he frantically flipped through each document. *There it is!* He pulled the bundle of pages towards him. The others got up and joined him. His eyes fell on the heading at the top of the page: LETTERS TO MARIE MONTH. He frowned. Was that the title of a book? *I've never heard of it.*

Pulling out his phone, he opened his browser and searched the title but nothing showed. There was silence as they all stared at the page. *I've got nothing.*

"Oh my giddy aunt!" Perry's voice was loud and excited.

"I think it's *The Mentor*, one of Simon's books."

Where did he get that from? Fitzwilliam leaned in and looked at the title again. T..H..E..M..E..N..T..O..R. Yes, *The Mentor* was in there definitely. He was a big fan of Simon Lattimore's thrillers and remembered reading *The Mentor* last summer while on holiday. But how does Perry know it's Simon's book? There must be more than one book called that.

Bea, shook her head. "How did you work that out?" she asked Perry, her eyes wide in astonishment.

Perry blushed. "Well, er."

"What is it?" Bea asked gently.

"Okay. It's a little embarrassing, but I was thinking of ideas for my wedding vows, and I thought it would be cool to make up some words out of Simon's full name. You know, see if there was something cute in there I could use. Anyway, after what seemed like hours fiddling around with the letters, one of phrases I was left with was 'to Marie'. It's in the name Lattimore. So..." He shrugged. "When you take Lattimore out, then it's easy to work out the rest."

Of course! An anagram. Fitzwilliam returned to the word. LATTIMORES THE MENTOR.

"That's brilliant, Perry," Bea said, grinning.

"Yes, well done Mr Juke," Spicer added.

Perry beamed and wiggled his phone in his hand. "Shall I call Simon and see if we can translate it?"

"Yes, please," Fitzwilliam said, clearing space for them at the end of the table. Soon, Bea and Perry were going through each line with Simon at the other end of the phone.

———

"Sir?" Fitzwilliam looked up from the crime scene photos he'd gone back to. Hardwick sat opposite him, holding a photo, a frown creasing her make-up. "Who's this?" She pushed the photo of a youngish man with a shaved head towards him.

"That's the man Carmichael brought in in connection with the duke's kidnapping. Dean someone or other. His name should be in the file. I think he's connected to THC. Why?"

She rummaged in the green folder in front of her. "Dean Foxley. He looks familiar, but I can't place him. I just know I've seen his face somewhere recently." She shrugged and slid the photo back, pinning it to the top of the folder. "It'll come to me."

"Daisy!" Spicer cried in surprise as the little dog suddenly jumped up onto her lap. "You nearly made me spill my cup of tea," she said, laughing as she patted the terrier. "You only have to ask, you know…" She rubbed Daisy under her chin.

Fitzwilliam caught his breath. *Cup of tea!* He started furiously, searching through the crime scene photos again. *Where are the ones of Street's desk?* He found one. His eyes scanned the items on Street's desk. No cup or mug. He looked at the next one, taken from a slightly different angle. *Nope.* "Do you have Ruth Ness's statement there?" he asked Spicer urgently.

"It's on the app—"

"I know. I know. But there should be a printed version there, in that folder," he said, pointing to a light-blue folder in the pile closest to Spicer.

She picked it up and passed it to him, a scowl on her face. "The whole point of the app, sir, is to avoid all of this. If you would just—"

"Tina!" he hissed, conscious Bea had glanced over at them. "I like paper, okay? I like the feel of it. I like that I can spread it out and move it around. But what I particularly like is I can *see* it." He grabbed the folder from her outstretched hand. "It's too small for me on that blasted phone. I can barely see more than a dozen lines at a time..." He felt like a naughty schoolboy making excuses for why he'd not done his homework.

Spicer flipped her hands up in front of her. "Okay, I get it," she said. Then she grinned. "You don't like change, and your eyesight is going. It's alright, sir, don't worry. We'll keep doing it the old-fashioned way..."

Ha! He laughed out loud. He could always rely on Tina Spicer to get him off his high horse. "When you've quite finished being insubordinate, I think I've found something." He pushed the photo of Street's desk towards her. "What's missing?"

Spicer frowned as she leaned over Daisy's head and studied the photo. "I don't know."

He turned to Hardwick, who was now peering at the photo too. She shook her head.

"His cup of tea!" he told them triumphantly. He flipped open the file. "See here, Ruth Ness said, 'I followed Mr Rockcliffe into the office with a cup of tea for the chief superintendent.'" He closed the file with a flourish. "So what happened to it? It's not in any of the photos taken of the crime scene."

Spicer and Hardwick stared at him for a moment, then Spicer said, "Could Street have moved it?"

Fitzwilliam pushed the rest of the photos towards the two sergeants. "You have a look through them and see if you can spot it anywhere in his office." He rose. "Meanwhile, I'll make a few calls." He picked up his mobile. "I'll be in my office." He glanced over at Bea and Perry, busily scribbling away on the other side of the long table. He caught Bea's eye, and she smiled lazily at him. *Focus, man! Catch the killer first...*

43

LATER, SATURDAY 6 FEBRUARY

"That's it!" Perry exclaimed proudly as Bea wrote down the last letter of the message and let out a sigh.

Thank goodness that's done. She stretched out her right hand and wiggled her fingers.

"Thanks, love," Perry said into the phone.

"So it was hard from here when I'm just giving you letters, but it seems like it's some sort of list?" Simon Lattimore asked, letting out a sharp breath through the mobile's speaker that sounded like someone opening a can of fizzy drink.

Perry looked over at the paper in front of Bea. "Yes. It looks like a list of names of people, what they do, and who they work for."

Bea leaned towards the phone. "Simon, I think it's organised crime members. A bit like the list from James. Did you notice Jacky Prince's name is on it?" Jacky Prince had been arrested during their last investigation at Drew Castle. He was a member of The Hack Crew.

"Well, that makes sense," Simon said at the other end of the line. "Street must have been compiling it over the years as some sort of security blanket. He could use it to bargain with if he ever got caught."

Bea looked across the room. Hardwick and Spicer, with Daisy still on her knees, were sorting through pictures at the other end of the long meeting table. But Fitzwilliam hadn't come back yet. *Where did he go?* While Perry and Simon were still chatting, she rose and walked towards the two sergeants. "We've finished decoding Street's papers," she said, holding them up. "Will the chief inspector be back in a minute? Or…" *Should I go and find him? He'll want to know about the list as soon as possible, won't he?*

Tina Spicer smiled and held out her hand. "I'll take it, my lady, thank you."

"Indeed," Bea replied, trying to keep the disappointment out of her voice. "It looks like a list of names, roles, and other information. Jacky Prince from THC is on it."

Spicer nodded as she scanned the list. "I'll get it uploaded to the database to cross reference everything on it with the suspects, then pass it on to Intelligence," she said, gently placing Daisy on the floor, then brushing down her navy-blue trousers.

"Sorry about that," Bea said, sending Daisy a look. "White dogs are a bit of a nightmare when you wear dark colours."

Spicer smiled down at Daisy, then picked up the papers. "Ah, but they're worth it." She looked up. "Thank you, Lady Beatrice. To you and Mr Juke. I think this is going to be a vital document."

Spicer flipped open her laptop, and Bea walked back to Perry, who was just saying goodbye to Simon. "I could do with a coffee," she said.

Perry nodded. "Me too. And maybe a piece of cake?"

She smiled. "Indeed."

44

AT ABOUT THE SAME TIME, SATURDAY 6 FEBRUARY

"So you didn't see it on the desk when you found Street's body?" DCI Richard Fitzwilliam asked DI Madeline Carmichael on the other end of the phone.

"No. I'm fairly sure I would have noticed if there'd been a cup or mug on his desk."

"Well, thanks. I just wanted to check. Sorry to bother you on a Saturday."

"No problem. If you need anything else, don't hesitate."

He ended the call and ticked her name off the list on his desk in front of him. He moved to the next name and grimaced. George Rockcliffe. *Is there any point asking? No doubt his lawyers will have told him not to say anything to PaIRS or the police without them present.* He sighed and moved on to the next one. Ruth Ness. He tapped her number into his phone and waited. After ringing several times, the line clicked, and her voicemail message kicked in.

"Hi. This is Ruth. I'm either kicking someone's butt or reading a book. Please leave a message after the tone." *What an odd message.* He left her a message to call him at her earliest convenience and moved on to the final name. DCI Bird.

"Fitz!" Bird answered the phone before Fitzwilliam heard it ring at the other end.

"Sorry to disturb you on a Saturday, Henry. But can I ask you a quick question, please?"

"Sure. No problem. I'm hanging around while the missus is trying on dresses. I'm glad of the distraction. She won't ask me what I think if I'm on the phone. I always seem to say the wrong thing," he said, sighing.

Fitzwilliam smiled. "Best just to nod, mate, and say yes." Bird chuckled. "So when you first went into Street's office, you know, after you heard Carmichael cry for help, did you notice where Street's cup of tea was?"

There was a pause, then Bird said, "I did see it, but not in his office."

Fitzwilliam's belly fluttered. "Where was it?"

"In the sink in the kitchen. Well at least it was when I went to get Maddie Carmichael a glass of water when the police arrived."

"And neither you, Ruth, nor Maddie picked it up off his desk when you first discovered the body?"

"Nope. Ruth didn't even get that far into the office, and Maddie didn't have anything in her hands when she took Ruth out. As you know, I did a quick visual check of his desk, looking for my appraisal, and I definitely didn't see it."

So someone removed it from Street's office and put it in the kitchenette. But who and why?

"What does it look like?"

"It's a mug. White, with 'World's Okayest Boss' on it in black. It was his secret Santa present from Christmas. I know because I was the one who bought it for him." Again he chuckled.

Fitzwilliam glanced down at his list again. Why would any of them have moved it? "Great, thanks, Henry. Good luck with the dress shopping. Just smile and say something nice."

Fitzwilliam pressed end, then immediately opened the message app to text Carmichael.

DCI Fitzwilliam (PaIRS): *Did you notice a white mug with 'World's Okayest Boss' on it in the sink when you went into the kitchen to get Ruth Ness a glass of water?"*

He pinched the top of his nose and closed his eyes. Had it been the murderer who'd removed the mug? But why?

DI M Carmichael (City): *There was a white mug in the sink, but I didn't read what it said on it.*

He smiled and typed: *Thanks,* before opening up a new message for Spicer.

Fitzwilliam: *I'm going over to Street's office to look for the mug. Someone moved it from Street's office between the time Ruth Ness took it in and before Carmichael found his body. It was in the sink in the kitchen by then.*

He put his phone down and ticked Bird's name off the list with a sense of satisfaction. He had something to go on now.

He was fairly sure whoever had moved the mug was the killer. But for the life of him, he couldn't think of why they would've done it.

45

ALSO... OVER HERE, SATURDAY 6 FEBRUARY

"So now we wait," Detective Sergeant Tina Spicer told her colleague Detective Sergeant Arabella Hardwick as she leaned back against the chair. "The program will take all the names I've just scanned in from Street's list that Lady Beatrice and Perry Juke have collated and as I've set the 'match' function running, it will look at all of the notes, both uploaded automatically from the app we use or anything input manually, and it will see if any of the words or phrases are a match to the ones on the list. Then it will look at the list and check it against anyone in the PaIRS database and see if *they* match. It also pulls additional information from public records to see if—"

A box flashed up saying 'possible match'. *That was quick!* "It normally takes longer than that," she told Bella, clicking the box. Spicer's pulse quicken. *Could we be that lucky and already have a connection?* Her eyes sparkled as she read the information on her screen.

. . .

POSSIBLE CONNECTION: Ruth Ness (Suspect) + John Travers (Street List) married Joan Travers née Ness (Marriage Register). Click for more information...

Bella swore under her breath and leaned over to click the link before Spicer recovered. The additional information gave a summary of what had been on the input list regarding John Mark Travers (bent cop, City Police, related to the Peck brothers), then a date he'd married Joan Ellen Ness and a note saying she had a young daughter at the time. Gently moving Bella's arm out of the way, Spicer open up the PaIRS HR system and searched Ruth's name. "Let's see if we can corroborate that." When the record came up, she clicked the attached documents and pulled up Ruth's birth certificate. Bingo! "It says father unknown, mother Joan Ellen Ness." *Well, that's a turn up.* "Although Ruth has an alibi – in fact, you," she said, turning to Bella. "So she..." She halted when she saw Bella's face.

Bella's eyes were wide, and her mouth hung slightly open. She gasped. "That's it! That's where I've seen him before," she cried.

Spicer frowned. *Seen who?*

"Dean Foxley," Bella continued. "The one from THC that Carmichael pulled in on suspicion of being involved in the duke's kidnapping attempt. I was just staring at the screen, and it came to me. I saw his face on Ruth's computer screen when we were doing a video call briefing last week. She shared her screen with me then; I remember seeing his face for a split second on her screensaver before she closed the window."

Wow! Spicer's head was reeling. Not only was Ruth's stepfather on Street's list, but now there was a connection between her and Dean Foxley. Suspicions began circling around in her head again. Could Ruth Ness be working for THC? She swallowed. *Did she kill Street?*

"But you were on the phone to her when—" Her mobile beeped.

Fitzwilliam: *I'm going over to Street's office to look for the mug. Someone moved it from Street's office between the time Ruth Ness took it in and before Carmichael found his body. It was in the sink in the kitchen by then.*

But they needed to tell him about Ruth Ness....

Spicer*: Wait, boss. We've found out something important about Ruth Ness. We're coming to your office now.*

"Come on," she said to Bella, slamming down her laptop screen. "We need to tell the boss."

———

Spicer's mouth went dry when she saw Fitzwilliam's door was open. She hurried forward and shoved her head around the door. She huffed. *Why didn't he wait?* Then she saw his mobile phone on his desk. This time, she swore. How could he have left his phone? Of course, if he was using the app the whole time like he should be, then he wouldn't let his phone out of his sight. *He's such a dinosaur sometimes!* She ran in and grabbed it off the table. "Carol!" she shouted as she exited his office. "How long ago did the chief inspector leave?"

Carol looked from her computer. "Oh, only a few minutes ago. He's going to…"

Spicer knew where he was heading. "Thanks, Carol. Come on, Bella. We may be able to catch up with him."

———

Fitzwilliam strolled along the corridor. His brows were knitted together in concentration, his lips pursed tightly. His hands tucked into his pockets, his steps echoed in the dark hallway. *Why would someone feel like they needed to remove Street's cup of tea from his office after they killed him?*

He made his way past closed offices, silent hallways, and deserted lobbies. *It doesn't make any sense. Maybe Ruth Ness can help?* She hadn't rung him back yet. Should he ring her again? He stopped suddenly, his hand shooting to his jacket pocket. *Where's my phone?* His heart raced as he realised it wasn't there, then sank as he remembered he'd left it back in his office. *You idiot!* Should he go back? Or should he carry on to Street's office? It was only a few minutes away. He would go there first and then go back for his phone after-wards. *I hope Spicer doesn't find out…*

———

Bea drained her coffee cup. "I needed that," she told Perry. He nodded, absently stirring his tea, his gaze distant like he wasn't really in the canteen with her. His brows were drawn together, and he'd gone a little pale.

What's wrong? He'd been so proud when he'd figured out the code for Street's list, but he'd been unusually quiet since they'd left the office. She reached out and touched Perry's arm lightly, her eyes softening with concern. "Perry, are you okay? You seem...distracted."

Perry turned to her and forced a smile, but Bea could see the worry in his eyes. "I just... I don't know. I have this feeling something bad is going on, and I'm worried we're caught up in it all now," he said with a sigh. "That list of big-time gangsters was serious stuff, Bea. Someone killed James, then that guy Preece, and now Street. It seems they'll go to a lot of trouble to cover their tracks." He looked around the half-empty room, then leaned towards her. "How do we know we're not next?" he whispered.

Bea stifled a giggle at his overreaction. "Oh, Perry!" she said, trying to keep a straight face. "You know it's not an episode of *CSI*. We're not going to get targeted by the under-world here. We're in a palace." She squeezed his arm. "Don't worry, I'm sure Fitzwilliam will figure it all out soon," she said with more confidence than she felt. He'd looked perplexed when they'd been in the meeting room together. And tired. *I hope he solves this murder soon...*

Perry huffed. "I much prefer it when it's a straightforward murder like our previous cases. You know, when the motive is love, money, or revenge. I don't like all this complicated spy and baddies stuff."

She knew what he meant. This case had an edge to it the others hadn't. Hopefully next time— *What am I talking about? There will be no next time!*

She tapped Perry's arm and rose. Daisy got up and stretched. "Come on. Let's see if those deliveries have arrived yet." She looked for the door out of the security staff canteen. "I hope you know how to get back to the main house from here as I have no idea."

46

ABOUT THE SAME TIME, SATURDAY 6 FEBRUARY

"But she has an alibi," Spicer said as they rounded the corner and turned into another dreary, empty corridor. "You were on the phone to her the whole time, so how could she have—"

Bella Hardwick slowed down. "What if she did it while she was on the phone to me? Oh my g—" She halted abruptly, the blood draining from her face.

The hair lifted on the back of Spicer's neck. *Was it possible?* She met Bella's gaze. "What?"

Bella stared, her eyes wide. "She uses a bluetooth headset. I've seen her wearing it so many times when I've been waiting to go in to see Street. There are no wires. She wanders around the outer office, talking to someone on the other end like—"

Spicer stopped too. "Like what?" she asked, her skin feeling clammy.

"This one time she got up and went into Street's office and came out with his empty mug and took it to the kitchen, all the time on a call." Her lips trembled as she blew out her breath.

Spicer started to move again, feeling a sense of urgency.

Had Ruth Ness calmly choked the chief superintendent while on the phone to Bella, then cleaned away his mug like she always did? *It seems so extraordinary, but...* She sped up.

"Why the hurry?" Bella asked as she caught up with Spicer.

"Fitzwilliam's on his way to Street's office now."

"I know, but it's a Saturday. Ruth's not going to be there today, is she?"

"You never know," Spicer said, yanking open a door and hurrying through it. "The office was secure while it was listed as a crime scene, but SOCO has finished with it now. She might have come in to clear up anything we've missed."

Bella swore. "Let's go!"

────────

Fitzwilliam turned the corner and opened the door leading to Street's outer office. He halted suddenly. Ruth Ness's head shot up from where it had been buried in her desk drawer. *What's she doing here on a Saturday?*

"Ruth. I wasn't expecting to see you here today. Is everything okay?"

Ruth looked flustered as she pointed to the shredding machine by the side of her desk. "Just having a tidy up, you know, before I move on," she said in a shaky voice.

Fitzwilliam's eyes narrowed. Something about it didn't feel right. He checked himself. She was probably just upset and didn't want to be clearing her desk during the working day with everyone watching her. He smiled. "Well, don't let me stop you," he said as he looked away and headed for the small kitchen.

Walking into the kitchenette, he scanned the shelves and counters for the white mug he was looking for. There were several colourful mugs arranged in a neat stack near the coffee machine, but nothing white was among them. He looked further, and then he spotted it. Tucked away in a corner, behind a box of teabags was a white mug with black writing on the front. *Got it!* He whipped out a pair of blue gloves from his pocket and grabbed the mug. He was clutching at straws that it might still have prints on it, but it was worth a shot.

Fitzwilliam left the kitchenette, still holding the mug, and entered the outer office. He noticed that Street's office door was open. He frowned. *What was Ruth doing in Street's office?*

Suddenly his attention was drawn back to the outer office by Ruth's gasp. He spun around to face her, and she immediately averted her gaze from him but not before he caught a glimpse of fear in her eyes.

———

"Could you have been having a conversation with her while she was moving around?" Spicer asked Hardwick as she marched down the corridor.

Bella, trotting beside her, held her hands out, palms up. "I suppose so. I was concentrating on reading her my conclusion. Apart from a few words of encouragement, I suppose she didn't really say much. I did most of the talking."

Spicer's knees felt weak, like they would crumble any minute, and she would collapse in a heap on the floor. *Please don't let her be there...*

———

"Why have you got the chief superintendent's mug?" Ruth Ness asked, standing by her desk, a wad of papers in one hand. Her eyes were fixated on his hand.

"Well, maybe you can help me there, Ruth. In your statement, you said you took CS Street in a cup of tea when George Rockcliffe arrived for his meeting, but when we searched his office after his death, the mug wasn't there. Someone must have removed…" He trailed off. Ruth was clutching at her throat.

Fitzwilliam's mind was slowly turning. *Why is she so afraid?* Suddenly he was hit by a recent memory. Carol had been in his office one afternoon. Just as she'd left, she'd picked up his dirty mug and taken it out with her, presumably to wash it, as it had reappeared later in the day on his desk, clean. *She does that a lot.* Then it struck him. Who was the most likely person to have removed it from Street's office on the day of his murder? His EA, of course!

He clenched his jaw. *Could Ruth Ness be Street's killer?* Staring at her now in joggers and a top rather than her usual business suit and blouse, he could see her well-defined shoulders. Her biceps and triceps were bulging out from the sleeves of her tight T-shirt. *She must work out a lot.* A thought crossed his mind. *Does she do martial arts?*

He took a deep breath. He was getting carried away. She'd been on the phone to Hardwick when Street had been killed. He glanced down at her desk, the black headset lying on its side by the small switchboard. *They're wireless! Oh my—*

Following his eyes, Ruth suddenly moved, darting for her bag. "Ruth," he barked, his legs feeling heavy as he moved slowly towards her. "Stay where you are."

She ignored him. Diving into her bag, she grabbed something black and metallic. She lifted it up with both hands.

Fitzwilliam couldn't speak. His limbs seemingly turned to jelly. His brain told him to move, but his body had gone deaf. Time stopped. All he could hear was the rushing of blood in his ears. He felt strangely calm. Surely she wouldn't shoot him? *She will*, a voice in his head replied, *and stop calling me Shirley*...

———

Bang! Spicer jumped and wheeled around to look at Hardwick. "Was that a shot?" she shouted above the thundering of her heart, already knowing the answer. Bella nodded. They streaked down the corridor towards Street's office.

47

AT ABOUT THE SAME TIME, SATURDAY 6 FEBRUARY

"So will you ever tell Sam what really happened?" Perry Juke asked Lady Beatrice as they made their way through the labyrinth of the dark corridors of the security wing on their way back from the canteen, Daisy trotting between them.

This place is a maze, Bea thought. *Will we ever find our way back to the main house?* "I think I will, but not yet. I want to make sure he's mature enough to understand." Perry nodded. "But I *will* send James's old school trunk to James's parents so his father can go through it with Sam. They'll both love—"

Bang! An abrupt loud sound like a split second of thunder shattered the peace of the narrow corridors, echoing off the walls and reverberating deeply in Bea's eardrums. Daisy barked. Bea's heart pounding, she stopped and turned to Perry. *What the—*

"Oh my giddy aunt! What was that?" Perry asked, his voice trembling as he stared at her, his eyes wide.

Bea put a shaky hand on his shoulder. "It sounded like a gunshot to me." Her eyes frantically searched up and down the corridor. *Where is everyone?* "Do you think we should go and see what it was?"

Perry shook his head vigorously. "It could be dangerous. We should wait here for security."

He's probably right. But…. "What if someone needs our help? We should go and see." She bent down and grabbed Daisy, hoiking her into her arms. "Come on. Let's go. We'll be careful, I promise."

Holding on to each other, they made their way cautiously down the corridor. As they turned the corner, they heard voices. Urgent and anxious. A woman began shouting. Bea sped up, dragging a reluctant Perry beside her. She couldn't make out the words, but she could tell the woman was in distress. "We have to help," she said, starting to run towards the noise, her heart thumping wildly in her chest. Perry, still holding on to her, was running too.

As they got closer, Bea could just make out what was being said, "Call an ambulance! Sir, can you hear me?" It was a female voice. *Spicer?* Bea's heart raced. *Sir?* Her heart pounded. *Fitzwilliam!* She swung around, shoving Daisy into Perry's arms. "Look after Daisy," she shouted to him as she bolted towards the door.

After bursting into the room, it took her a moment to make sense of the scene before her. The room was in disarray — furniture askew, a broken mug, and papers strewn around. A woman lay on the floor by an open office, her hands hand-cuffed behind her back, kicking her legs out wildly. Another woman, who Bea recognised as Spicer's student Bella Hardwick, was sitting next to her, holding the woman down as best she could while talking urgently into her mobile phone. A gun was strewn on the floor just a few metres away. Bea's head was pounding, and there was a whooshing in her ears. *Oh my gosh, what happened?*

"Sir!" Her attention was drawn to the middle of the room where Spicer was huddled over a body on the floor. Bea's heart stopped. Everything slowed down. *Fitzwilliam!*

The chief inspector was lying motionless on the floor in a pool of blood, an ugly wound just below his chest. Spicer, leaning over him, was taking off her jacket, which she then balled up and pushed onto him.

Behind Bea, Perry, holding a wriggling Daisy, gasped. Bea wanted to move, but she couldn't breathe. Then suddenly she got the air she needed and launched herself in Spicer's direction.

Throwing herself down beside Fitzwilliam's body, she noticed the shallow rise and fall of his chest, the faintest of motions indicating he was still alive, though barely conscious. Her eyes widened. Tears welled up behind her eyelids. *Come on, Fitzwilliam! You're going to be alright. You have to be alright!* She pushed away the tears that were threatening to fall and focussed on the task at hand. She took off her jumper and carefully placed it under Fitzwilliam's head. She looked over his prone form to Spicer, who was holding her jacket in place to stop the bleeding.

Spicer looked up, her eyes pleading for assurance. Bea nodded. "Keep up the pressure. You're doing great."

Spicer gave her a weak smile in return. "Bella's calling an ambulance."

"Indeed," Bea said, glancing up at Bella Hardwick, who was still holding on to the woman thrashing around on the floor and talking to Perry. *She seems to have it under control.*

She looked back down at Fitzwilliam. What more could she do? *Talk to him. Reassure him.* She leaned towards his bloodless face. "Fitzwilliam, can you hear me?" she murmured softly. He let out a low groan and opened his eyes slowly. Tears of relief flooded her eyes, and she brushed them away with one hand and grabbed his blue-gloved hand with the other. The plastic was cold and clammy, but she felt his hand clench around hers as she looked into his eyes. *Come on, Fitzwilliam, you can do this.* He managed a weak smile, and she tightened her grip on his hand.

"Help is coming," she whispered. "You're going to be alright, I promise."

"Ruth..." he croaked. "Button on her blouse sleeve. Tell Elmes..." His eyes flickered. *Fitzwilliam!*

At that moment, there was a loud clatter outside the room, and the paramedics arrived, pushing a trolley. Bea gave Fitzwilliam's hand a final squeeze, then dropped it as she stood up. She stepped away as they rushed towards him, carrying medical bags and equipment.

Spicer rose, brushed herself down, and moved out of the way too, coming around to join Bea. "I need to deal with Ruth Ness. Will you ring me when you have news?"

Ruth Ness? So that's who the woman on the floor was. Hadn't she been Street's assistant? *Was she the killer?* Bea nodded. "Of course. What happened?"

Spicer took in a breath, then exhaled. "I think the boss caught her trying to destroy evidence. She had a gun. She shot him." She paused and swallowed, then continued, "Hardwick and I jumped her and wrestled the gun..." She stopped again and took another breath in. "He'll be okay, won't he?"

Bea gave her a reassuring smile. "I'll make sure he gets the best possible care."

"Thank you, my lady." Spicer crossed the room. Taking a bag out of her back trousers pocket, she bent down over the gun and picked it up with the bag, then with a flick of her wrist, she dropped it inside and zipped up the top. She moved to join Hardwick. Between them, they pulled Ruth Ness up from the floor and wheeled the still-wriggling handcuffed woman out of the room.

A paw on her shoulder made Bea start. Perry was beside her, Daisy straining to get out of his arms. Their presence brought a calm over her as she opened her arms and enfolded Daisy into them. The warmth of her furry little body caused Bea's muscles to relax. *It's going to be alright.*

The paramedics, efficient and professional, worked with an urgency that made Bea's heart swell with admiration. She let out a deep breath when Fitzwilliam's colour began to slowly return and his breathing deepened. They placed an oxygen mask over his face, then carefully lifted him and placed him on a stretcher. As they wheeled him across the room, she went to hand Daisy back to Perry so she could follow, but Perry shook his head, holding her back. She turned to him, frowning. *I want to go with him.*

"Bea," Perry said gently. "You can't go with him."

"But—"

"For a start, you're covered in blood."

She looked down. There were brown stains on her white T-shirt and the knees of her jeans.

"But also," Perry continued, "think about how it will look if people see you arriving with him at the hospital. It will cause all sorts of trouble for you…and him."

She sighed. *Perry's right.* The last thing she wanted to do was make it worse for Fitzwilliam. She nodded.

"Go and get changed," he said, steering her towards the door. "Then if you feel you need to go to the hospital, do so discreetly."

48

AFTERNOON, SATURDAY 6 FEBRUARY

The Society Page online article:

<u>*BREAKING NEWS Billionaire Rudy Trotman and His Wife Missing After Killer Avalanche Hits French Ski Resort*</u>

Reports are coming in that business man, Rudy Trotman (68), and his wife Sheri (66) are among the seven people missing following a deadly avalanche yesterday on the upper slopes of the French ski resort of Val'Nes. The couple, whose eldest son Otis Trotman (41) is married to Sybil (36), step-daughter of well-respected businessman and star of television's The Novice, *Sir Hewitt Willoughby-Franklin (68), reportedly made a last minute decision to go skiing for the weekend, following a visit to London to see Sir Hewitt and his wife Lady Grace (61).*

A statement issued on behalf of the family by Otis Trotman, who flew out to Val'Nes last night, reads: 'It is with great sorrow, I can confirm Rudy and Sheri Trotman are missing following the avalanche in Val'Nes yesterday. Our parents loved skiing, and we believe they flew to the resort for a short break. We have been unable to contact them since the avalanche was reported, and they have not returned to the ski chalet where they were staying. We have organised additional help to support the local rescue teams who are searching for survivors and will continue to hold out hope that they may be found.'

Rescue attempts have been hampered by the threat of further avalanches and had to be called off when it got dark at four yesterday afternoon. They resumed at eight this morning. Also missing are a local guide and four students, who were known to be descending what was considered to be a relatively safe slope as a group when the avalanche occurred at lunchtime.

We will bring you updates as we have them.

49

ALSO AFTERNOON, SATURDAY 6 FEBRUARY

"Lady Rossex!" A pretty dark-haired woman cried as she rushed towards Lady Beatrice along the hospital corridor lined with fluorescent lighting that cast a faint blue chill on the walls and floor. Her eyes were filled with anxiety as she pushed her dark curls out of her face and stopped right before Bea. "I had no idea you would be here," Elise Boyce said breathlessly.

"How is he?" Bea asked, swallowing down the bile that had risen in the back of her throat. *Please let him be okay.* Glimpsing over Elise's shoulder, she noticed a woman wearing a dark-blue outfit speaking in a low voice to three others — one person dressed in a pink uniform and the other two attired in lighter shades of blue. *Aren't they nurses? Why aren't they with Fitzwilliam? Shouldn't they be looking after him?* Elise whimpered softly, and Bea turned her attention back to Fitzwilliam's sister and a thick-set man with short brown hair who had joined them.

"They're not really saying much," Elise said in a shaky voice. She lifted her hand to her mouth, then turned to the man and sank into his arms. "Rhys?" Bea addressed Elise's husband. "Is he still in surgery?"

Rhys shrugged as best he could with his wife clinging to him. "They took him down over three hours ago, and we've heard nothing."

A wave of nausea washed over Bea. Three hours? *Why so long? Is there a complication?* She looked at Elise. She'd only met Fitzwilliam's sister and brother-in-law once before, back last summer when they'd come to visit Fitzwilliam for a weekend while he'd been working on a case in Fenshire. She remembered Elise as a bubbly, chatty person. She didn't recognise the broken woman before her. Bea glanced over towards the nurses' station again, and this time, she caught the eye of the woman in the dark-blue uniform. Her entire appearance changed as she noticed Bea, her eyes widening and her mouth dropping open. She hurriedly whispered something to her colleagues before making a beeline towards Bea, Elise, and Rhys.

The woman stopped, clasping her hands in front of her. "My lady," she said, looking panicked. "I am Matron Hathaway, head nurse of the ward. Forgive me, but I...I didn't recognise you at first." Bea looked down at her black sweatshirt with 'Give me some love' written in a red heart on the front, a pair of black joggers, and her running shoes. *What a mess I must look.* But when she'd changed out of her bloodstained T-shirt and jeans, she'd just grabbed the first things she could find. *No wonder she doesn't recognise me.* "I had no idea you were here." She scanned the area behind Bea, clearly wondering where her entourage was.

Bea cleared her throat and smiled at the woman as she held out her hand. "My apologies, matron." Bea said, trying to keep her voice calm despite her desperation to find out where Fitzwilliam was. "I'm here in a private capacity as a friend of the family." She glanced at Elise and Rhys. "One of the senior police officers who works at Gollingham Palace was brought in here after he was shot. Chief Inspector Richard Fitzwilliam? I'm trying to find out where he is."

The matron looked at Bea for a few seconds, studying every inch of her face, then returned her handshake and nodded. "Let me go and make some enquiries. Please excuse me, my lady." She pivoted on her heels and hurried back towards the nurses' station.

"Should we follow her?" Rhys asked. Bea shrugged. "I suppose so." They headed slowly towards where Matron Hathaway was now talking animatedly on the phone. *Please let this be good news...*

The matron put the phone down, her face grim as she walked towards them. Bea was vaguely aware of the other staff hanging around the station watching her. She should go over and greet them. Say hello. Be friendly. Thank them for their hard work. But she couldn't. Her heart felt like it had stopped beating. She couldn't breathe. She grabbed Elise's hand and almost recoiled when Elise crushed her fingers.

Matron Hathaway stood before them. She swallowed. Bea's head was spinning. *Oh no... Please no...* "They've removed the bullet from Mr Fitzwilliam's body. He's lost a lot of blood, but it appears not to have damaged any vital organs. He's currently in the recovery room and will be taken from there to a room in the intensive care wing where they will monitor him closely. He's not out of the woods completely, but all the signs are good that he'll make a full recovery."

Tears welled up behind Bea's lids. *He's going to be alright...* She wanted to say something, but she couldn't seem to find the right words. Elise let out a cry next to her and released her hand. Bea wiggled her fingers and licked her dry lips. Smiling at the woman before her, whose face was still intensely serious, she said, "Thank you, matron." Then added in her head, *And you might want to work on your bedside manner...*

———

"So it might be a while before he's back at work," Lady Beatrice told her silent audience of Emma and Izzy McKeer-Adler, Perry Juke, and Simon Lattimore. "But the doctor was quite positive about his ultimate recovery."

"And this is the doctor you spoke to who did the op?" Adler asked. Bea nodded. She had left her number with Matron Hathaway and asked her very nicely to ask the surgeon to contact her when they had a chance. The doctor had rung about twenty minutes later when Bea had been in the car being driven home, having left Elise and Rhys Boyce to go to the room allocated to Fitzwilliam to wait for him.

"It was a close run thing, your ladyship," Doctor Ayesha Bhait had said, making Bea's insides wobble. "Fortunately, the trajectory of the bullet was such that it missed all his vital organs and exited through his side. He's got a lot of tissue and muscle damage in his lower body but nothing that won't heal over time with rest. He's lost a lot of blood as you know, so he'll be weak for a while, but he's a strong healthy man, so as long as he doesn't pick up an infection in the wound or push his recovery too hard too soon, he'll be right as rain in twelve weeks or so." Bea had had to wipe away the tear that had trickled down her face.

She smiled at the memory and took a sip of her red wine before returning it to the dining room table. "Yes. She was very helpful."

Adler leaned in and rested her hand on Bea's arm.

"Thanks so much for ringing from the hospital and letting us know how he was. I can't tell you how worried I was..." Her voice cracked, and she picked up her wineglass. Bea nodded. She'd rung Adler and Izzy, then Spicer, and finally Perry and Simon as soon as the matron had told them Fitzwilliam would be alright. Elise had gone to ring her mother. Bea had never really thought about Fitzwilliam having family other than his sister. Did he have other siblings? Was he close to his mother? There had been no mention of a father. *Is he dead or simply not around?* she wondered.

When Bea had rung Adler, she'd immediately asked her over for dinner tonight along with Perry and Simon. She'd said she had more information about what Ruth Ness had told the police since her arrest. Bea was keen to hear it but also knew her friends wanted an update on Fitzwilliam first.

"Will they keep him in long?" Izzy asked, her eyes still full of concern.

"They don't know yet. Apparently with muscle damage, there's a lot of inflammation, so they'll keep him comfortable until that starts to ease and he can move okay."

"But is he safe?" Adler asked, her fingers gripping Bea's arm. "I mean, after what happened to Preece..." She trailed off and dropped her hand as she took another sip of alcohol. Across the other side of the dining room table, Izzy pushed the remaining bottle of wine towards her wife.

"Yes. Don't worry. He has around the clock protection from Surrey Police. He's perfectly safe," Bea said reassuringly, then glanced over at Simon opposite her and raised an eyebrow.

He nodded. "I spoke to Lord Fred just before we arrived, and he said that by the morning, they will have arrested all the major players. I think then they'll have bigger things to worry about than a PaIRS police officer who caught one of them out."

Adler's eyebrows rose. "Like finding Rudy Trotman before he can talk?"

About to open her mouth and tell them that Rudy had already talked, Bea stopped as Perry jumped in. "But he's dead, isn't he? He and his wife were caught up in the avalanche in France. I read it in the paper."

"Well, technically, they're just missing at this stage," Simon said, pushing his chair away from the table. He leaned back and crossed his legs.

"If they're there to be found," Adler said, placing her elbows on the table.

Bea turned to face Adler sitting next to her, frowning. "What are you suggesting?"

Adler pulled a face. "Don't you think it's a bit odd Rudy Trotman is due to spill his guts about his involvement with some of the most powerful organised crime families in the western world, and the next thing you know, him and his wife disappear?"

Oh my goodness! They were killed for betraying them.

Izzy gasped. "You mean these gangsters had them killed?"

Adler shook her head. "No, I don't think so. MI6 wouldn't be that sloppy in protecting them. I think Rudy Trotman must have made it a condition that once he and his wife made their sworn statements, giving all the dirt the police needed to arrest and charge everyone, he'd want to ensure they would be safe from retribution. And what better way to do that than disappear...for good," she said with a dramatic flourish of her hands.

It sort of makes sense... But how do you arrange a natural disaster?

Perry's eyes were shining. "So you're saying MI6 started the avalanche and pretended the Trotmans were—"

"No, Perry," Simon interrupted, trying to hide a grin. "I think what Em's suggesting is once MI6 heard of the disaster, they retrospectively arranged for it to look like the Trotmans had been there for the weekend."

"So you think that's what they did, do you?" Bea asked him.

"I think it's possible."

Adler said, "Thanks," and raised her glass towards Simon.

Wow. Bea shook her head slowly. She'd have to ask Fred when she spoke to him next. Although, of course, he wouldn't be able to tell her directly. She suppressed a smile. She was confident she would be able to tell from how he answered as to whether it was true or not…

50

SHORTLY AFTER, SATURDAY 6 FEBRUARY

Izzy McKeer-Adler stood and began to clear away their plates from the dining table. "I'll get coffee," she said as she disappeared out of the room.

"You promised you had more to tell us about Ruth Ness," Perry Juke said to Emma McKeer-Adler, leaning over the table, his eyes fixed on her.

"I did, you're right." Adler gave him a cheeky grin as she picked up her wineglass and slowly took a sip.

"Em, come on," Perry whined.

"Okay, okay. So it seems Miss Ness is prepared to do a deal to save herself from a lifetime behind bars by telling the police everything she knows about THC and their links with other organisations, including the Grazzi Family."

"Ohhhh…" Perry raised an eyebrow at his other half. "You were right, love, when you said she would crumble."

Simon winked and held his wineglass up in a salute.

So Street's list is verified, Bea thought. The Grazzi Family *had* arranged for THC to kill James to stop him from revealing the corruption that had gone on in Miami around the Olympic Games. "So how does she fit in with THC?" she asked.

Adler shook her head. "Her real father disappeared when she was young. Her parents weren't married, and her mother raised her on her own until Ruth was about eighteen months old. Then her mum married a man called John Travers. He was a second cousin to the Peck brothers — Leo, Logan, and Charlie. He didn't ever work for them as such, but he was a police officer and helped protect them by giving them advanced warning of raids on the raves they ran, so they'd switch venues at the last minute. Stuff like that. He died in the line of duty, pushed by an abusive husband when John tried to pull him off his wife. He hit his head and never recovered. They had to make the decision to switch off his machine. Ruth was ten years old.

"Apparently, Charlie kept an eye on her and her mother. His daughter Lilly was only five years older than Ruth, and she sort of took Ruth under her wing. Ruth's mother was diagnosed with cancer when Ruth was in her mid-teens. The Peck family, through Charlie, got her the best care possible, and she survived for another six years until the cancer came back. There was nothing anyone could do. Ruth was an orphan by the time she was twenty-one." Adler paused as Izzy came in with coffee.

Once they all got a cup, she continued, "She went off to college and got an admin qualification. Of course Ruth was eternally grateful to Charlie and Lilly for all they'd done for her, so when Charlie suggested she use her stepfather's police contacts to get her a job at City Police, she went along with it. She told the guys interviewing her she had no idea they were going to then ask her to pass back information when she took the job.

"After a while, she was occasionally asked about cases

being worked on, and she passed the information on to Charlie. She says she felt she owed it to him. Apart from that, she worked hard, kept herself to herself and slowly got a reputation as an effective and efficient admin assistant. About six years ago, not long after Charlie Peck died, Lilly Peck asked her to apply for a move to PaIRS. She didn't say why other than she thought it would be a good career move for Ruth. She says she looked up to Lilly Peck and wanted to impress her, so she agreed.

"As we know, she got the transfer and went to work as a general team support assistant. When the vacancy for Street's EA came up, Lilly again encouraged her to apply, and she did. She got the job. Lilly asked her to 'keep an eye' on her boss Street. Lilly told her he was working for them but that she didn't completely trust him. Ruth agreed. Then a year ago, she met Dean Foxley after Lilly introduced them." Adler stopped and took a sip of her coffee.

Come on! Bea, her right leg bouncing up and down under the table, moved her hand onto her knee and steadied it. *Get on with it...*

"A few months ago," Adler continued, "Lilly called her and said she was worried Street was going to double cross them. She laid it on thick that Street could jeopardise their whole business as he, in her words, 'knew too much'. Lilly also said Dean had told her he wanted to marry Ruth but was worried he would be put in prison if Street caused them trouble. Ruth told the officers that by this time she was in love with Dean and wanted to settle down with him. Lilly was also making noises that if Ruth helped them, then she could come and work for Lilly as her right-hand person. She would be well paid, enabling her and Dean to buy a nice house and settle down. Lilly told her to keep an ear out for any mention of a DI Preece from City or a City DI called Carmichael. If either of them got in contact with Street, Ruth was to let Lilly know straightaway."

So now we're getting to it.

"When Carmichael made the appointment to meet with Street, Lilly told Ruth she had to kill him before the meeting in case he said anything incriminating, especially about his relationship with Preece."

"So the plan was for Ruth to kill Street before he had a chance to talk?" Simon asked.

Adler nodded. "But here's the thing. It was supposed to look like suicide. That's why she took his gun from his office the afternoon before and why we found a partly shredded suicide note after she was taken away."

Ahh... "She had typed it up, ready?" Bea said.

Adler nodded. "But it went wrong for her. Street had arranged off his own back to meet with George Rockcliffe before his arranged meeting with Carmichael. Ruth only found that out at her briefing with Street first thing that morning. So she'd hit a snag. She no longer had time to set up his suicide. She called Lilly, who told her she would have to find another way of getting rid of Street, or they would all be done for. That's when she came up with the idea of the blood choke. It was something she had learned at her martial arts classes at the gym she goes to."

"But she took such a risk," Perry said, shaking his head. "She only had a short window of opportunity to do that between Rockcliffe leaving and Carmichael arriving."

"That's why she moved Carmichael's appointment that morning. She wanted to give herself a little more time," Adler explained. "She told them at the interview she felt she had no choice. She was fighting to preserve her future life with Dean and return the favour she owed Charlie to protect Lilly."

"Wow," Perry said, putting down his empty coffee cup

and picking up his wineglass. "I almost feel sorry for her."

"Well don't." Adler said, an edge to her voice. "I'm only telling you what she told them before she gave them all the names of the people she knew who worked with Dean and Lilly and signed a statement saying she'd been coerced into killing Street. My mate who sat in on the interview with her said he didn't believe a word of it. He thinks she's a cold-blooded murderer who had her eyes on being Lilly's right-hand woman and would do anything to make that happen."

They sat in silence for a few minutes. Bea held her wineglass in front of her and swirled her wine. Watching the red liquid spin around the bottom of her glass was how she imagined the thoughts in her head were right now. It seemed so extraordinary. "Fitzwilliam mumbled something about a button just before they took him to the hospital. Do you know what that was about?"

Adler nodded. "Yes. Spicer heard him say that too. He said to tell Elmes about a button on her blouse sleeve. He's the pathologist. Spicer rang him earlier. Apparently, there was a small indentation on Street's neck. When Spicer delivered the message, Elmes said that the mark could have been the result of a small button pressing into his neck when he was being held in a chokehold. Spicer recalled Ruth Ness was wearing one of those blouses where you can roll up the sleeves and secure them with a tiny button on the day Street was killed. They'll search her house to try and find what she was wearing that day and see if they can match the button from the blouse to the mark on his neck or if Forensics can get anything off the item. It's a bit of a long shot, but worth a try."

"But she's confessed, hasn't she?" Perry asked frowning.

Adler smiled. "Yes. But the more evidence we have against her, or at least she and her lawyers *think* we have against her, then the more likely she is not to get cold feet at the last minute and refuse to testify against the Pecks."

"I have a question," Perry said. They all looked at him expectantly. "Why did he do it?"

"Who, Street?" Adler asked.

Perry nodded. "Why did he get involved with these people in the first place? Was he related to the Peck family or something?"

Adler tipped her head to one side. "Well, funny you should say that. Bella Hardwick did some background on Tim Street, and it turned out he was born in Hackney."

Indeed. So he must have gone to school with someone connected to THC—

"But," she continued, "his father got a new job when he was three and they moved to Wimbledon."

Oh. Not that then...

"However, she did find out something that had happened to him twenty years ago that might have some bearing." They all leaned towards her. She took a sip of coffee and continued, "Street has two sons. When his youngest was fourteen years old, he was with his mum, Street's now ex-wife, on their way to a dentist appointment when a car mounted the pavement and hit him."

Perry raised a hand to his mouth, mumbling, "How awful."

A shiver went down Bea's spine. *His son was the same age that Sam is now...*

Adler nodded. "He survived but suffered severe brain damage. He's thirty-four now and needs twenty-four hour care."

Bea swallowed. *Perry's right; that's awful.* She could only imagine what his parents must have gone through. *If anything like that happened to Sam...*

"Did they catch who did it?" Izzy asked.

Adler shook her head. "There was an investigation, of course. They traced the car to a young lad, Michael Spears, but he said it had been stolen that morning, and one of his mates confirmed it. There were two witnesses: Street's wife and a man who'd been coming out of a shop nearby. But their descriptions of the driver were muddled and didn't match. In the end, with contradicting witness statements and insufficient evidence to prove the car hadn't been stolen, the CPS refused to prosecute."

Bea could only imagine how soul destroying that must have been for Street and his wife.

"Street's marriage only survived for a year or so after that." Adler leaned in and gave a wry smile. "But," she said, her voice low, "only a few months after Street and his wife split, the suspect, Spears, was fished out of Regent's Canal just by Victoria Park in East London. The inquest concluded he'd fallen in after a drunken night out."

Perry gasped. "But you think Street killed him?"

Adler gave a dry laugh. "I've no idea. But Hardwick has a theory that someone might have done it for him and then held it over him."

"Like blackmail?"

"Or a bit like how a protection racket sometimes starts. You have a problem. Without even asking, someone solves it for you. Then they come and tell you they're the ones who fixed it and can you now do them" —Adler air quoted— "'a little favour' in return."

There was a short silence, then Simon, who had been quiet throughout Adler's speech, asked, "Isn't Victoria Park near Hackney?"

Adler raised an eyebrow. "Exactly."

51

FIRST THING, SUNDAY 7 FEBRUARY

The Society Page online article:

BREAKING NEWS Arrests in UK, Europe, and US of Suspected Organised Crime Syndicates

City Police late last night arrested members of an organised crime group called The Hackney Crew, better known as THC. The arrests were made all around London, as well as in Birmingham, Leeds, and Manchester. In a related incident, a woman was disarmed and arrested at Gollingham Palace yesterday afternoon. A senior PaIRS officer injured during the arrest is now out of intensive care and expected to make a full recovery. A spokesperson for Gollingham Palace stated that the arrest of the unnamed woman took place in the security wing, and there were no official functions taking place at the time. Their Royal Highnesses the King and Queen are currently at their private residence Fenn House in Fenshire.

At the same time, coordinated via Europol, arrests were made in Amsterdam, Rome, Valencia, and Monaco of members of the notorious Peck Family, including brothers

Leo and Logan Peck, along with their sons Alfie, Harry, and Jay. A warrant has been issued for the arrest of the late Charlie Peck's daughter Lilly, who is believed to be in the UK.

Meanwhile in America, the resignation of the Governor of Florida, the State Commissioner of Police, the Mayor of Miami, and various officials across the state yesterday have been followed by the arrest early this morning in Miami of Aldo Grazzi (72), the alleged head of an organised crime cartel known as the Grazzi Family, along with his eldest son Silvo Grazzi (48). There is also a warrant out for the arrest of Aldo's youngest son Vittario (45), who was last seen two days ago in New York.

A spokesman for MI6 said, "An international collaboration between MI6, City Police, Europol, and the FBI has resulted in the biggest clean up of international organised crime for decades. Charges being brought against those arrested range from nuclear weapons smuggling to assassinations, with numerous charges of money laundering, human trafficking, sale and distribution of drugs, and illegal gambling in between. We expect to make further arrests over the coming weeks."

―――――

"Lady Beatrice! How lovely." Elise Boyce got up from her chair and walked around her brother's hospital bed to greet Bea. She lowered her voice. "Rich is asleep, my lady. They said he'll sleep a lot over the next few days. It's the anaesthetic wearing off, apparently. Rhys has just gone to the loo and then he thinks we should go for a coffee, but you know, I don't like to leave Rich in case he wakes up, and he's all alone. He might need something…" Tears welled up in her eyes, and Bea grabbed her hand. Looking over at Fitzwilliam, she stifled a cry when he opened his eyes and winked at her. He quickly closed them again as Rhys walked into the hospital room.

"Elise," Bea said, holding her hands. "Firstly, please call me Beatrice or Bea. You almost broke my hand yesterday, so I think we can cut the formalities, don't you?" She grinned at Elise and got a beaming smile back in return. "And secondly, you deserve a break. So let your husband take you for a coffee. Have some cake too. I'll stay here with your brother."

"Are you sure?" Elise looked over at Fitzwilliam, who was seemingly in a deep sleep.

"Come on, *cariad*." Rhys gently placed his arms on his wife's shoulders. "We both need five minutes away from this room." Bea dropped Elise's hands, and Rhys steered her out of the room before she could protest further.

Bea walked around the bed and sat down in the chair Elise had vacated. She found her gaze lingering on him. His face looked so peaceful compared to yesterday when it had been tense with pain. Now it was relaxed, he looked ten years younger. *Handsome even...*

He shifted slightly and opened his eyes. They were a little hazy, but he was clearly awake. "Thank you," he whispered hoarsely as he smiled up at her. "I love my sister dearly, but boy can she talk."

Bea smiled back at him. "You're welcome. How are you doing?"

He nodded slowly. "I'll live."

A cold wave washed over her, and she pushed away the memory of yesterday when she'd thought the matron was going to tell them he'd not made it. She'd spent a considerable amount of time last night when she'd got home from dinner at Adler's, thinking about why she'd felt the need to

rush to the hospital yesterday to be by his side. Was it grati-
tude that he'd helped her find out the truth about James's
death and more importantly James's feelings for her? Or was
it simply the concern of a friend? Or was it something more?
She hadn't wanted to dig any deeper. All she knew was she
desperately hadn't wanted Fitzwilliam to die. There was a
warmth in her chest, and she smiled at him. "I'm glad you're
going to be alright," she said softly.

Fitzwilliam attempted to sit up, wincing as he did so. "It
would seem I also have you to thank for my luxurious
surroundings," he said lightly, though there was something
serious in his eyes as he looked at her. She blushed. Before
she'd gone to change, she'd given the ambulance clear
instructions to take him to the nearby Gollingham Infirmary,
the private hospital used by her family, following it up with a
call to her uncle's private secretary asking him to make sure
the senior PaIRS officer injured in the line of duty was given
the best possible care.

She looked around the light and airy room, taking in the
large television on the wallpapered wall opposite the bed.
There was a large plush sofa and two armchairs laid out
around a low coffee table by the window looking out over the
extensive gardens and a discreet door in the corner, presumably leading to an ensuite bathroom. If it wasn't for the large
white hospital bed and the array of machines beeping on the
table on the other side of the bed next to a vase of fresh-cut
flowers, it could be an expensive hotel room.

She shrugged. "Well, it's the least we can do to say thank
you for..." She trailed off.

He looked up at her, his eyes full of understanding and
finished the sentence for her. "For my help?" he asked
quietly. Bea nodded, unable to speak as a lump formed in her
throat. He shifted slightly to get more comfortable, and she

noticed the way his hospital robe pulled tight against his chest, revealing the muscular outline beneath. She looked away quickly, heat burning through her cheeks. *Oh my goodness, I hope he didn't see me look at him like that!*

Fitzwilliam cleared his throat. "Are you alright, Lady Beatrice?"

Lady Beatrice? She suppressed a sigh. Was she fooling herself that she and Fitzwilliam were becoming friends? After all, he still used her title. Well, maybe it was up to her to change that. She took a deep breath. *Here goes...*

"Erm, no," she said, looking down at his pale face. "When we're alone or you're not working, I'd like you to call me Beatrice or Bea, whichever you prefer."

He raised an eyebrow. "Are you sure?"

Was he worried about the protocol? After all, he belonged to the organisation tasked with protecting her and her family. "As long as it doesn't put you in an awkward position." A pit opened up in her tummy. *Oh no, does he think I'm flirting with him?* She added hastily, "I'm going to ask Adler and Izzy to drop the title Lady as well."

He smiled. A smile that lit up his face and instantly made her want to smile back. "I only have one condition." His grin radiated warmth and acceptance, and she felt the tension leave her shoulders.

She smiled. "A condition? I'm not sure; it depends..."

"You have to agree to call me Richard or Rich, whatever you prefer...but—" He paused and held up his hand— "*not* Dick."

Heat crept up her neck, and she looked away. She couldn't believe how rude she'd been last year when he'd resurfaced unexpectedly in her life. She'd been so mad at fate for bringing the only other person who'd known the contents of James's letter back into her life that she'd punished him for

287

it. *Shall I apologise?* She raised her eyes and met his, which twinkled with mischief. The corners of his lips were curled into an inviting half-moon. *Two can play at this game…* "How about Dickie?"

He threw his head back and laughed out loud, then winced.

"Careful," she cried. "You have to take care not to…" She stopped. *I don't want to sound like his mother.*

Fitzwilliam shifted slightly, and the pain cleared from his face. "So you've settled on Dickie, have you?"

So we're still playing, are we? "Or Chuck. I believe that's a popular shortening in the United States?" she said.

"Really?" Fitzwilliam grinned.

I haven't finished yet… "Or Ric…kaaaaay!" Bea said, doing her best impression of Bianca from the television show *Eastenders*. "Or Chard," she said in a sloaney voice. "That's very posh and in keeping with you having a bachelor pad in Surrey."

"Okay, okay." Fitzwilliam held up a hand, still grinning. "You clearly have options. Let's hope you make a wise choice." He held her gaze, and her heart skipped a beat.

She looked away. *Oh my giddy aunt!*

Fitzwilliam cleared his throat. "So Rhys tells me they've arrested a whole bunch of organised crime families then?"

With a sense of relief that they were back onto the case, she nodded and brought him up to date with what had been reported in the press, including Rudy and Sheri Trotman's disappearances, presumed dead. "Adler thinks they aren't really dead, and it's all a cover to keep him safe after he revealed all to MI6."

Fitzwilliam raised an eyebrow. "Witness protection sort of thing?" She shrugged. He grinned. "I don't quite know how they would engineer an avalanche though."

She grinned back, and their eyes met for a moment before Bea quickly looked away, her stomach fluttering. *What's going on with me?*

"How about Ruth Ness? Did she say why she killed Street? I presume she was working for the same people he was…"

Bea repeated what Adler had told them last night. When she finished, Fitzwilliam shook his head, then winced. "You need to rest," Bea pointed out. He gave her a weary smile as he slowly sank back into the pillows.

"You know, if you need somewhere to recuperate, there are plenty of empty places at Francis Court," she blurted out. *What are you doing, Bea?* "I mean, and other places too, like er…Fenn House… I just meant if you need somewhere quiet to —" *Stop talking!* "—get better…"

Fitzwilliam's smile had a warmth that made her heart skip a beat. "I'll bear it in mind," he said softly. His eyes were still locked on hers, a smile playing at the corners of his lips. Her heart raced as she tried to make sense of what was happening between them. She had to stop herself from leaning into him slightly, as if drawn by a force greater than herself, their closeness both comforting and exciting. She licked her lips. *Oh goodness!* Fitzwilliam's eyelids fluttered as if he was fighting the sleep that wanted to take over. "Bea, I, er…"

Bea raised her hand and cut him off. "You need to rest. If you don't take your recovery seriously, then I will have no choice but to start calling you Dick."

52

AFTERNOON, SATURDAY 20 FEBRUARY

The Society Page online article:

Popular TV Show Bake Off Wars *to be Filmed at Francis Court*

Francis Court estate, the home of Her Royal Highness Princess Helen and her husband Charles Astley, the Duke of Arnwall, is reportedly buzzing at the announcement it is to host the next series of Bake Off Wars.

The competition, which sees twelve bakery teams compete over ten weeks to win the coveted title of Bake Off Warriors and a twenty-five thousand pound reward, starts filming in April and will be aired later in the summer. Following the controversy surrounding the sacking of judge Mike Jacob (45) at the end of the last series, renowned pâtissière Vera Bolt (66) will be joined by TV chef Ryan Hawley (31) as the second judge. In another change, comedians Hamilton Moore (38) and Summer York (33) will take on the task of presenting the show after comedy duo Claudia Sharp and Kit North chose not to renew their contract with the show. An announcement by the show's production company stated they were excited to have an injection of new blood into the show, and they expect this eighth series to be the best yet.

"Ryan Hawley is one of the most popular chefs on television and will bring a newer, more cutting edge perspective to the judging. Hamilton Moore is a well-known foodie and hosts a chart-topping podcast called Moore Food Please! *Summer has just completed a sellout tour of her standup show* A Season of Me *and is, in her own words, 'totally addicted to chocolate'. Vera and all here at Eat Cake Productions are looking forward to welcoming Ryan, Hamilton, and Summer to our* Bake Off Wars *family."*

In other news, Princess Helen and her daughters, Lady Beatrice and Lady Sarah Rosdale, have been frequent visitors to Fawstead Manor to comfort Sybil Trotman (36), who is staying with her mother Lady Grace Willoughby-Franklin (62) at the family home in Fenshire. Sybil's husband Otis Trotman (41) and his brother Jed (39) are due to fly back from France today and will join them at Fawstead Manor. Their parents Rudy and Sheri Trotman are still missing, now presumed dead, following the avalanche in the French ski resort of Val'Nes two weeks ago. Although the rescued local guide and his four students told the search and rescue teams that they were not aware of any other skiers on the same slope as them at the time of the disaster, two witnesses have since come forward to confirm they saw a couple, since identified from photos as Mr and Mrs Trotman, in the area above the group just as the avalanche hit. Having completed as thorough of a search of the area as they can in the current conditions, rescue teams have now been stood down.

Meanwhile, Lady Beatrice, the Countess of Rossex, and her business partner Perry Juke have completed the refurbishment of several guest suites at Gollingham Palace in

Surrey. The King and Queen are said to be delighted with the results. Rumours are that the pair's next project is closer to home as Lady Beatrice and her son Samuel prepare to move back to The Dower House in the grounds of the Francis Court estate, where she lived with her husband James Wiltshire, the Earl of Rossex, before his untimely death fifteen years ago. A little dickie bird tells us Lady Beatrice is keen to update the interior of the seven-bedroom home and move in as soon as possible. No doubt her business partner Perry will be pleased to be back home as he'll be busy organising his upcoming nuptials to crime novelist and celebrity chef, Simon Lattimore, due to take place at Francis Court in March.

———

I hope you enjoyed *I Spy With My Little Die*, If you did then please consider writing a review on Amazon or Goodreads, or even both. It helps me a lot if you let people know that you recommend it.

Will Lady Beatrice get caught up in the middle of a Bake Off war? Find out in the next book in the *A Right Royal Cozy Investigation* series *Dying to Bake* available on preorder in the Amazon store or wherever you get your paperbacks.

Want to know how Perry and Simon solved their first crime together? Then join my readers' club and receive a FREE short story Tick, Tock, Mystery Clock at https://www.-subscribepage.com/helengoldenauthor_nls

If you want to find out more about what I'm up to you can

find me on Facebook at *helengoldenauthor* or on Instagram at *helengolden_author*.

Be the first to know when my next book is available. Follow Helen Golden on Amazon, BookBub, and Goodreads to get alerts whenever I have a new release, preorder, or a discount on any of my books.

A BIG THANK YOU TO...

As I publish more books, this section gets shorter! Not because I'm any less grateful to the support network who surround me, in fact the opposite is true, they become more valuable each step of the way, but more because I don't want to repeat myself at the back of every book. So I'm just going to say a huge appreciative thank you to my friends and family who continue to offer encouragement and support. I couldn't do it without you.

To my beta readers Ann, Ray, and Lissie — your vital feedback in the early stages helps me refine my story, so thank you.

To my editor Marina Grout — you continue to encourage and correct me. Both of which I need. Thank you for your patience and knowledge.

To Ann, Ray, and my lovely friend Carolyn I appreciate your additional set of eyes for me before I publish. Error free is impossible, but thank you for helping me get closer.

And the biggest thank you goes to you, my readers. Your emails, social media comments, and reviews mean so much to me, and I appreciate your time and attention. Please continue to get in touch, I'm always keen to hear from you.

I must mention two readers in particular, Jane Litherland and Cinnamon Mason, who won a competition to name a character each in this book. Thank you both for taking part, and I hope you enjoy seeing your name in print.

As always, I may have taken a little dramatic license when it comes to police procedures, so any mistakes or misinterpretations, unintentional or otherwise, are my own.

CHARACTERS IN ORDER OF APPEARANCE

Ethan Preece — Detective Inspector at City Police.

Prince David — Duke of Kingswich, brother to the king. Lady Beatrice's uncle.

Lady Beatrice — The Countess of Rossex. Seventeenth in line to the British throne. Daughter of Charles Astley, the Duke of Arnwall and Her Royal Highness Princess Helen. Niece of the current king.

Perry Juke — Lady Beatrice's business partner and BFF.

Simon Lattimore — Perry Juke's fiancé. Bestselling crime writer. Ex-Fenshire CID. Winner of cooking competition *Celebrity Elitechef.*

Daisy — Lady Beatrice's adorable West Highland Terrier.

James Wiltshire — The Earl of Rossex. Lady Beatrice's late husband killed in a car accident fifteen years ago.

HRH Princess Helen — Duchess of Arnwall. Mother of Lady Beatrice. Sister of the current king.

Sam Wiltshire — son of Lady Beatrice and the late James Wiltshire, the Earl of Rossex. Future Earl of Durrland.

Charles Astley — Duke of Arnwall. Lady Beatrice's father.

Lord Frederick (Fred) Astley — Earl of Tilling. Lady Beatrice's elder brother and twin of Lady Sarah Rosdale. Ex-Intelligence Army Officer. Future Duke of Arnwall.

Emma McKeer-Adler — Detective Chief Inspector, investigations team PaIRS.

Isobel 'Izzy" McKeer-Adler — Emma's wife.

Richard Fitzwilliam — Detective Chief Inspector at *PaIRS (Protection and Investigation (Royal) Service)* an organisation that provides protection and security to the royal family and who investigate any threats against them. *PaIRS* is a division of City Police, a police organisation based in the capital, London.

Gill Sterling — the late wife of Francis Court's estate manager. Passenger in car accident that killed her and James Wiltshire.

Alex Sterling — the late Francis Court's estate manager.

Brett Goodman — CIA Agent.

Tim Street — Detective Chief Superintendent at PaIRS.

Nigel Blake — Superintendent at *PaIRS*. Fitzwilliam's boss.

Ruth Ness — Detective Chief Superintendent Tim Street's executive assistant.

Henry Bird — Detective Chief Inspector at *PaIRS*, Intelligence.

Madeline 'Maddie' Carmichael - Detective Inspector at City Police, Organise Crime Unit (reader suggestion from Jane Litherland).

Tina Spicer — Detective Sergeant at *PaIRS*.

Arabella 'Bella' Hardwick — Detective Sergeant at *PaIRS (*reader suggestion from Cinnamon Mason)

Mrs (Maggie) Fraser — cook/housekeeper The Dower House.

Fraser (William) — butler/handyman The Dower House.

George Rockcliffe — building contractor.

Carol — DCI Fitzwilliam's EA at *PaIRS*.

Dr Dominic Elmes - Pathologist at *PaIRS*.

Rudy Trotman — owner of Fortune US Corp. Billionaire.

Rory Glover — ex-private secretary to Lady Beatrice and her husband James.

Dean Foxley — member of *The Hack Crew (THC)*.

Joseph Peck — hitman and member of *The Peck Family* who run *THC*.

Sir Hewitt Willoughby-Franklin — well-respected business mogul. Star of TV show *The Novice*.

Duncan Neal — Forensics at *PaIRS*.

Ward/Mr Ward — the Astley family's driver and overseer of maintenance at Francis Court.

Elise Boyce — Richard Fitzwilliam's sister

Rhys Boyce — Elise's husband. Richard Fitzwilliam's brother-in-law

Matron Hathaway - Head nurse at *Gollingham Infirmary*.

Doctor Ayesha Bhait — Surgeon at *Gollingham Infirmary*.

Lilly Peck — member of *The Peck Family* who run *THC*.

ALSO BY HELEN GOLDEN

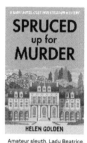

Can Perry Juke and Simon Lattimore work together to solve the mystery of the missing clock before the thief disappears? FREE novelette when you sign up to my readers' club. See end of final chapter for details.

Amateur sleuth, Lady Beatrice, must pit her wits against Detective Chief Inspector Richard Fitzwilliam to prove her sister innocent of murder. With the help of her clever dog, her flamboyant co-interior designer and his ex-police partner, can she find the killer before him, or will she make a fool of herself?

Lady Beatrice, must once again go up against DCI Fitzwilliam to find a killer. With the help of Daisy, her clever companion, and her two best friends, Perry and Simon, can she catch the culprit before her childhood friend's wedding is ruined?

When DCI Richard Fitzwilliam gets it into his head that Lady Beatrice's new beau Seb is guilty of murder, can the amateur sleuth, along with the help of Daisy, her clever westie, and her best friends Perry and Simon, find the real killer before Fitzwilliam goes ahead and arrests Seb?

A Prequel in the A Right Royal Cozy Investigation series.
When Lady Beatrice's husband James Wiltshire dies in a car crash along with the wife of a member of staff, there are questions to be answered. Why haven't the occupants of two cars seen in the accident area come forward? And what is the secret James had been keeping from her?

Snow descends on Drew Castle in Scotland cutting the castle off and forcing Lady Beatrice along with Daisy her clever dog, and her best friends Perry and Simon to cooperate with boorish DCI Fitzwilliam to catch a killer before they strike again.

ALL EBOOKS AVAILABLE IN THE AMAZON STORE.

PAPERBACKS AVAILABLE FROM WHEREVER YOU BUY YOUR BOOKS.

Printed in Great Britain
by Amazon

28289589R10175